*Black Wall Street New Dream Publishing*

TH

# NEVER

# GIVE UP

# ON YOUR

# DREAMS!

RONALD GRAY

# MY CALL III

*The spirit of hell Unleashed*

RONALD GRAY

# MY CALL III

## The Spirit of Hell Unleashed

### Ronald H. Gray

**BLACK WALL STREET NEW DREAM PUBLISHING**

*Owned by*

**MY PROVIDER PRODUCTIONS LLC**

www.myproviderproductions.com

blackwallstreetnewdream@yahoo.com

RONALD GRAY

My Provider Productions LLC
My Call III The Spirit Of Hell Unleashed
Copyright © 2015 Ronald H. Gray
**Revised Edition: 07/20/2021**

Library of Congress Control Number: 2015909293
ISBN-10: 0692467661
ISBN-13: 978-0-692-46766-4
Author: Ronald H. Gray
Cover Design/Graphics: Ronald H. Gray
Printed in the United States of America

*This is a work of fiction. Any references or similarities to actual events, real people, living or dead, or to real locales are intended to give the novel a sense of reality. Any similarity in other names, characters, places, and incidents is entirely coincidental.*

Distributed by Black Wall Street New Dream Publishing
My Provider Productions LLC
www.myproviderproductions.com
blackwallstreetnewdream@yahoo.com

RONALD GRAY

# Dedication

*This book is dedicated to family and friends who continue to believe in me and the vision and still tell me the same thing, "Never Give Up!"*

RONALD GRAY

# ACKNOWLEDGMENTS

First and foremost, I would like to thank God once again in the name of King Jesus for giving me this gift and opportunity to share another powerful story.

I continue to thank all who stood by me in this journey. Because after all has been said and done, I never gave up.

All the betrayal, lies, deceit, pain, and tremendous love I have experienced in my life's journey continue to compel me to write with hopes that the messages in the books will have a positive effect on other people's lives.

To some, this may be just that a story, to others it may be their life. But if you are truly honest with yourself, I think we all can see just a little of us somewhere in this story. It will make you laugh, cry, and think about your life and others as well, it will move your mind and spirit.

Another raw untold story...Until now!

RONALD GRAY

**THE BOOK THAT SET IT OFF**     **ALSO BY RONALD GRAY**

RONALD GRAY

# CHAPTER ONE

*The return of the Devil*

Leon and Carter are thirty-eight-year-old homeless drunks living in Washington DC. They were sleeping in an alley littered with trash and boxes and sleeping inside two large boxes and using old newspapers as pillows. Leon was six-one, two-hundred-forty-pounds, brown-skinned complexion with a deep baritone voice. Carter is six-two, two-hundred-sixty pounds, dark-skinned complexion. Both are veterans who served in the army for ten years and have been friends for six years. Leon and Carter travel together going from shelter to shelter and place to place. Making money how and when they can and drank every day.

Leon carried his green duffle bag everywhere he went, and Carter carries a brown one. It was three o'clock in the morning when it started thundering and lightning and they woke up. Leon got up and walked down the alley and started pissing against one of the old buildings. Carter watched Leon and decided to take this opportunity to open his duffle bag to see what is in it. When he opened the bag and reached inside, he heard a click. He looked up and saw Leon holding a large knife.

"Did you lose something in that bag boy?" He stared at him with eyes full of rage. "I told you, never go in my damn bag and I never go in yours. Do you want me to put this blade in your big fat stomach?"

Carter knew his friend well and hoped he would not stab him.

"Relax partner, I was checking to see if you had a bottle," he held his trembling hand out for Leon to see. "I woke up with the shakes. I need a drink really bad this morning to calm my nerves."

Leon reached down and snatched his bag from Carter.

"I don't give a damn about your shakes fool. You go into my bag again and I am going to put this blade in your gut and slide it up to your neck." He reached into his bag, pulled out a bottle, took a drink then threw the bottle to Carter. "Here fool, take a drink before your ugly old ass passes out."

Carter took a drink and looked up at Leon smiling.

"Thanks, partner I needed that," he patted the ground with his hand. "Come on and take a seat so we can talk."

Leon stared at him then leaned over and snatched his bottle from him and took another drink and put the bottle back in his bag and then sat down.

"Leon, I remember when you had it going on big time after you got out of the military. Luxury cars, pretty women, and pockets full of money, and you always looked out for me. What happened to you?" How did you go from sugar to spit?"

Leon stared at Carter wondering if he should tell him the truth.

"Do you remember when I went to South Carolina after I got out of the military to visit a root worker name doctor Eyes that we heard so much about? Well, he was the real deal and then some. Anyway, he gave me this small pouch and told me to carry it with me everywhere I went, no matter what. I started gambling and the first month I made four-hundred and fifty-thousand dollars, I was rolling after that for years. I became a professional gambler and traveled all over the country. I could count five-hundred-thousand dollars in any given week, all mine. I was balling until two women changed all that in one night. I was with two fine ladies in bed, bodies so curvaceous they would make a preacher sin, repeatedly. We did all kinds of freaky things that night," he started laughing then stopped and became angry. "But the following morning when I woke up, I noticed the sluts robbed me. They took all the cash I had in my pockets, thirty-grand, and watch, my necklace, and my ring. Those three pieces were worth over six-hundred-eighty grand. They took my three-hundred and forty- thousand-dollar Bentley which I always kept five-hundred-thousand dollars in cash hidden in the trunk. But the worst of it was they took my pouch and my luck turned bad after that. My bank accounts got frozen by the feds and the IRS audited me saying I owed them over five million dollars in back taxes. They took my other cars and houses and I was ass out. So, I went back to visit the root worker and found out he was dead. He got burned up. I went to his house and found some things and have carried them around with me for years, afraid to mess with it."

Carter was not paying attention to him but he leaned forward hearing this news.

"What, what did you find partner? I would do anything to get out of my situation. Ain't no fear in me. Hell, the devil can have my soul I am going to hell anyway," he started laughing. "So, show me what you got?"

Leon knew this day would come and besides he was tired of living like an animal on the streets. He reached inside his duffle bag and pulled out a cane, a black pouch, and a small jewelry box. He handed the jewelry box to Carter and held the cane and black pouch in his hands. He tapped Carter on the arm with the cane.

"Stand up."

They both stood and Leon stared at Carter.

"I know this is bad stuff we are about to do, I can feel it."

Carter looked at the box in his hand and looked at Leon and saw the fear in his eyes, but he does not care. He wanted off these streets.

"Look man, damn all that conversation. What do you know?"

Leon looked up.

"Lord forgive me for what I am about to do." He started tapping the cane on the ground, suddenly his body began shaking and he let go of the cane which stood up by itself. He reached into the black pouch and removed some bones and laid the bones on the ground in a circle around him and Carter. The bones started vibrating and the cane began taping itself on the ground repeatedly. He stared at Carter. "Open the box, Carter."

He opened the box and saw two eyeballs which made Carter drop the box and the eyeballs rolled out and stayed inside the circle of bones.

"What the hell, two damn eyeballs?" He looked at the eyeballs and saw an envelope inside the box, so he picked up the envelope and stood up. He opened it and saw a stack of one hundred-dollar bills and counted it and its five-thousand dollars in cash. He laughed and began jumping up and down. "Leon, it's on baby, we are back. Five grand partner and I am going to split it with you because you always looked out for me."

"Read the note inside the envelope Carter."

He pulled the note out and stared at it.

"It says, repeat these words on the paper six times and you can have whatever you want." He looked at Leon. "What do you think partner?"

He stared at him.

"Read it now Carter."

Carter reached into his pocket and pulled out his glasses and looked at Leon then at the paper.

"Yeah okay. It says the spirit of darkness come to me. That's it? "I can say that. This is too easy." He repeated the words six times, but nothing happened. "Damn man, I was hoping something was going to happen. This is some damn game but we got some money."

The air suddenly became very still, and a thick black cloud appeared hovering over them. Lightning struck Carter in his eyes and his eyeballs fell out and explode on the ground. He started screaming and his body began to shake hard and he leaned back. The eyeballs that fell out of the box floated up in the air and went inside Carter's eye sockets. He yelled and his skin turned a shade darker and seconds later he started laughing.

"Yes, the spirit of darkness is back." He continued to laugh and then grabbed the cane and screamed. "Ahhhhhhh, so much power." His clothes changed colors to all black and the circle of bones floated up and landed in his hand. "I am back, all evil is back. You can kill the body but not the spirit," he mumbled some words. Immediately, he and Carter began to float up in the air. "Damn, it feels good to be back. We are coming for you Chosen Boy. The spirit of hell has been unleashed." He mumbled some more words and a black cloud appeared over them, and they disappeared.

# CHAPTER TWO

*Dream come true*

This is the day Stacy has looked forward to for years, her wedding day. After Keith gave his heart to the Lord he wanted to focus on nothing but positive things for his life. One of them was to marry Stacy, his only ride-or-die lady. He wanted to leave his past in the past, but he and Ron were able to keep all their legit businesses including their club. They started working on planning and building their dream entertainment complex which would be the headquarters for their empire. They would name it, *My Provider Productions,* a multi-entertainment business complex. The *Young Wolves* kept their hands clean, so they were still in business. But Keith kept ten of the *Young Wolves*, his very loyal and elite ten. The other twenty he let go after giving them a severance package of fifty-thousand dollars apiece.

Keith purchased a large four-car garage, five-bedroom mansion in Potomac, Maryland which would be his and Stacy's home after they got married and it was close to Ron's house They wanted a small private wedding with their closest friends attending and wanted it to be somewhere tropical. They picked the Cayo Espanto resort in Belize. The resort was rented a week for their wedding. The wedding day was a beautiful, eighty-five-degree temperature and a light breeze with a spectacular ocean view.

Keith and Stacy decided to wear all white for this day. Keith wore a three-piece, tailor-made tux, and white shoes. Stacy wore a tailored form-fitting off the shoulder beautiful gown that hugged her curvaceous body. White flowers were everywhere, and they finally stood next to each other to say, I do.

Ron, Diana, Sheila, Grandma Harris, Zechariah, Christine, Sandra, Pastor Williams, and the ten Young Wolves stood by watching this precious moment. Everyone was dressed very well. Keith arranged for a pastor on the island to perform the ceremony but wanted Pastor Williams to be there as well to pray over them and give his blessing.

Zechariah stood next to Sheila as Stacy and Keith said their wedding vows and he grabbed her hand gently and smiled. Sheila smiled back feeling his sincere care for her and others noticed this and smiled as well. Grandma Harris was so happy Zechariah was here, in her heart she knew he was the one for Sheila. They listened as Keith and Stacy exchanged vows and their words were perfect for what they have shared.

Both Pastors stood in front of them as Stacy and Keith faced each other. Keith stared into Stacy's eyes as he spoke knowing she was his heart. They exchanged rings then stared at one another smiling.

"Stacy, I promise to love you, respect you, protect you, and watch your back until my last breath."

"Keith, I promise to love you, respect you, be your queen and ride-or-die lady for life baby, for life." Her eyes were bright and full of love as she stared into Keith's eyes.

The Pastors say at the same time.

"We now pronounce you husband and wife. Keith, you may kiss your bride."

They stared at each other with a degree of love anyone could feel. As if they moved in slow motion their lips finally touched with enough love to heal the world. Keith whispered in her ear.

"Now can I have some booty?" He smiled.

Stacy slapped him playfully.

"All you can handle my husband; all you can handle." She kissed and hugged him tightly. Everyone started clapping their hands, hugged and congratulated them. This is a day they will never forget and a long time coming.

# CHAPTER THREE

*A day to remember*

After the wedding ceremony, Keith and Stacy went back to their hotel suite to shower and change clothes. They showered and changed in separate places so they would not see each other to increase the anticipation of what was to come. Wearing shorts, T-shirt, and custom sandals from *Doogie Fun Apparel*, Stacy and Keith walked on the beach holding hands and enjoyed the beautiful view. Stacy wanted to talk but had no words to fully describe how she felt because her emotions were overwhelming. All she could do was look at Keith as they walked hand in hand and she was finally where she desired to be, married to the man she deeply loved beyond words.

Keith looked at Stacy with the same intensity as if he could read her thoughts. He stopped walking and pulled her closer to him and held her hands.

"Some things in life, words alone will never be able to express. I love you Mrs. Stacy Washington."

Stacy squeezed his hands and stared at him with tears building in her eyes.

"I love you more than I could ever show you in one lifetime baby, but I will try every single day, Mr. Keith Washington." She smiled and pulled his body into hers wrapping her arms around him and kissed Keith with love from her heart and soul.

Keith caressed her hips as they kissed feeling his desire for her increasing with each passing second.

"I want you so bad Stacy." He was grinding slowly into her so she could feel his growing erection.

Stacy smiled and pushed him back.

"I am glad you are a man who does not hold back but we need to go to our room to finish this before I let you take me right here and now." She kissed him and they walked away holding hands.

The sky turned very cloudy and the wind began to blow hard. Carter and Leon appeared in a cloud of grey smoke on the beach close to some large boulders not far from where Stacy and Keith were walking. Leon had his cane and pouch in his hands and they were dressed in all black and stared at Keith and Stacy walking away. Leon pointed his cane at them.

"Look at those fools all happy and in love. Enjoy it while you can because hell is coming and we ain't taking no prisoners."

Carter's eyes turned coal black and waved his hand through the air.

"You are damn right. But in the meantime, who can we kill and take to hell today? Somebody's got to die."

There was a couple on the other side of the boulders lying down naked on a blanket having sex. They were so into pleasing each other they never noticed Leon and Carter standing next to the edge of the blanket watching them. The man finally noticed them, rolled over quickly, and reached for his clothes and the women started screaming and reached for their clothes as well.

"Oh God, who are you?" She said, quickly getting dressed covering her shapely figure.

"Jesus, you can't just walk up on people. You two fools got a death wish." He said, getting dressed, and stepped closer and pointed his finger at them. He was tall and muscular.

Leon's face became eerily contorted and pointed his cane at the man.

"Now you want to call on Jesus. I hope the sex was good boy," he pointed his cane at the lady. "And you want to call on God. You two were cheating on your mates out here in Belize where you thought no one would see you, committing adultery. Woman, you are a big freak, sucking this man's dick and you do not suck your husband's dick. You were sucking it good too, slobbering all over it. I saw you, nasty dirty dog, spitting all over it and licked his balls." He leaned his head back and laughed.

The man stepped toward Leon.

"Enough of this." He swung at Leon.

Leon pulled the sword from his cane so fast it looked like a blur and cut the man's arm off then his head. The woman ran away screaming but Carter pointed at her.

"My serpent, attack!" He yelled.

A large king cobra snake appeared in front of her and lunged forward and bit the woman in her throat and wrapped itself around her body and pulled her to the ground. Then bit her in the neck and on top of the head. She started convulsing and foaming at the mouth and her skin began melting from her body until all you saw was her skeleton.

Carter walked over to Leon and looked at the man's cut-up body and laughed. Leon looked at Carter

"Damn, killing him felt good."

"Killing her felt better. It is what we do. Trick people, give them what they want, and destroy them. Fuel for hell is increasing as time goes on. Keith and Stacy better enjoy their time because soon, hell will visit them."

Leon's sword was dripping with blood. He swung it through the air shaking the blood off and tapped his cane on the ground twice. He and Carter disappeared in a cloud of smoke.

A mist lingered at Keith and Stacy's hotel door then slid under it and moved slowly inside their room rising and taking on the faces of Leon and Carter who stared at Keith and Stacy in bed making love but they could not see the mist.

Stacy and Keith were making love since they arrived back in their room after taking a shower together. They have known each other for years and had sex in every position and every way but tonight was very different. It was clean and pure for them. Tears of joy and peace flowed from their eyes as they exchanged the spirit of lovemaking in the Lord. Everything they did, every touch was extremely intense, and felt it in their soul and spirit. They laid in bed giving themselves to each other repeatedly. Not realizing, evil spirits were so close watching them and waiting.

# CHAPTER FOUR
### New Beginnings

The club was closed for renovations because Ron and Keith wanted a new look and image for the club's name, *New Beginnings*. The club interior is beautiful. Ron, Keith, the Young Wolves, and an interior decorator and his helpers did most of the work. It is Monday afternoon and several people walked around the club adding final touches getting ready for the club's grand opening. The club's entire staff was new which was what Keith and Ron wanted and they did interviews for a couple of days for various positions within the club.

Ron, Keith, and Zechariah sat at a table in the lounge area of the club dressed in suits and having a business meeting. Ron wanted nothing but the best for his friend Zechariah, so he and Keith offered him the job as head of security for the club. Zechariah was hesitant to accept the job at first because of the environment he would be in, but he needed a job. And it is extremely hard for a convicted felon to get a decent job, especially one that paid well. His starting salary would be eighty thousand dollars plus bonuses, company credit card, and company car. How could he turn down such an offer? They all shook hands and Zechariah walked out of the club, but Ron had a surprise for him. A new dark blue S550 Mercedes Benz was being delivered in front of the club on a rollback tow truck. The driver walked up to Zechariah and put the keys in his hand and drove away. He was surprised and became emotional as he sat in the car and prayed giving God the glory and drove away smiling.

A stretch Benz limo drove up in front of the club. A female driver got out, opened the door and five attractive women wearing shades and dark blue expensive business suits stepped out and stood next to the car. They looked around and Leticia Wilson stepped out of the limo dressed as if she were walking down a fashion show runway. She was stunningly beautiful with an exotic look. Her skin was flawless and caramel toned, she was five feet nine, one-hundred-forty pounds, jet long black hair wearing a tailored twelve-thousand-dollar dress that hugged her body well. She was the epitome of a *FULL SEVEN*, pretty in the face, slim in the waist, hips, lips, pretty painted fingertips, big butt, and a pretty smile. As she walked toward the club, every move of her flawless body looked as if she moved in slow motion. The other four women walked behind her. She looked around and stared at the club frowning then smiled.

"Enjoy this club and your lifestyle while you can boys because your time is coming and hell ain't far away."

Leticia and the other five ladies walked toward the limo and a Cadillac Escalade drove up behind the limo. Stacy, Shantai, Cynthia, and Tonya stepped out and all four were casually dressed in heels, tight jeans that hugged their curves, and blouses. They looked at Leticia walking and Shantai shook her head and spoke softly.

"Wow, who in the world is that lady, the next Miss America?" Lustful thoughts immediately came to her mind.

Stacy looked at Shantai and read her facial expression.

"Keep your mind on Jesus Shantai." She fought her lustful thoughts as well. *She is one of the finest-looking ladies I have ever seen.*

Leticia looked at the girls and locked eyes with Stacy as if she read her thoughts. They all got into the limo and drove away. Music played in the limo and the woman drank wine. Leticia licked the rim of her wine glass slowly and looked at her associates.

"The erotic-looking girl was Keith's wife. No one touches her, she is mine. I have some special plans for her young hot ass. I am going to find out how much she loves the Lord." They all laughed and continued drinking.

Stacy, Shantai, Cynthia, and Tonya shook their heads as they walked in the club towards the table where Ron and Keith sat.

Keith and Ron stood as they approached. Stacy hugged and kissed Keith.

"Hi, baby," she looked around. "The club looks great and so do you. Hi, Ron." She kissed Keith again.

"What's up Stacy?"

Keith knew when Stacy was trying to persuade him to do something and this is one of those times, he felt it.

"You look great, now what's going on. All of you did not come here for nothing. I know you are up to something, so what is it?"

Shantai, Cynthia, and Tonya waved and spoke to Keith and Ron.

"Hi Keith, Hi Ron."

Ron walked over and hugged them and Keith did the same.

"It's good to see you all again and you look good. So, what is going on?" Ron said as he looked at them.

Stacy walked to the table and sat down and waved her hand at the girls.

"Girls, have a seat please, we need to discuss some business."

Everyone sat down and Keith looked at Stacy because she had a mischievous smile on her face.

"Business, what business Stacy?" Ron said.

"Yeah, what business my beautiful wife?" Keith smiled at her.

Stacy thought and planned this ever since Keith said he was getting a new staff for the club.

"I do like the sound of being called, wife. Okay straight to the point. Keith, you and Ron need people you can trust to work here, and I brought three you can trust. They need good jobs and I know you will treat them right and pay them well."

Keith and Ron looked at each other then looked at the girls.

"Cynthia, what happened to your job at the car dealership? After all the cars we purchased at one time, your commission should have been good and you on easy street." Ron said.

"Well, I was for a while, but the owner kept trying to get in my pants and I refused, so after a while, he said I was not doing my job well enough, and fired me, and here I am."

Stacy waved her hand in the air.

"I have seen the owner. He is a rich, arrogant snob who thinks his money can buy him anything. He pushed up on me, but I laughed in his face and walked away."

Keith's temper immediately began to rise but his face did not show it as he looked at Stacy.

"You should have mentioned this to me Stacy when it first happened." He looked at Ron. "Ron let's go."

They stood up and so did Stacy. She held her hand out in front of Keith.

"No Keith. I know what you are thinking, that is the old you. You have given your life to the Lord and you have to trust God to handle things in your life from now on." She stepped closer and kissed him on the lips. "Please baby, you are not a gangster anymore. That part of you is dead."

Ron walked over to Keith and put his hand on his shoulder.

"She is right my brother. *If any man is in Christ, he is a new creature. Old things have passed away, behold all things are become new.* You are new, let it go, pray, and keep it moving."

Keith looked at Ron and then at Stacy

"Yeah, you are right." He sat down. "Let's get back to business. Girls, my sisters in Christ, what do you want to do here?"

Ron and Stacy sat down.

"Well, I am good with mixing drinks so I would like to be a bartender." Tonya said.

Cynthia leaned forward.

"I am not bragging, but I work well with people and have a degree in business and I know the club scene well. I would like to be considered for club manager."

"The manager." Stacy stared at Cynthia. Yes, she knew Cynthia changed her life living for Christ, but she was very protective concerning Keith and what they shared and almost lost. If Cynthia were manager she and Keith would be spending a lot of time together and she does not want that, but she does not want her possessiveness to show. "Being a manager in a club is a big responsibility, can you handle all that?"

"I know I can." She looked at Stacy then Keith.

Shantai saw something in Cynthia's eyes when she spoke, and did not like it.

"Ambition, I like that. Well, I would make a good hostess. I have the personality, the brains, and the looks." Shantai said.

Ron felt them all and wanted to hire them.

"Bartender, hostess, and manager, we do need. What do you think Keith? It works for me."

Keith looked at Stacy knowing what she thought but he has changed and will treat her better and spend more quality time with his wife. He looked at Ron.

"It works for me. You three are hired. Be professional always please and we will get along well. I know we are all friends and love the Lord, but business is business." He stared at them.

The girls started clapping their hands then hugged Ron, Keith, and Stacy thanking her for the help.

"Great, that is settled so let's all go out someplace fancy to eat and celebrate our family in friendship and business." Ron said.

"Sounds great Ron and where is Diana? How come she is not here as well?" Stacy said.

Ron knew this was coming.

"Short story, Diana does not like the club scene at all, but she is supportive of what I do and will be with us when we go out."

"Great, because I miss her." Stacy said.

"Yeah, I do too. So, let's leave and meet up tonight. I have some business to take care of at home with my baby."

"Yes, you do. Go handle your business my brother." Stacy said and smiled at Ron.

They all walked out of the club with Keith holding Stacy's hand. Stacy loved all his attention and kissed him on the cheek and kept walking but could not get Leticia off her mind. She felt a strong desire to fast and pray soon.

Shantai stared at Tonya's butt as they walked out and thought of Leticia and what she would like to do to her. She caught herself and repented, *Lord help me, help me to stay focused on you.*

Cynthia looked around the club as they walked out then looked at Stacy and Keith seeing how happy they were together. She thought, *yes, hold on to him Stacy while you can because if you slip, he is mine.* Her thoughts bothered her and she repented to herself quickly, *forgive me, Lord.*

At that exact moment, unbeknownst to them, Leticia, and the other women in the back of the limo held hands and chanted an unknown language. Everyone began taking their clothes off and began caressing and kissing each other until it became an all-out orgy. Lips, tongues, fingers, hands, and bodies touched everyone, everywhere, and intertwined with one another repeatedly until every woman was sexually satisfied and exhausted. They held hands again and called out the names of Keith, Stacy, Ron, and Diana. Their chanting increased to cursing louder and louder using various hand signs at the same time.

Diana was home laying on the sofa asleep when she woke up suddenly and got on her knees and started praying and rebuking the devil and its demonic forces and calling on God to protect all her loved ones.

She had no idea what was about to come her way!

# CHAPTER FIVE

*Leticia Wilson*

Leticia Wilson is thirty-four years old and the younger sister of Sherry Wilson. Sherry was Victor Augular's club manager who Stephanie killed. She and Sherry had the same mother but a different dad. She was born in the United States and was very close to Sherry until their continued arguing caused them to separate. Leticia moved to Belize when she was twenty-one, got a job in a high-class strip club as a dancer, saving money for college. She went to the best Universities and earned a double Masters' in finance and business. Sherry called and wrote to her often talking about her life and later talking about Victor. Leticia was concerned for her sister and often told her so, especially when hearing about Victor Augular whose path she would later cross.

When Victor acquired so much money so fast in the billions of dollars, Belize was one of the main places he would travel for business and pleasure. He had ten billion dollars in a bank in Belize that was kept in a secret account. When he was killed the Feds shut down all his businesses and confiscated all his assets which came to a total of twenty-five billion dollars. But his account in Belize was unknown to anyone except Sherry. Before sherry was killed, she sent many pictures of Victor to Leticia and copies of Victor's business paperwork and money locations. Leticia never opened any of these legal papers and always put them in a locked suitcase she kept under her bed. One day when she walked out of the bank, Victor and his security team walked in. Leticia recognized him immediately from his pictures and had to admit he was a very handsome man, but she saw the evil in his eyes and knew he was not a man to mess with.

The day Leticia found out Sherry was dead she fell on the floor in her bedroom and cried for hours. She knew somehow Victor was responsible for her sister's death, so she got the suitcase from underneath the bed and started reading every business letter sent to her. She discovered Victor had ten billion dollars in the bank. Leticia's heart turned cold and her only desire now was revenge, but on whom? Victor and his team were dead. She saw paperwork concerning Victor's club being sold to Keith Washington and much information on him and Ron O'Neil. These two and anyone close to them became the target for her extreme hurt and revenge. She thought about the ten-billion dollars and how to get it. Simple plan, use her brains and looks to seduce the bank owner. He was very wealthy also from various oil investments.

This was no simple plan as she thought. She had to marry the man and then figure out a way to get rid of him for good. Easy, he had a weak heart, so she had rough sex with him daily. One day she rode him ridiculously hard during sex and he began having breathing problems. She continued riding him hard and put a pillow on his face and smothered him to death. He came and went at the same time. It looked like he had a heart attack. After his death, the rest was easy. Leticia transferred the money from Victor's secret account and put it in her dead husband's name she had legal access to and then put the money in her name in Belize and other banks across the country. Now, she was worth ten billion legal dollars and needed a plan to invest it. After thinking and studying for weeks what business she wanted to get involved in, it came to her. A large five-star hotel and casino combined, offering the best of services and accommodations in the world.

Leticia was very smart and highly skilled in martial arts from years of training in Belize. A pretty woman alone in Belize had to be able to take care of herself. She traveled to other countries to study their different fighting techniques. Leticia favored, *Systema,* Russian martial art that includes hand-to-hand combat, grappling, knife, and firearms training. It focuses on breathing, relaxation, and fluidity of movement, as well as, utilizing an attacker's momentum against them to control the six body levers (elbows, knees, waist, ankles, and shoulders) through pressure point application and striking weapons applications.

It has become more and more popular among police and security forces, including the US Secret Service. Her favorite was knife fighting and she spent years studying and perfecting until she could fight blindfolded and kill several attackers at the same time. She had exceptional quickness and incredible speed with knives in her movements.

She knew her overall task would not be easy even with all her skills and abilities, so she recruited the best looking and highly skilled women she could find as her private security team. Leticia was now very smart, lethal, and extremely rich with a cold heart. Her heart was so full of pain and revenge she performed a blood oath, so private it could never be spoken again once it was done. It was perfect for what she was about to do, get close to Ron and Keith and destroy them, along with anything or anyone they love or cared about.

# CHAPTER SIX

*Double Team*

Leon and Carter watched Keith, Stacy, Ron, and the entire O'Neil family. They stood outside close to the club day and night. Not because they physically had to but it was their desire and the main objective, corrupt and destroy the O'Neil family along with anyone attached to them and whoever got in their way.

With the spirit of darkness possessing them, Leon and Carter could not lose. They went to Vegas the same day of being possessed and Carter started playing Blackjack as Leon stood next to him. He was dressed in dress shoes, slacks, and a dress shirt and Leon wore all black holding his cane and pouch. After six hours of playing, they walked away from the table with stacks of chips to the cash-out window. They left with a six-hundred and twenty-thousand-dollar check. That was the beginning of them making money going from casino to casino until they had over eight million dollars.

They moved out to Brandywine, MD, and purchased an old large five-bedroom house on three acres and was close to a graveyard, just what they wanted. In the driveway were two black Bentleys, two pickup trucks, and two dump trucks. They also purchased sixty acres of commercially zoned land in Brandywine and started an aluminum and steel recycling business called. *Your Choice Recycle LLC.*

Carter continued to gamble until he made over twenty million dollars which they used to finance their business. They purchased all the necessary equipment and hired people that knew the business and had a good marketing team. Word spread fast, and trucks, cars, and people came to their site daily with so much aluminum and steel they had to buy more and larger equipment to recycle everything. The business made a fortune in a short period of time, but all this was part of their plan to get next to Keith and Ron and destroy them. They needed a legal business as a front to do business with them. Their motto, *embrace your enemy as a friend, build trust, and then destroy them.* This is how the devil works.

They had forty employees, and all was going well until several workers began complaining they were being worked too hard. Leon and Carter called the eight workers that were complaining into their office. Leon threw his bones at them and their bodies exploded on fire immediately and he gave Carter his cane and he pulled the sword out and cut them into pieces. The workers screamed and ran around the office on fire. Blood and body parts were scattered throughout the office when all was done. A women's head laid on the floor and Leon kicked it and it hit the wall and exploded into a pile of worms. Carter looked around the room and shook his head.

"Look at this mess. Stupid fools complained about making money, now they are dead and going to hell, greedy bastards."

Leon mumbled some words and stomped his foot, smoke engulfed the entire room, and when it cleared all the blood and body parts were gone.

"Damn, I love all this power and sending people to hell, I love it." He laughed and looked at Carter. "We will tell the other employees the complainers quit and left and kill anyone else that complains."

They started laughing. There was a company meeting the next day and the employees were told the eight workers quit. No worker complained after that and business increased quickly.

Three o'clock in the morning smoke appeared in front of Ron's and Keith's houses and Carter and Leon stood there looking. They spoke at the same time and pointed at each house.

"Hell has been unleashed, it's coming, and its name is Death."

Carter held his hand out in front of his eyes and hit himself in the back of his head and his eyeballs came out and landed in his hand. He threw them at Ron's house and the eyeballs shook the house when they hit it.

Ron and Diana slept close to each other when the house shook and they sat straight up in bed sweating.

Leon mumbled some words and threw bones at Keith's house and they too shook the house.

Keith and Stacy were wrapped in each other arms when their house shook, and they sat straight up in bed sweating.

Carter's eyes floated back in his head, and he started laughing and pointed at the house then disappeared in a cloud of black smoke. Leon mumbled some words and started laughing while pointing at the house. Smoke came from underneath his feet surrounding his body and he disappeared in the smoke.

# CHAPTER SEVEN
*Keith's House*

**K**eith has an eight-foot metal fence around his entire house and a long driveway leading to the front. The front exterior of his house is stone, and the other three sides are brick. There is a large deck and swimming pool in the back with a large pool house and a grill area with an overhang. The area could easily seat twenty people.

It is mid-June, and the weather is a nice eighty degrees. Keith and Ron sat at a table by the pool area grilling steaks, lobster, and pork chops, with white potatoes wrapped in aluminum foil slow cooking. They wore sandals, sweatpants, and a short-sleeved shirt sitting in the shade and discussing business.

Stacy and Diana walked out of the house toward the pool area carrying two different salads and homemade iced tea. When Keith and Ron saw the girls coming, they stopped talking and stared at them. Their eyes were captivated by the raw sexiness of these two women. Stacy and Diana were so exotic looking they would make anyone lust. They wore Doogie Fun Apparel sandals, short tops showing toned stomachs, and tight shorts. They placed everything on the table and Stacy sat in Keith's lap and Diana sat in Ron's, they started kissing. Stacy was grinding hard on Keith purposely teasing and getting him aroused. Diana was laughing and kissing Ron when they looked up and saw what Stacy was doing to Keith in his chair.

"Stacy, you and Keith do have bedrooms for all that grinding you are doing. We are grilling and relaxing not having an outside sex party." Diana said, and laughed.

"Speak on it baby. You two need to go in the house if your hormones are raging that hard." Ron said as he leaned back in his chair and held Diana.

Stacy kissed Keith slow and passionately and then looked at Diana and Ron.

"The last time I checked this is my house and grinding on my husband is a regular." She pointed at them. "You two need to mind your own business and do your own grinding." She stuck her tongue out at them.

"That's what I am talking about. Tell them again baby. It's booty grinding time." Keith laughed.

"Yeah, maybe but you two are nasty anyway." Ron said.

Keith kissed Stacy and caressed her leg then looked at them.

"True that but the best part about all this is we got a license to grind and be nasty," Keith and Stacy said at the same time. "We married now." They kissed and looked at each other smiling.

Stacy stood and walked over to the grill.

"Well, I need to check this meat before you two men burn it by getting distracted from all this grinding. Speaking of grinding, Diana you can't point the finger at me. What about you and your tight shorts showing your butt cheeks and grinding on Ron. Poor baby, I know he's ready to bust."

"Stacy, you are something else with your nasty filthy mouth. However, I would never dress like this in public, I am a Christian and a queen, and some things are for my baby's eyes only." She kissed Ron and hugged him while still sitting on his lap.

"I respect that, but you are still an undercover closet freak." Keith said and started laughing.

Diana looked at Keith and rolled her eyes at him then she and Ron stood and he grabbed her hand.

"Hold it baby. Don't go off on the brother. Pray for him sister, pray."

Suddenly, the grill started shaking and a large flame of fire shot up from the grill. Stacy screamed and jumped back quickly and walked toward Keith who was standing. The grill rose twelve feet in the air and exploded sending food, flames, and metal pieces everywhere. Ron, Diana, Keith, and Stacy hit the ground. The water in the pool started bubbling and became boiling hot. They stood up, looked around, and stared at the water.

"In the name of Jesus, what in the world is going on?" Diana said.

Ron walked closer to the pool and looked at the water.

"I think I know but it can't be, no way!" He turned around and looked at Diana, Stacy, and Keith.

"No!" Diana yelled. "This can't be happening. Lord, what is going on? Not again. We all need to pray."

A large cloud of black smoke appeared in the yard twenty feet from them. Out of habit, Keith reached into his waist for his guns but he gave that up and Stacy reached into her shorts for her razor, but it was not there.

Leon and Carter appeared after the smoke dissipated. Leon wore all black holding his cane and pouch and Carter was dressed in all black. His eyes were so red they were on fire in his sockets shooting out small flames of fire.

Diana pointed at them.

"In the name of Jesus."

"In the name of Jesus." Ron said.

Without thinking, Keith ran toward Leon and Carter but when he was within arms distance, Carter's eyes spat fire towards him temporarily blinding Keith. Carter smacked Keith so hard it lifted him off his feet and he landed on the ground unconscious.

"Keith!" Stacy yelled and ran over to him and kneeled and began shaking him. "Keith, are you alright? Wake up baby." She stood up quickly and looked at Leon and Carter with rage.

Ron grabbed two chairs and threw one at Carter and the other at Leon. Leon pointed his cane at the chairs, mumbled some words and the chairs stop moving in midair and began melting towards the ground. He pointed his cane at Ron.

"You young foolish boy. Have you not learned anything? You can't fight spiritual warfare with material things."

"Who are you two and what do you want?" Diana yelled.

Ron walked closer to them.

"I don't know who they are, but I know what they are. Two bodies doing the devil's work. I have done battle with you and God destroyed you."

Leon pointed his cane at Ron again.

"You are so dumb boy. You were used to kill the body but you cannot kill the spirit, you dumb foolish boy. Now there are two of us and this time, we will have no mercy. You and your whole family will die boy. Time is short and hell has been unleashed to kill and destroy every damn body, burn baby burn."

Carter spat towards Stacy, and it landed close to her feet.

"That is how I feel about you, sorry dick sucking, pussy licking slut. Yeah, I know all about your freakish ways. You ran to God and he spared your life but this time before we are finished, you will be on the corner selling your ass just to eat," he spat towards Diana and it landed close to her feet as well. "Diana, we are going to possess your body turning you into the

ass licking freak you are, then we will kill you, fake Christian."
He stared at her.

"Shut up devil, hold thy peace." Ron said.

Leon mumbled some words and waved his hand through the air which made a loud smacking sound. Ron, Diana, and Stacy were smacked so hard they were lifted off their feet and landed on the ground unconscious.

Carter shook his head laughing.

"I like that. Can we kill them now? Damn, I want to kill them. I hate praying, faith-believing people. Time to go to hell everybody."

Leon turned toward him and waved his hand.

"No, not now it's too early for that. We must torture all of them first and make their life a living hell. We will send various demonic spirits their way. Sadness, depression, hopelessness, doubt, strong lust spirits, and finally thoughts of death." He walked over and spat on all four of them speaking curses at the same time. "Demonic lust to your mind, body, and soul." He started laughing.

"I like that. The fury of hell is coming."

Leon tapped his cane on his leg and smoke appeared then he and Carter disappeared in the smoke.

# CHAPTER EIGHT

*Coming together*

Ron, Diana, Keith, and Stacy laid on the ground unconscious. Zechariah was at Sheila's house and Jazz music was playing, and they sat on the sofa next to each other. They finished eating fried chicken, mashed potatoes, collard greens, and corn bread.

Zechariah looked at Sheila and smiled.

"What are you smiling so hard for?   Am I missing something?"

Zechariah shook his head, picked up Sheila's hand gently and kissed it and put it back down.

"No, you are not missing anything. I am smiling for several reasons. I am sitting here and not in prison, which is wonderful. You are a great cook, and I am enjoying your company very much. And for the record, you are a very attractive lady."

Sheila lowered her head then looked at him.

"Zechariah, you have so much to be thankful for. And I must admit, I am drawn to you for various reasons but please take it slow with me. I know David has been dead for many years, but he was the only man I have known. He was my best friend besides God.  Now here you are, and I feel like a schoolgirl being courted by her high school sweetheart." She smiled at him.

"Sheila, I understand, and in no way will I put any pressure on you. We are not in high school, but we can have a courtship taking things one day at a time. We were connected by the act of God so there is no need to rush into anything because we will become closer, and things will naturally happen as the spirit of God moves."

"I agree with all you said and we must be careful and very honest with each other. You have not been with a woman in a long time, and I have not been with another man since David. Yes, I can feel the strong spiritual and physical attraction between us. So, we have to be careful with our affections toward one another".

"True that. You keep a brother praying. Sheila, you have a very nice figure, and you are sexy."

"Thank you for the compliment but you can't focus..."
Before Sheila could finish her sentence, Zechariah leaned over and kissed Sheila on the lips. This caught her off guard and her first instinct were to pull away and slap him, but his lips felt so good and her emotions became overwhelming. Without thinking about it, she kissed him back and opened her mouth to allow their tongues to taste each other. It has been so long since Sheila felt this way. She moved closer and put her arm around his neck and kissed this man with a passion that has been buried deep within her for years. He was such a good kisser and feeling his tongue in her mouth was making her body hot, until a moan escaped her lips. Sheila became caught up in the moment and rubbed his leg until she felt his erection. She pulled away immediately and lowered her head in shame.

Zechariah enjoyed Sheila's warm mouth and touch, causing him to become aroused quickly. Now, he felt embarrassed for her and himself. He lifted her head slowly.

"Sheila, please look at me. I apologize for getting caught up in the moment, we both did at the same time, but I am not going to beat myself up about it. We are two adults who have feelings and desires. Yes, they need to be kept in check but do not ask me to pretend I am not sexually attracted to you because I am. I will respect you, okay?" He leaned closer kissed her on the cheek. "Are we good?"

"Yes Zechariah, we are good and on the same page," she exhaled and looked at him. "I have to be prayerful and careful around you." She smiled and kissed him on the cheek.

Grandma Harris pulled up in Sheila's driveway in her Lexus SUV and saw a new S550 Benz. She smiled knowing it belonged to Zechariah and it pleased her knowing he and Sheila were getting to know each other better. She had a good feeling about him and wanted Sheila to have a good man in life after losing David so early in their relationship. She got out and knocked on Sheila's door and walked in. She saw Sheila and Zechariah sitting on the sofa.

"Good afternoon Sheila and Zechariah. You two look real cozy sitting on that sofa and I smell food. Sheila, you cooked for this man? What else did you do for him," she said smiling, "you two did not go back in the bedroom and do the nasty did you and come out here and sit on the sofa like nothing happened? Sheila O'Neil, did you give up some kitty cat?" She laughed and sat on the sofa across from them.

Sheila shook her head because she was used to her smart comments and nasty mouth.

"Grandma Harris, hello to you and just walk into my house, why don't you? I see some things do not change; your mouth is still dirty. No, we did no such thing, and you know it, so stop being carnally minded."

"Hello Grandma Harris. It is always good to see you."

She pointed her finger at him.

"It is good to see you baby. I know it has been a long time for you but do not come over here trying to get into Sheila's panties. God does not like ugly so keep your hands to yourself and do not rub on her butt either. I saw you looking at it." She laughed.

"Grandma Harris, don't you have any shame for what comes out of your mouth especially being a Christian woman?" Sheila said with a serious attitude.

Grandma Harris waved her hand at Sheila.

"Child please, you better be glad God smiled on you and sent you a good man. You know you want him to rub on your booty. It has been years since you had that booty rubbed. Oh, and I noticed Zechariah has big hands too," she looked up, "Lord Jesus help me." She looked at Sheila and Zechariah and leaned back on the sofa and started laughing hard.

# CHAPTER NINE

*Keith's House*

**K**eith, Stacy, Ron, and Diana laid on the ground unconscious and there was a very foul odor in the air. Keith woke up first, raised his head slowly and looked around seeing everyone else on the ground. Diana laid on her side in the fetal position, not far from Keith and her thong underwear, and a portion of her butt was exposed. Keith's stared at Diana's butt and became aroused and whispered to himself.

"Damn, she got ass."

Stacy woke up and heard what Keith said. She looked around and noticed how Keith stared at Diana's butt and saw the outline of his erection on his sweatpants. Keith turned his head and saw Stacy looking at him, but no words were exchanged, just the look of anger from her. Ron and Diana woke up and everyone stood up and looked around in total amazement at what took place. Keith walked over to Stacy.

"Baby, are you alright, are you hurt?"

With everything that took place the only thing Stacy could focus on right now is how Keith stared at Diana's butt and became aroused. The look of disgust she gave Keith spoke for itself. She stepped closer and spoke softly to him.

"No, Keith I am not alright," she turned her head to look around the yard and up in the air. "What is that horrible smell?" She looked at Keith and bit her lip with emotions of controlled anger. "The damn devil attacked us and all your nasty dirty mind can focus on is Diana's butt crack and your dick got hard. God, I can't believe you. You better be glad I gave my life to Jesus."

Keith moved closer to Stacy and whispered in her ear.

"Keep your voice down. I woke up and happened to see her butt exposed and got hard, so what. It is a natural reaction, so stop making a big deal out of it and let's focus on what happened to us. You are something else you know that."

Stacy snapped and without thinking she grabbed Keith's dick and squeezed it hard.

Keith's grimaced with pain.

"Ahhhh, are you crazy? Let my dick go, you ain't acting like a Christian wife."

"Shut up, who do you think you're talking to? Stop looking at Diana's ass, Christian husband." She looked at him with disdain and then let his penis go.

Ron walked over to Diana, they hugged and held each other then walked towards Keith and Stacy holding hands. Ron discerned something was not right with them and Diana noticed it as well. He put his hand on Keith's shoulder.

"My brother, are you two okay?"

"Yeah, partner we are fine, all things considered."

Stacy was still in her feelings and looked at Keith with anger then gave Ron a fake smile.

"Yes Ron, we are lovely." She turned to look at Keith, rolled her eyes at him, then hugged Diana.

They all walked into the house and sat down in the living room exhausted. Ron and Diana were on one sofa and Keith and Stacy on the other. Keith wanted peace with his wife, so he kissed her lips, and as angry as Stacy was at him, his touch always affected her as it did now. The love for him caused her to give in and she kissed him back with heart-felt passion and desire.

Diana shook her head when she looked at them.

"Are you two kidding me? Is that all you can think of right now, sex? Truly unbelievable. The devil attacked and almost killed us but no big deal for you two. Let's come in the house and have sex. Don't you ever get enough? Good God."

"Don't be a hater Diana." Stacy stuck her tongue out at her then grabbed Keith's hand, and they walked away.

"Where are you two going? We need to talk." Ron said.

"Partner, this day has been a nightmare. I know we need to talk but we need to release some stress. You two make yourself at home and do whatever." He kissed Stacy. "Come on baby." They walked toward their bedroom but Stacy turned her head to the side, looked back, caressed her butt, and winked at them.

Ron watched Stacy's every step and had lustful thoughts. Diana noticed but said nothing to him because she was fighting her inner lust demons. They continued watching them walk away then looked at each other in total amazement.

"Ron, I love and desire you tremendously but there is a time and place for everything. First, I can't believe what happened outside, and now these two act like dogs in heat and seem oblivious to what happened."

The moment Keith and Stacy entered the room and closed the door, Keith kicked his sandals off, snatched his sweatpants and underwear off, and stood there staring at Stacy with a hard dick. He began sliding his hand back and forth on his dick.

"You know I am sprung, and I am about to put all kinds of dick in you." He continued stroking his dick while smiling.

Stacy looked at him like he lost his mind.

"What! What in the world is all kinds of dick Keith? Boy, you have lost..."

RONALD GRAY                                                    37

Keith grabbed Stacy and pulled off her sweatpants and underwear. They looked at each other with lust burning in their heart. Stacy kneeled and started sucking Keith's dick like it was the best tasting lollipop in the world. She licked, tasted, caressed, and sucked his dick while stroking it back and forth, and then used her mouth with such skill it would make a man pay all her bills, and more. Keith was in another world and knew he couldn't hold back much longer, so he grabbed Stacy by the shoulders and moved her body facing the wall. Stacy knew what was coming as she braced herself with her hands. Keith put his hands on Stacy's hips and slid inside her. This was not making love, this was straight fucking each other to the physical limit and they held nothing back. All you heard was their loud moaning, screaming, and Diana's hands hitting the wall at times from such intense pleasure. For the first time, Keith pictured Diana's ass as he slid in and out of Stacy. He felt bad but this did not make him stop.

Diana and Ron heard Keith and Stacy and it was not long before they were naked and going at each other like they were in heat. Ron had Diana bent over the sofa making her climax continually as he slid inside her. He thought about Stacy's hot body and Diana had images of Stacy's face and warm tongue between her legs each time Ron brought her to orgasm.

For the next two hours, all four explored each other sexually in so many different positions until exhaustion caught up with them. Ron and Diana ended up in one of the other bedrooms. They took a shower and laid down to rest, then prayed, repenting to themselves for their evil thoughts because the guilt was overwhelming. Keith and Stacy did the same and the house was finally quiet.

A mist came into the house and slid under their bedroom doors and landed on Diana's and Stacy's chest as they slept. Both had nightmares of perverted sexual acts. An hour later they woke up and walked quietly out of their bedrooms naked and closed the door behind them. Neither said a word, they kissed, hugged, and caressed each other's body slowly with passions thought to be long gone. As they looked into each other's eyes when caressing each other, they spoke at the same time.

"Soon."

For the next ten minutes, they kissed and their hands caressed one another's body completely. Tears flowed from their eyes because of guilt but they seemed unable to stop. They climaxed simultaneously while kissing and fingering one another and then walked back into their bedrooms and closed the door. They laid next to their husbands and prayed as tears flowed from their eyes, each wondering, *how did this happen.*

# CHAPTER TEN

*Church*

It was a beautiful Sunday morning, and the spirit of peace was felt throughout the church. As the choir sang, people were coming in clapping their hands to the music as the ushers were seating them. Sheila, Zechariah, and Grandma Harris sat together and embraced the joyful spirit and music. Ron and Diana drove up in their Bentley, Keith and Stacy drove up in their Bentley, and Cynthia, Shantai, and Tonya drove up in their new company rented C300 Benz. All three of them sat together. Sheila and Zechariah visually flirted with each other like teenagers in love and Grandma Harris noticed all this and loved it. She wanted things to work out for them and felt they would. Rick walked in and sat behind Cynthia and as a polite jester he tapped her on the shoulder. Cynthia turned around and smiled at him, but Shantai gave Rick a dirty look because she knew what happened between them and did not desire Cynthia to go back to her old ways. She wanted her to stay focused on serving God. Rick ignored her mean look and smiled at her. The church was full now and everyone was seated.

Pastor Williams walked up to the pulpit clapping his hands and praising God. He raised his hands for everyone to stand.

"Good morning everyone and to God is the glory. Can I get an Amen church?"

"Amen." The church said.

Pastor Williams made a jester for everyone to be seated.

"I am glad and blessed to see all of you wonderful people this morning. You are in the right place at the right time. Now, I am sure some of you ladies in here were in the club last night twerking and dropping your body like it's hot and all that. And I am sure some of you men in here were in the club last night watching the ladies and trying to get your Mack on. Well, be that as it may, that was then, and this is now. It's time to get your praise on and give God his due. The fact is, every second of the day it is time to give God his due. Amen to that. Now in the times we live in, we all deal with various life temptations to distract us from living the life that God desires for us to live. After you submit to the will of God the devil will still try and use anyone and anything to pull you back to your old ways."

Shantai could not help but look at Cynthia when the pastor said that, but Cynthia rolled her eyes at her and pinched her on the leg. Shantai jumped and pinched her back. Tonya saw all this and leaned over and whispered to them.

"You two grow up and stop playing in church."

Pastor Williams continued to bring forth his message.

"My subject for today is, God will reveal who and whatever you are. Coming from the book of Luke, Chapter 12, verses 2 and 3. And it reads as such, *For there is nothing covered that shall not be revealed, neither hid that shall not be known. Therefore, whatsoever ye have spoken in darkness shall be heard in the light, and that which you have spoken in the ear in closets shall be proclaimed upon the housetops.* To make this simple for everyone, I know there are some very slick-talking, fast-moving people in this world but the fact is, the real you, will be revealed to all and you could never fool God. Get healed and delivered today. Do not leave here the same way you came in, in Christ or out."

The pastor continued preaching and then invited the congregation to the alter. What he did not know was on this very morning, God had a master plan to do only what he can do, Deliver souls. Today there would be many. Fifty people came up for alter call, including Ron, Keith, Diana, Stacy, Shantai, Cynthia, Tonya, and Rick. All desired a closer walk with God and to feel His Holy touch. The Pastor did not expect so many and his heart was overwhelmingly touched. He and the entire ministry team were praying for people. Some were praising God while others were going through their spiritual deliverance time. The devil was busy trying to keep people spiritually bound but he is no match for the power of God. This deliverance service went on for over an hour until everyone was touched by the hand of God and received great blessings. Later, after the church service was over, Pastor went to his office to spend quality time with the Lord in prayer because he felt so much evil when praying for some of the people. He knew some of them were about to enter the fight of their life and he felt some strong lust spirits oppressing Stacy, Diana, Ron, and Keith. So, he decided to protect them all through intercessory prayer continually because he knew they would need it soon

# CHAPTER ELEVEN

*The Battle of Evils*

With the amount of money Leticia Wilson had she could live anywhere in the world. She purchased a twenty-million-dollar, 35,000 square foot, six-car garage, twelve-bedroom house on seven acres in Potomac, Maryland. This house was beyond luxurious and had every amenity you could want, including an indoor and outdoor pool. There were six, white 2015 Rolls-Royce Phantoms in her garage. One for her and each security team member. She lives with her five-person security team, and they go everywhere and do everything together, including martial arts training five days a week. When Leticia was not traveling by car she traveled on her private hundred-million-dollar plane and 200-ft mega yacht. She could travel anywhere in the world at any time with just a phone call, her staff was on twenty-four-hour call seven days a week.

She researched finding the right location to have her mega hotel-casino built and chose Brandywine, MD. It was close to Leon and Carter's recycling business. She wanted to own it only because of the land and its proximity to her chosen sixty-acre site for the casino. Even with all her money and connections, she knew getting rid of Leon and Carter would not be an easy task. Leticia was fully aware of who or shall we say what they were and their powers. But did not care because they walked around in the flesh, and all flesh could be destroyed. You destroy the flesh and allow the spirits oppressing or possessing the body to have you. If she could accomplish this, it would make her unstoppable and put her on the path to do anything at any time. Destroying Ron and Keith would be a walk in the park.

Leticia made an appointment to see Leon and Carter at the recycling plant on a Sunday when they were closed so there would be no witnesses to what she planned to do. She knew defeating these two directly would be impossible without some type of distraction, so she arranged for two of her security members to leave early. They laid on the rooftop of a building a mile away from the recycle plant, each holding an Accuracy International's L115A3 sniper rifle with custom-designed explosive bullets.

Leticia and her three other security members drove to the site in a white stretch Benz limo. They stepped out of the limo, wearing white pants and jackets. Leon and Carter were dressed in all black, holding canes. The women walked towards them with Leticia in front. Leon and Carter looked at the women and laughed, considering them to be nothing but dumb pretty females.

"So, miss Wilson, I understand you desire to have our land and business. You should have stayed away from us and enjoyed your very wealthy lifestyle. You and your playmates are just another piece of ass for men and women to enjoy, nothing more and you mean nothing to me." Leon said as he looked at them with hate.

"I came here to discuss business with you two, but you chose to insult me because you believe you are the superior ones. This attitude has been the downfall for so many people. Now, can we act like civilized people and talk please." Leticia said smiling while she and the others walked closer to them.

"It is a shame to kill such beautiful women, but this will be the first day of the rest of your lives. You sorry pussy and ass licking sluts. Time to go to hell." Carter said then spat on Leticia, leaned his head back, and laughed.

Carter and Leon mumbled some words and pulled swords from their canes. The two women on the roof watched all this and the moment they pulled their swords out, they pulled the trigger and hit both in the back. The bullets exploded their mid sections on impact, and with incredible speed, Leticia and the other three women pulled knives from their jackets and lunged forward, and stabbed Leon and Carter in both of their eyes. What happened next was almost a blur. The women pulled two more knives out and stabbed Carter and Leon twenty times in five seconds. With a hole in their midsection and multiple stabbed wounds, Leon and Carter were still standing and alive and their wounds begin to quickly heal. All four of the women took two steps back and got on one knee. Leticia looked up and shook her head. The two women on the roof fired two more shots hitting Leon and Carter in the head which exploded on impact. Their bodies were still standing holding their canes and Leticia snatched both canes and sliced their bodies into several pieces.

The four women looked at the bloody mess and laughed at their unbelievable conquest, but the laughing came to a halt when the wind suddenly begins to blow hard, the sky turned a dark grey, and lightning begins to strike the ground around them. Wolves appeared out of nowhere and ran towards them but the women on the roof never left their post. They started shooting the wolves one by one in the head killing all thirteen of them. The sky cleared, and the winds and lightning stopped. Leticia looked down and saw two eyeballs on the ground for which she felt compelled to pick up. Seconds later her body felt like it was on fire, and she started screaming. One of the three women slapped Leticia hard in the back of her head and her eyeballs popped out and hit the ground. Leticia put the eyeballs in her hand in her eye sockets.

Leticia's body shook and looked like she was having convulsions and she screamed from pain as she has never experienced. The three women stepped back and looked at her, but they felt no fear. Leticia stopped shaking and screaming feeling power like she has never known in her life. It was far beyond all her deep meditation and martial arts training. Holding the cane, she raised it high in the air.

"You can kill the body but not the spirit. The spirit of Mr. Bones is back and in me. Long live Mr. Bones. I am back, I am back." She yelled repeatedly.

The two women on the roof saw all this but said nothing to each other as they left the roof and ran towards them. All five women stood in front of Leticia. She walked towards each lady mumbling words and kissed each one with passion then stepped back and looked at them. The five women said at the same time.

"We serve you as you serve the spirit of Mr. Bones." Each lady kissed Leticia again.

"I thank each one of you for your discipline and loyalty. Now that I have the spirit of Mr. Bones, we will be unstoppable. Time to go ladies," she looked around and laughed then looked at the women. "All this and so much more will be ours to run and control. Look out world, the trained killers are coming, and we are fucking men and women, licking pussy, ass, sucking dick, taking dick in the ass, telling lies, and tricking you straight to hell. This is what the devil does." The women laughed as they walked to the limo and drove away.

Four wolves came from the woods and ate the body parts of Leon and Carter until nothing was left, not even one drop of blood on the ground. The wolves began howling and ran back into the woods.

# CHAPTER TWELVE

*Two Years Later/ Leticia's Grand Opening*

It was a beautiful spring night and Brandywine Maryland will never be the same because of what Leticia Wilson, her security team, and the best lawyer's money can buy were able to get accomplished despite all the negativity she experienced. Today was the grand opening of, *Leticia's Palace,* the most luxurious twenty-four-hour hotel/casino in the Nation. Many wealthy businesspeople, politicians, and government officials worked against her because of jealousy and control. Those she could not buy, seduce, bribe, or blackmail she killed in various ways making every death look like a timely accident.

The sixty acres of land the recycled plant sat on was torn down and Leticia purchased forty more acres next to it and it became her hotel/casino site. Building permits that would normally take years to get approved, was approved in weeks, getting the land re-zoned to mixed-use took years sometimes. It took Leticia one month. No one knew, including her lawyers, exactly how she was able to get so much done so fast, but people had their suspicions. But no one dared to talk about it. Leticia was named, the untouchable business woman, that treated everyone like VIP, until you crossed her. She was able to get a seven-day, twelve-hours-a-day construction labor approval, which is how she finished construction in only two years. The company created 4,000 full-time jobs and 1,500 part-time jobs. There were no outside funds used for this project from the city or state which was another way she bypassed political red tape and hold-ups. Leticia invested two billion dollars of her own money.

*Leticia's Palace* has forty floors, 350ft high, and 7,500 rooms with rates from $180 to $20,000 per night. It offered limo, helicopter, and private jet service, three lounges, exquisite restaurants, clothing stores, and offered more table games and slot machines than any casino in the country. The hotel offered twenty-four-hour concierge service and massages. If the *Palace* did not have it, they would get it for you, and quickly with a smile. Company policy.

You saw the lights shining on the hotel from miles away. Camera crews and various news station representatives were all over the place. People came by the thousands from other states and countries to attend this two-week grand opening. Leticia was determined this was not going to be a typical hotel/casino grand opening, so she contacted the most elite private adult escort services around the world. The best-looking women and men in the business had their travel fare paid by Leticia's staff to stay in town for two weeks. A total of ten thousand escorts ranging from $250hr to $500hr to $1,500 to $20,000 per night with Leticia getting forty percent of every transaction. Every hotel in the DMV area was booked. Using social media and other media outlets, the word was out internationally concerning this event and the people came.

This was not just a grand opening but a place of total euphoria to the highest level. Two tons of marijuana and cocaine were shipped in. The best lodging, sex, and drugs, for the next two weeks, compliments of Miss Leticia Wilson. During the grand opening, between the gambling, sex, and drugs, Leticia made five-hundred-million dollars.

After two weeks of being persistent, Keith and Ron talked Diana and Stacy into visiting the hotel but said they would not go into the casino. On this Saturday night, all of them were dressed to impress. Diana and Stacy's clothes were not as revealing or tight because of their commitment to the Lord but they looked nice. They drove up in front of the hotel in Keith's Bentley and gave the keys to the valet. As they walked into the lobby of the hotel, they had to admit to being impressed, the place was beautifully decorated in every way. Although they lived in mansions, they checked into the hotel in two, $1,500 a night large suites. Stacy, Keith, Ron, and Diana walked away from the desk and saw Leticia Wilson and five other women walking towards them. The five women wore white business dress suits and Leticia wore a white dress that hugged her curves with a long slit on the side. All the women were very attractive, but Leticia was definitely a FULL SEVEN, stunningly gorgeous in every way. Keith could not help from lusting over her and whispered.

"She is fine."

Stacy elbowed him in the side and looked at him like he was crazy, and then whispered to him.

"I heard that Keith. Don't forget who I am, and who you are, Christian husband."

Keith looked at her and smiled. Ron and Diana looked at them both and shook their heads. Leticia walked closer.

"Mr. Ron O'Neil, his wife Diana and Mr. Keith Washington and his wife Stacy. It is a pleasure to finally meet the proteges of the legendary Victor Augular. I hope you all enjoy your stay at the Palace and if you should need anything, please don't hesitate to inform anyone at the concierge services. Whatever you desire, is yours at the Palace. Today, for all of you while in the casino, there are no limits at the tables, and I will gladly extend you a line of credit if you so desire." She stared at Keith.

Stacy wanted to leap on this lady and beat her down because she felt the strong seducing spirit coming from her and did not like how she stared at Keith. She prayed and God gave her peace in her mind and spirit.

"You seem to know a lot about us Miss Wilson, the past that is." Ron spoke with boldness as he looked at her with confidence in Christ.

"Thank you for your invitation but we will not be gambling. We are here to relax and enjoy this lavish hotel you have built." Stacy said with an attitude.

"Well, I appreciate your visit and please enjoy yourself," she and her security team stared at them then walked away but Leticia stopped walking and turned around and looked directly at Stacy. "Sometimes, a person may not know what they want until it is offered to them. And here at the Palace, we offer so much more, enjoy." She walked away exuding sexuality with such grace, making sure to shake extra with each step. Her dress hugged her ample hips and butt and she did not have any underwear on.

Keith and Ron could not help but stare at her body when she walked away. Stacy and Diana looked at them stare at her. They stood directly in front of them and spoke at the same time with attitude.

"What are you two looking at?" Their expressions revealed anger.

"I felt that woman's evil spirit, and she is very nasty. She was purposely shaking her body and walking nasty so everyone could see she had no underwear on. Nasty trifling dog. Diana looked up. "Lord Jesus, keep me this night so I don't snap on my husband."

"Amen to that sister," Stacy stared at Keith feeling her anger increasing. "Hold me Lord so I don't have a flashback."

Keith and Ron looked at each other as if reading one another's thoughts, they did the same thing at the same time. Both grabbed Diana and Stacy by the waist and pulled them closer and kissed them.

Diana and Stacy were caught off guard but kissed them back and then smacked them playfully and walked away.

"Come on Stacy, let's go see what clothing stores are in this place," they continued walking away and winked at each other, knowing what they were about to do. They put an extra shake in their walk to purposely teas their husbands.

Ron and Keith looked at each other and smiled.

"Partner we have been blessed with the best women in the world and thank God for them but Miss Leticia Wilson is all that."

"As you would say Keith, she is a FULL SEVEN walking, but so are our wives."

"Amen to that my brother."

They laughed and walked quickly to catch up with their wives, kissing them and putting their arms around their waist.

Leticia was in the main security room with her team watching the monitors. Every angle of the Palace on every floor could be seen on one of the monitors. She saw Ron, Diana, Keith, and Stacy walking into one of the many clothing stores and zoomed in on Diana and Stacy.

"Very nice and I am going to get them both by divide and conquer and Mr. Ron will suffer greatly. Ladies, listen to me. Yes, I know all the details of Ron's life. His birth, his unbelievable release from prison, and the chosen call on his life he tried to run from. His involvement with Victor Augular almost got him killed. Now, he, his wife, Keith, Stacy, and some of their friends rededicated their life to God. But we are going to separate them by using the woman to weaken the men. We turn the women out after we weaken their faith and then destroy them all. We are going to see just how much they love the Lord and how protected this Ron O'Neil is. In the meantime, we will make money and have fun." She hugged and kissed each of them and they looked at one another shaking their heads and smiled.

Ron, Keith, Stacy, and Diana walked around the hotel admiring the beautiful artwork and decorations. Diana and Stacy wanted to do some shopping but Keith started complaining and Ron co-signed it. So, they went to Keith and Stacy's hotel suite to relax. Keith wanted to see the casino, but he knew Stacy would not want to and Diana would never go for it, so he gave Ron a specific look and nod they always understood.

"Diana, let's go to our room and leave these two married people to handle their business."

She looked at Keith then at Ron.

"No problem baby but I think you and Keith are up to something but let's go." She walked over to Stacy and hugged her.

"I know they are up to something Diana and I saw that look they gave each other but no matter because as soon as you two leave, I will be rocking my husband's body. Believe that." She looked at Keith and smiled.

Diana waved her hand in Stacy's face.

"Too much information my sister. Bye, you two." She grabbed Ron's hand and they walked out.

# CHAPTER THIRTEEN
*The Set Up*

$R$on and Diana were in their hotel suite taking a shower, playing, and washing one another and then they began making love. Because of the powerful spiritual connection, the chemistry, and the bond they have for one another, each time they made love was always beautiful and emotionally explosive. Ron always made sure his wife's needs came first and were satisfied. While the warm water cascaded over them, their kissing and caressing only intensified their desire. Not only to sexually satisfy their burning fire within but to touch each other's mind, spirit, and soul. Diana loved her husband beyond words and often meditated on what it took to bring them together. The various trials and tribulations and all the prayers but everything was worth it. They are husband and wife, bone of my bone and flesh of my flesh, they were one. Ron has Diana up against the wall holding one of her legs up, thrusting in and out of her. Diana's eyes were locked into his and enjoyed his every thrust. She put her arms around his neck and pulled him into her and kissed him with a spiritual passion that brought tears to her eyes.

"Ohhh Ron, baby I love you so much and you feel so good inside me. Please don't ever stop loving me. Ron, keep fucking me baby, ahhhhhh you are going to make me cum. Ahhhhhh, Ron, I am cummming baby, I'm cumming," she wrapped both of her legs around his waist as he held her up giving every ounce of her desires to him. Diana's body was trembling with satisfaction from such an explosive orgasm but her spiritual desire was much more. Ron put Diana's legs down and the moment her feet hit the shower floor he put his hands on her hips and tried to turn her around. Diana placed her hands on his chest. "No Ron, not like that. I want to see your face as you cum inside me," she began to cry. "I want a baby Ron. Give me a baby, please give me a baby."

Ron saw and felt his wife's overwhelming desire to share something priceless between them and this intensified his need for her. After he kissed Diana's lips ever so slowly they stepped out of the shower, he picked her up and carried her to bed and laid her down. His eyes engulfed her beauty.

"I love you deeply Diana." He kissed and licked her soft lips and his mouth left traces of his warm tongue on her neck, breasts, and stomach and then lifted her legs and kissed the inside of her legs until his tongue slid across her wetness. For the next hour, Ron tasted and licked every inch of Diana's body front and back. He sexually appreciated and positioned Diana on her stomach and back, and gripped her legs firmly as his mouth pressed between her legs. She climaxed several times and then laid there exhausted, but Ron was not finished because this was a night they would never forget. Diana had beautiful breasts and her nipples were sensitive to touch and he enjoyed taking advantage of them. Ron's hands caressed her breasts and licked them all over until his tongue dragged across her nipples slowly, repeatedly. Her moans motivated him to slid his finger inside her, moving it back and forth. He licked her juices off his finger and slid it back in, rotating and bending it repeatedly while it was inside her.

Diana was so extremely turned on by everything Ron did, it caused her to have several intense orgasms but knew she could not take much more and was close to another powerful orgasm.

She placed her hands on the side of his face and lifted it to look at him.

"Ron, I can't take anymore but I want you inside me. I want your seed inside me. Put a baby in me Ron and I will give you a son. Make love to me."

Their tongues met each other with fire. He slid down her body and penetrated her, never taking his eyes off hers as he began making love to Diana. His body moved slowly and Diana loved looking down seeing his dick move back and forth inside her.

"Yes Ron, it feels soooo good. Faster baby, fuck me Ron."

Their eyes touched emotionally and he lifted Diana's legs until her toes almost touched the headboard. Ron knew he was so close, so he pulled out and pressed his face between her legs and sucked on Diana's clit until her body jerked as she climaxed hard. He continued sucking as she covered his face with her juices.

"Ohhhhhhh Ron, now baby, now. Put it back in, please."

Ron smiled and gladly slid inside his beautiful wife with the desire to put every drop of his seed inside her.

"Ahhhh Diana, you are making me cum baby. You are so good, ahhhhh Diana."

"Yes, that's it. Don't stop Ron. I want it. I want your baby. I am cuming again Ron, ohhhhhhh."

Diana and Ron's eyes never left one another as they came simultaneously and gave each other all they had.

As Ron and Diana made love, Keith and Stacy enjoyed each other's company as well. Their desires for each other were equally as strong and loving. Keith's hands were underneath Stacy's butt, lifted her in the air, maneuvered each of her legs on his shoulders, placed her back against the wall, and buried his face between her legs. Stacy had three orgasms from Keith's skills but this was taking her over the edge and all she could do was place her hands on his shoulders and hold on. Stacy screamed so loud when climaxing, she could be heard from the hallway. Keith carried her to the bed and for the next thirty minutes, they kissed and made love until falling asleep from satisfaction and exhaustion. They woke hours later, and took a shower together and went to sleep.

What Keith, Stacy, Diana, and Ron did not know was, they were being watched from Leticia's Wilson private floor. The entire fortieth floor belonged to Leticia and her five personal bodyguards. Access required coded key, fingerprint, and voice command. This floor was specifically designed with the best security. The floor, walls, and ceilings had reinforced concrete with heat and vibration sensors. The windows were made of special layered plastic that looked like glass but could stop a round from a fifty-caliber rifle. The floor had a weapons room resembling what you would see on a military post. There were special fire, gas, and chemical protection measures and a private escape route known only to them. The designers of this floor were no longer alive. Each security team member had a very large suite, but Leticia's room was one side of the entire floor. A section of it had hidden walls within the walls that revealed multiple monitors. This allowed her to view and hear in every room in the Palace with a click of a button on the panel. This is how she learned so much about every guest and used this to her advantage. Leticia sat in a ten-thousand-dollar custom-made lounge chair as she watched Ron, Diana, Keith, and Stacy having sex. For the next three hours, she watched the tape of them repeatedly and pleasured herself many times, and learned a great deal. Now, she knew their weaknesses and how she was going to destroy them. Revenge and hate were coming in the body of a woman who was a FULL SEVEN. It is the spirit in the person, that is by far, the most dangerous.

# CHAPTER FOURTEEN

*James and Catarina*

Attorney James Reed has dealt with many things of a negative nature for years, and now he needed a change in his life and a long vacation. He was forty-nine years old and looked great from healthy eating, years spent in the gym and running. For years his legal practice has done well financially and he made investments in various areas. James invested a total of three million dollars in the stock market, film and music production, oil, and real estate companies. Today he has a net worth of twenty-eight million dollars.

He decided to take a short break from his legal practice and do some international traveling and was currently in Brazil. He stayed in a two thousand dollar-a-night Penthouse suite at the luxurious Belmond Copacabana Palace in Rio de Janeiro. James sat in the lobby this afternoon relaxing and sipping a glass of wine. He wore a five-hundred-dollar pair of *Crockett & Jones Albert* casual dress shoes and a thirty-five-hundred-dollar *Isaia Aquaspider* base two-button suit. His mind was at peace, and he thought, *Lord, I thank you for saving me and how blessed I am, all because of your grace and mercy.* He smiled and looked around the lobby appreciating where he was at this point in his life. Then he saw a beautiful looking lady walk in with two other women and four men. She was breathtaking! James has seen many attractive women since being here, but this woman could raise insurance premiums by just walking down the street.

Catarina Silva walked in gracefully with all her erotic beauty wearing heels and a snug-fitting dress. She was thirty-six years old, five-feet-seven, one-hundred-thirty-eight pounds with an incredible body thanks to good genes and the love for overall physical fitness. She had smooth brown skin with shoulder-length brown hair and green eyes. Catarina was of mixed heritage of black and Brazilian, the daughter of Mr. Clemente Silva of Silva Management Corporation (SMC). His corporation has a net worth of twenty-six-billion dollars and owns a conglomerate of businesses across the globe. Catarina was his only child and has been the hotel manager for the last seven years. She has an MBA in accounting and speaks English, Spanish, French, Italian, and Portuguese. She was the only person her dad fully trusts. Catarina loves her dad but was torn between her association with the business and her walk with Christ. SMC also owned the largest and most prestigious adult escort agency in Brazil, operating in more than 40 countries around the world. Offering select and luxurious international companionships across the globe. This branch of her father's business generates more than a billion dollars annually attracting clients from around the world. She hates this part of her dads' business because it's seedy and dirty, attracting men and women of vast wealth that manipulate and use people to get whatever they want by any means necessary.

Catarina was making her rounds through the hotel which is her daily routine when she noticed James sitting in the lobby. There was something about him that stood out, he had this aura of tranquility and raw confidence. After talking with her staff and talking with some of the guests walking by, she made her way over to James and he watched her every step. James buttoned his suit jacket as he stood up to greet her.

"Good afternoon sir. I hope you are enjoying your stay here and find everything to your liking."

"Yes, I am very much so. The hotel is beautiful and has wonderful accommodations, and you are?"

Catarina was trying hard not to show her attraction to James. She extended her hand out to him.

"I am Catarina Silva the Hotel Manager, and I am glad you are enjoying your time here. And your name is?" She spoke calmly but the moment their hands touched she felt the incredible warm spirit and chemistry between them.

The four men who walked in with her were part of the security team that followed Catarina everywhere she went. Despite the repeated attempts asking her father not to do this, he did not accept his daughter's request for something he considered so reckless.

As James shook her hand he looked into her eyes and saw so much love and having her hand in his caused him to lust.

"My name is James Reed, I am sure you heard this many times, but you are stunningly beautiful. Forgive my directness and I am sure you are a busy lady, but will you join me for dinner tonight, please?" He still held her hand and looked into her eyes.

Catarina enjoyed this man's touch far too much and she was approached by men every day but there was something very appealing about him. She let his hand go and was grateful to do so and gave him the warmest smile.

"Mr. James Reed it is a pleasure to meet you sir. And thank you for the lovely compliment. Yes, I am very busy, and I do not spend personal time with guests, but for you, I will make an exception. If you would meet me here in the lobby at eight o'clock tonight we can dine in one of the hotel's wonderful restaurants."

"Thank you for making me feel special and I will be here. Enjoy the rest of your day Miss Silva. Oh, and by the way, I like your name, what does Catarina mean?"

"Thank you Sir, Catarina means *Pure.*

"I like that and will not forget it." He smiled and extended his hand to her.

She did not want to, but she shook his hand and smiled.

"Please, call me Catarina and I will see you tonight." She let go of his hand and walked away from him trying hard not to shake her hips and butt because she did not want James to think negatively of her.

James could not help from staring as she walked away so gracefully in her tight dress accentuating her small waist, ample hips, and butt. It would be impossible for him or any man not to desire her. He repented to God for his thoughts and walked back to his suite to change clothes and go for a long swim to relax and cool off. After spending some time swimming and relaxing on the beach, it was time for James to leave and prepare for his dinner date. There were many good-looking women on the beach with tight bodies who wore the skimpiest bikini possible. Everywhere James looked women walked around in sexy thongs, but he could not get Catarina off his mind. She was captivating in body and spirit, and it was her spirit and mind he wanted to get to know on a personal level if she gave him the opportunity.

The first thing he did when he got back to his room was open his laptop and research Catarina and her family. He learned a great deal and came across many articles on her dad. He remembered seeing Mr. Silva's name on some paperwork during the investigation on Victor Augular. James was hoping she was nothing like him and he would be on guard during their dinner date. He was not impressed with very wealthy people because in his experience most were very arrogant, obnoxious, and self-centered. He did not feel this from Catarina but now that he knew her dad was worth twenty-six-billion dollars, he was more interested in getting to know her. Not because of the money but having that much money and not allowing it to corrupt her mind and spirit. She seemed confident but humble at the same time and this impressed him the most about her. It was close to his date time, so he hurried and showered, and got dressed. Keeping it simple, he dressed appropriately wearing *Salvatore Ferragamo Normand Balmorals* shoes, *Armani Collezioni* triple pleated dress pants, and an *Alexander McQueen* short-sleeved shirt. He wore one piece of jewelry, a *Rolex Oyster Perpetual* watch worth seventy-thousand dollars, given to him as payment from a client. He sprayed on *Oud Wood, Tom Ford* cologne at five- hundred dollars for an eight-ounce bottle, another payment from the same client. James learned early on in his legal practice not to turn down any form of payment if it was legal and had value to him. Now he was ready to leave.

Catarina was focused on her work and protective of her dad's business so, she did not go out on dates too often, but she had to admit seeing James tonight was something she looked forward to. Her walk with God was very important to her and the image she portrayed was part of it. She never dressed slutty but wanted to look nice for James. She had a closet full of clothes from every designer a woman could want. She chose a pair of *Prada* heels and a dress that fit her figure but was not too tight. Catarina laughed to herself as she walked out of her private suite because she felt a little nervous but could not figure out why.

James sat in the lobby when the elevator door opened, and Catarina walked out looking more attractive than earlier today. Their eyes met when walking towards each other and as if reading one another's mind, they hugged, and she kissed him on the cheek. They walked away hand in hand as if they knew each other for years. This was the beginning of a blissful night for them. They ate a wonderful meal while talking and laughing getting to know each other. And then went to a Jazz/Reggae lounge, enjoying the old and new sounds coming from the band. They played James's old school song, *Try Jah Love,* by *Third World* and everyone got up to dance. When she and James were not talking, they were laughing and dancing. Catarina could not remember feeling this comfortable and having this much fun with any man. She was careful when dancing because she did not want to give him the wrong impression but the connection and chemistry between them was far too strong to ignore. When they left the dance floor the band began playing a slow song and James pulled her back. Catarina did not think this was wise, but she did desire to be in his arms. As they danced, what she did not want to happen, did happen. Their lips touched and she embraced this man by allowing his tongue to penetrate her mouth and they held and kissed during the entire song. James tried not to, but he became aroused and pressed his body into Catarina and the moment she felt his erection, it made her jump. Her desire for James was so overwhelming, she called on the Lord to stay focused. She pulled slowly away from James.

"James, you know I am having so much fun, but we need to stop and it's time to leave."

"It's not a problem Catarina and forgive me for, well, you know, allowing myself to..."

She kissed him.

"It's okay James and perfectly understandable, embarrassing but okay." She smiled.

They walked out of the lounge the way they walked in, hand in hand, knowing this was the beginning of what they were about to share.

# CHAPTER FIFTEEN
*Becoming Closer*

Zechariah was very thankful to Ron for his new job and for helping him get on his feet, but it was important for him not to forget where he comes from and how God delivered him. Things were working out well in the club and he enjoyed being independent. After spending so much time in prison and being told what to do every day for so many years, he was beyond grateful. He made good money, his credit was excellent, so he purchased a four-bedroom two-car garage house in Bowie, MD. Every time he came home and stuck the key in the door it made him emotional and extremely appreciative for the favor of God. Now he was more than ready to focus on his personal life.

He and Sheila spent a lot of time together getting to know each other better. They started going to the gym, running together, and going for walks in the park. They went to church together and had bible study at Sheila's house and Grandma Harris always desired to be present because she wanted to make sure these two remained focused. She felt the strong Godly anointing from Zechariah which pleased her dearly and she was so happy for Sheila, but she also felt the chemistry from these two. She prayed God would bless their relationship to blossom into marriage and they would refrain from sexual activity until such time.

Sheila never thought she would ever feel about another man the way she did for David until she met Zechariah. When she was on her knees praying this morning, she finally said the words out of her mouth because they came from her heart.

"Lord I am in love with this man. Please help us to remain Holy before you so we will be blessed to become one. Thank you Jesus." Sheila continued getting. dressed because Zechariah was coming to take her to the park which she likes a great deal. They acted like teenagers in love for the very first time. Sheila was always careful how she conducted herself around him which was not always easy. She was very attracted to him spiritually and physically and this man was fine with a serious physique. They walked and held hands while laughing and talking and after so many years, Sheila was in love again and wanted things to work out. But she began having hormones problems, desiring Zechariah sexually and keeping those desires to herself and under control.

It was the middle of Spring, and the weather was beautiful outside with flowers blooming, a soft wind blowing, and seventy-degree temperature. Sheila put on a colorful spring dress that made her look good and classy. She checked herself in the mirror when her doorbell rang. Grandma Harris was at the door singing to herself when Sheila opened the door.

"Grandma Harris, what a nice surprise! Please come on in and hug me." They hugged as she walked in.

"Praise the Lord Sheila, you know I should not have to be ringing no doorbell to get in. I practically live here so I need a key. You young women are something, as soon as you get a man, you forget us old folks."

"Miss Harris, I love you," she hugged and kissed her again on the cheek. "And just for the record I have not forgotten you and never will, so stop with all the acting you do, I love you."

Grandma Harris looked at Sheila, rolled her eyes, and walked over to the sofa, and sat down.

"Just because I am an old woman, you can't talk back to me," she looked up. "Lord Jesus keep me from sinning on this day in this house. Thank you, Lord. You look nice Sheila. Are you going out with Zechariah today?"

Sheila sat down on the sofa across from Grandma Harris and smiled at her.

"Thank you for the compliment and I am going to ignore your remark about me talking back to you. Yes, he is on his way over here to get me and we are going to the park, I think."

She hit the sofa with the palm of her hand.

"I knew God sent me over here for a reason. Baby, I am so glad God blessed you with a clean, Holy, good-looking man. Oh, he loves the Lord, and he is good-looking too. You better be glad I am not younger because I would give you a run for your money Miss Thang."

Sheila could not keep herself from laughing.

"Grandma Harris, only God knows how much I love you, but I will be glad when my baby gets here."

"What!" She raised her hand. "Your baby, so he is your baby now. Just for the record, you are a grown woman, and your babies are your children. Wait, the only time a woman calls a man her baby, is after they've had sex," she rubbed her head. "Oh my Lord, as hard as I prayed and you done gone and gave up the kitty cat. That man ain't had no kitty cat in years and he is strong too, I know he put something on you. Got you all sprung and out of your mind, talking back to me. I saw him looking at your butt, lusting. Help us Jesus."

Sheila leaned back on the sofa and waved her hand at Grandma Harris and laughed so hard water came to her eyes.

"Stop, just stop talking please. You are making my stomach hurt. I have done no such thing and you know it."

"Okay, if you say so but God knows all things. Oh, and one more thing. When a woman gets all heated in the body over a man, they stop wearing those big, comfortable, ugly underwear and start wearing dental floss for underwear. You know, the ones with the string going up your butt crack. Lord have mercy, I do not understand how any woman can wear something all day, in her butt crack. Some women don't wear underwear at all. You got any underwear on underneath that dress?"

Zechariah drove up to Sheila's house in his Benz and saw Grandma Harris' SUV. He walked to the front door wearing dress shoes, dress slacks, and a short-sleeved dress shirt. He rang the doorbell.

"You are unbelievable sometimes. Thank God, saved by the bell and you should be ashamed of yourself. That is my baby." She walked over and kissed Grandma Harris on the cheek and opened the front door.

"Praise the Lord Sheila," he walked in and hugged her, and kissed her on the cheek. "You look lovely, as always."

Sheila leaned back and stared at him.

"Praise the Lord to you handsome." She hugged him and kissed him on the lips. "I missed you."

Grandma Harris stood and waved her hands at them.

"Okay enough of that. Stop all that kissing. Kissing leads to rubbing each other's body and the next thing you know, you two will be on the floor butt naked, committing all kinds of sins. Sheila, once a lust spirit gets in your body, you will be giving it up regularly. You will wake up and go to bed with a penis on the brain. Lord help you after that happens child." She shook her head.

Sheila looked at Grandma Harris with her mouth open, not believing what she said and embarrassed her so much in front of Zechariah. She pointed her finger at her.

"In the name of Jesus woman, is there anything you will not say out of your mouth? God, I cannot believe you at times."

Zechariah walked over and hugged Grandma Harris, but she pushed him away.

"Don't hug me. I don't want any lust spirits attacking me at night."

Sheila laughed and hugged Grandma Harris and grabbed Zechariah's hand.

"Time to go baby," she looked at Grandma Harris and smiled. She grabbed Zechariah's hand and they walked towards the front door then Sheila turned around and looked at Grandma Harris. "Make yourself at home. Love you." They walked out.

"Sheila, you better not give that man none of your kitty cat. You two are not married, but I know you are in heat." She yelled at them as they walked out of the door.

They both laughed as they got in Zechariah's Benz and drove away. Zechariah drove to Baltimore Harbor, and they walked around and enjoyed the sites and each other. After two hours of walking, they sat in a nice restaurant. After eating they talked for a while and Sheila suggested it was time for them to leave.

"Sheila, I know we have not known each other long but I know in my heart this is right," he pulled a ring box out of his pocket and got down on one knee. "Sheila, I desire for us to spend the rest of our lives together getting to know one another day by day." He opened the box containing a beautiful three-carat diamond ring. "Sheila O'Neil, will you be my rib receiver and marry me?"

People in the restaurant were looking at this emotional occasion. Sheila was shocked and speechless, and tears began to flow from her eyes as she stared at him.

"Oh my God Zechariah, I can't believe this. Oh my God! Yes, yes, I will marry you. Yes, yes, yes."

Zechariah put the ring on Sheila's finger and they both stood and hugged each other tightly. She kissed him with passion and loved his tongue in her mouth.

Everyone started clapping and whistling. This noise was a much-needed distraction for Sheila, which brought her back to her present surroundings. She stopped kissing him and they stared at each other.

"I love you very much Zechariah." Tears flowed from her eyes.

Zechariah wiped Sheila's tears away gently and kissed her lips and hugged her.

"You are an answered prayer." They kissed again and Sheila looked at her ring as they walked away and shook her head in disbelief.

# CHAPTER SIXTEEN

*Meeting of Powers*

Catarina questioned her actions many times during her flight but thirteen hours later her private jet landed at BWI airport. She only slept a short time since leaving Rio because James was on her mind so much and she missed him greatly ever since he left. They talked on the phone every day, several times a day for weeks, and were very honest and direct about everything. This allowed them to become closer in a short amount of time. Catarina has worked hard at the hotel and told her dad she needed a break. Before James left, she introduced him to her dad who was not nice to him, but he was like this with any man who tried talking to his only daughter. With anyone, he had a background check done on James and when everything came back clean he was a little nicer to him and they all had dinner together.

As Catarina stepped off the plane she was all smiles and looked good wearing a matching jacket, skirt, and heels. She was in great anticipation of seeing James and being in his arms again. She only had a carry-on bag because James told her not to bring so many clothes because they were going shopping. As she walked through the airport she saw James standing there holding roses in his hand and wearing an *Armani* suit. Catarina stared at him as she walked closer thinking, *Lord this man is fine, keep me focused.* They embraced like they have not seen each other in years and James picked her up off her feet as he hugged her.

"Mr. James Reed, you better put me down." She was smiling and laughing and they kissed as their bodies pressed against one another.

Catarina's body slid down James's and she felt his erection and allowed the embrace to last longer than it should. Her spirit convicted her quickly, so she took the roses from his hand and he took her bag.

"Thank you for the beautiful flowers James, and the kiss was nice too." She smiled at him.

Two different worlds were about to collide. Leticia Wilson walked through the airport along with her five bodyguards, wearing blue dress pants suits. Leticia's suit fit her body well, revealing her incredible figure. She was there to meet three politically connected businessmen from Aruba. She recognized James from the newspapers and TV concerning legal cases.

Leticia did not know who Catarina was but found her to be extremely attractive with a regal aura. She whispered to one of her bodyguards to find out who this woman was. It was as if time slowed and everyone walked in slow motion as they passed each other. Leticia and Catarina's eyes met and Catarina felt her coldness and evil spirit but shook it off so as not to ruin this moment with James. His Bentley was parked out front and he opened the door for Catarina and put her bag in the back and drove away.

Leticia, her bodyguards, and the other three men got in a stretch Benz Limo, and it drove away. One of her bodyguards was on her laptop researching Catarina.

"Her name is Catarina Silva the daughter of Mr. Clemente Silva of Silva Management Corporation. It has a net worth of twenty-six billion dollars. She is his only child."

Leticia looked at her and smiled.

"Very interesting and who in the business world has not heard of Mr. Clemente. This is becoming more interesting indeed. I want to do business with him, and I just found my way in. Attorney James Reed is good at what he does but he walks with God. Well, we will test his faith and Miss Catarina Silva as well. I want him, her, and her father's business." She laughed and the laughter echoed throughout the car.

James reached the gate of his house, pushed a button, the gate opened, and he drove through. As he and Catarina got out she admired the design of his home and how meticulous the grounds were kept. James got her bag and the roses out of the car, they walked into his house, and he gave her the tour. She liked the house a lot but thought it was too much for just one person to live in. They were in his large basement and James could not help from admiring her beauty. He hugged and kissed her and tapped her on the butt which she didn't mind but did not want him to get the wrong intention.

"James, you promised if I came to visit, you would be a gentleman and behave yourself. Well, smacking me on my butt is not being a gentleman sir. So be nice. You have a lovely home, far too much for one person but it is very nice. Now, where do I sleep?"

He felt playful so it moved him to give her an answer he knew she would not like.

"That's easy, in my room of course, in my bed."

Catarina's mood instantly changed, and she became angry.

"What!" she yelled at him. "I don't know what kind of woman you think I am, but I am not about to sleep in your room or your bed. I did not fly thirteen hours to come here and be treated like some slut for you to use. If all you want is sex, then go find yourself a prostitute. I cannot believe you, and here I thought you were special. God, you are so typical. I am done with you, take me right back to the airport, now." She stared at him with anger and hurt.

James did not mean to push her this far, but she had fire in her and he loved it. He smiled and started laughing. This pushed Catarina over the edge because she thought he was mocking her, she tried to slap him, but he moved out of the way and continued to laugh as he raised both of his hands.

"Stop, I was only kidding. Lord have mercy, you look like you wanted to harm a brother. There are seven bedrooms in this house, so pick one, with your fine self." He leaned forward and kissed her on the cheek.

She tried hard not to laugh but did and pointed her finger at him.

"You have no idea sir how close you came to seeing the ugly side of me. Oh, you are something, but you got me," she exhaled hard and stared at him. "Now, lead me to my room please."

"Just for the record, I like the fire and passion in you. Anyway, walk up the stairs and to your right."

She rolled her eyes at him and smiled then walked up the stairs. James stared hard at her every step.

"That makes no sense for you to have all that goodness, and not share. Beautiful in the face, small in the waist, hips, lips, pretty painted fingertips, big butt, and pretty smile. An absolute FULL SEVEN."

Just as she was about to turn around and tell James about himself, she smiled because the compliment was nice coming from him and she knew he was trying to get a rise out of her again. Not this time. James put her bag on the floor in her room.

"Thank you. Now, if you do not mind, after getting up so early and spending so much time on the plane, I am a little tired, so I am going to lay down for a while. Will you wake me later please?"

He bowed in front of her.

"No question pretty lady. Anything you want, you can get. Just tell me what it is." He licked his lips and winked at her.

"I see this is going to be an interesting time with you," she stared at him and for some reason became emotional and wanted him to hug her. "James, will you hold me please."

Her tone and demeanor let James know she was serious. So, he embraced her. She kissed him and said thank you then he walked out. She took a quick shower, changed into her silk pajama set, and laid down. James changed into his gym clothes and went to the basement to his home gym to get a good workout. Afterward, he went to his room and showered, put on a T-shirt and sweatpants then laid down to rest.

It was nighttime and it began thundering and lightning. James and Catarina were still asleep but Leticia was in her private suite sitting on the floor, in deep meditation. Her body began to change slowly into a heavy mist then disappeared. The mist appeared in front of James' house and turned back into Leticia. She pointed her finger at his house and spoke curses. A neighbor happened to be driving by and saw Leticia and continued to drive but called the police. As Catarina slept, a mist came into her room and landed on her body. She started shaking and having a horrible dream of perverted sexual acts and then woke up but was unable to move. She started screaming James' name but could not hear herself and then repeated the name of Jesus over and over until she could move. The mist disappeared and she began crying.

The thunder woke James up and he heard Catarina screaming and calling his name and saying Jesus repeatedly. He grabbed his gun quickly from his nightstand, pushed a special button on the wall in his bedroom that instantly alerted the police, and ran up the stairs to her room. Catarina sat up in bed crying. James looked around the room then put the gun in the back of his sweatpants and held her.

Catarina looked at James with the most beautiful and caring eyes.

"Oh James, I had a horrible nightmare, unlike anything I have ever experienced in my life. It was..."

A buzzing sound came from the front gate that made Catarina jump but James knew it was the police. He caressed her face with his hand to comfort her.

"Relax, I am here and would never allow anything to happen to you. I will be right back, that is the police outside." He kissed her on the cheek and went downstairs to let the police in.

Three patrol cars were outside with two officers in each car. They all knew of James and his clean reputation and political connections, from the Mayor to the Governor's office. He let them in, and they explained to him along with his distress call, they received other calls about some woman standing close to his gate. Following the procedure, they searched inside his home and out, and before leaving he was told they would be making their rounds in the neighborhood. James thanked them and they left. He walked back upstairs to see about Catarina.

She was vertical in bed but as soon as James walked in, she sat up and he sat next to her.

"James is everything alright?" She looked at him with concern.

"Absolutely, everything is good. Someone was walking in the neighborhood that no one knew. How are you feeling?"

"Better now, but the dream was horrible, and I don't want to talk about it. We all have bad dreams sometimes. James, please don't take this the wrong way but can I sleep in your bed for the rest of the night?"

James kissed her lips and carried her to his room and laid her on his bed. He knew this was not a time to play so he kept his distance as they laid next to each other. Catarina did not want to send him any mixed signals, but she wanted to be held.

"James, will you hold me please?"

He rolled over, kissed Catarina on the cheek, and held her in his arms until they went to sleep.

# CHAPTER SEVENTEEN
*Long Time Coming*

It was a beautiful Saturday afternoon. A day Sheila and Zechariah prayed about and looked forward to but never knew what they felt now would be so great. One of the reasons it was so hard for Sheila to get over David after all these years, was because she held on to him and the intense connection they shared. Through prayer and fasting, she was finally able to let her past go. What she and Zechariah shared was very special and thank God for blessing her to be loved and give love. She knew her heart, spirit, and body were ready.

The church was beautifully decorated for the wonderful occasion of their wedding. Before all this took place, she had a long talk with Zechariah and explained to him it was not her desire to bring something new into her life, mixed with something old. Meaning, she wanted a completely new start for them. So, she would move in with him after the wedding and give her house to her two daughters. This was another prayer God answered for him as well. Sheila made it clear to Ron and everyone else she and Zechariah did not want a lavish wedding and not spend a lot of money. Her daughters talked her into having something a little more than what she initially desired. Pastor Williams was performing the wedding ceremony.

The colors were ivory and tan. There were seven bridesmaids Christine, Sandra, Diana, Stacy, Catarina, Cynthia, and Shantai, wearing ivory-colored dresses. The seven groomsmen, Ron, Keith, James, Detective Rick Matthew, and three *Young Wolves* wore tan tuxes. Pastor Williams wore a white robe as stood next to Zechariah on the main floor of the church. There were about three hundred people in the church and the choir began to sing *Stand By Me* by *The Drifters*, as the bridesmaids and groomsmen began walking down the aisle. Ron and Diana, Keith and Stacy, James and Catarina, Rick and Cynthia lead the procession, and Christine, Sandra, and Shantai walked with the Young Wolves. Shantai was very attracted to Tony, the guy she walked with and considered talking to him later. The choir stopped singing and everyone in the church stood as Sheila entered the aisle. *In the Still of the Night* by *Fred Parris and The Satins* began playing as Sheila began her walk. She wore an off-the-shoulder *Badgley Mischka* bridal gown with a long train attached. She had to hold back her tears with each step as she got closer to her answered prayer. As Sheila reached the front, Grandma Harris stood up to give her away. This was one of the happiest days of her life and they were such a wonderful couple, she could not hold back her tears of joy.

The Pastor moved forward, as Zechariah and Sheila began to exchange their wedding vows. Their best man Ron gave the rings to the Pastor. He prayed over the rings and smiled at Zechariah and Sheila.

"May God bless this union every day of your life. I now pronounce you, husband and wife. Brother Zechariah, you may kiss your bride."

Sheila stepped closer as Zechariah embraced her and kissed her lips.

"I love you Miss Sheila Brown." He kissed her again.

"I love you Mr. Zechariah Brown."

He leaned forward and whispered in her ear.

"Now can I find out what you are working with?"

Sheila laughed quietly as she whispered back to him.

"Take me home and you can find out."

Everyone in the church stood and started clapping their hands and the choir began singing.

In the other section of the church, a large meeting room was beautifully decorated and set up for the reception area. There were tables on both sides full of food. There was Soul food, Seafood, and various desserts. A three-tier cake was waiting for the couple to cut. Pastor Williams and Grandma Harris walked in the room first, followed by the Bridesmaids and Groomsmen, and then the church members. The servers were dressed in white and black and took care of the people as they came into the room. There were enough tables and chairs for everyone to be seated and several photographers were taking pictures and videos of everything.

Zechariah and Sheila walked into the room, and everyone stood and clapped. Grandma Harris walked over and hugged them tightly, trying to keep her emotions in check. She rubbed their faces gently as she looked at them.

"Sheila and Zechariah may God continue to bless you both and I am very happy for you two," she leaned closer and whispered to Sheila. "Sheila now it is time, so don't hold out on the kitty cat, give this man all he wants."

"Grandma Harris you are one in a million and this one time, I will agree with you." She whispered back to her.

"Amen to that." Zechariah said smiling.

"I love you both." She kissed them on the cheek and walked to her seat.

Christine and Sandra walked towards Zechariah and Sheila and hugged them, both saying how happy they are for them.

Tears began to flow from the lady's eyes and they hugged sharing a wonderful family moment, then they walked away.

James and Catarina walked over to Sheila and Zechariah congratulating them. Sheila told Catarina she was a beautiful woman and hope their relationship grows. They all hugged.

Sheila and Zechariah cut the cake and mingled with everyone and thanked them for coming. They eventually sat down as music played and people were eating, laughing, and having fun. Shantai sat at the table with Tony because she wanted to talk and flirt with him. He was so fine to her and built the way she liked her men, tight muscular bodies but not too big, clean-cut handsome face with a great smile. Yes, she wanted him but continued repenting of her sexual thoughts for this man and tried not to be too obvious of her desires. Rick watched Shantai, but she avoided him, so when she got up from the table to talk to people, he made his move and walked over to her.

"Hello Miss Shantai. As always you look lovely and it's good to see you again, although you have been avoiding me." He stepped closer to her.

Shantai avoided talking to Rick as much as possible because she felt a strong attraction to him and will never forget what they shared. However, all that was behind her and needed to stay there, in her past. Standing this close to him made her uncomfortable.

"Hello rick, you look nice in your tux. Yes, I am avoiding you because we need to keep our distance from each other and you know why, so don't start that smooth talk of yours."

"Okay, not a problem. Be blessed my sister and take care." He brushed up against her purposely as he walked away.

His very touch made her insides jump and this is another sign to stay far away from him if she could.

Three hours later the event was ending and the Pastor came forward to get everyone's attention.

"I wanted to thank all of you for coming to share in this wonderful, blessed occasion, and please keep our newly married couple in prayer that God continues to show them, his way. Be blessed and drive home safely. Again, we all thank you."

Sheila and Zechariah stood up holding hands.

"I thank you all for coming and God bless." Zechariah said.

"Yes, thank all of you for being here and it would not have been the same without you. Thank you so much."

People started leaving and taking the leftover food with them so it would not go to waste because Pastor William despised wasting food. Ron walked over to Sheila and hugged her and kept his emotions in check and then tapped Zechariah on the shoulder.

"My brother no words can explain how happy you have made my mom and how happy I am for you," he stepped closer and looked directly into his eyes. "Take care of my mom my brother she is the only parent I have left." He stared at him.

Zechariah knew where Ron was coming from and saw the look in his eyes and understood. He put his hand on his shoulder.

"Ron, I know where you are coming from, and I love your mom deeply my brother, and would protect her with my life." They hugged and gave each other dap.

Keith watched them talk and was happy for everyone, but he always had Ron's back no matter what. Pastor Williams was talking to Grandma Harris and promised to take her home. The only ones left in the room were the bride and groom and all the

bridesmaids and groomsmen. Sheila and Zechariah walked out and got into a chauffeured limo. Keith and Ron talked agreeing all the bridesmaids and groomsmen would meet back at Keith's house to finish celebrating this day with more food and music. Two limos waited outside as the bridesmaids got into one and the groomsmen into the other and drove away.

Shantai noticed Stacy giving her a dirty look.

"Stacy, why are you looking at me like I did something wrong?"

"You know why, I saw you talking and flirting with Rick, we both know you should not get involved with him again. Yes, you two have changed and are walking with Christ but some temptations are too great. Stop flirting with him. You are playing with fire."

"Thank you, mother," she rolled her eyes at her. "First, I was not flirting with him, and I do not plan on spending any time with Rick. However, the man is fine and got it going on."

"He is fine and got a tight body." Cynthia said.

All the ladies looked at each other and started laughing.

# CHAPTER EIGHTEEN
*Zechariah and Sheila*

Pastor Williams came to Zechariah's house and prayed inside and out, blessing it. Sheila made several visits as well to add her decorating touch. Everything she owned in her house except personal paperwork, she left or donated it. Nothing of the old was coming into her new blessings. She looked forward to her and Zechariah building together as one on every level.

When Zechariah and Sheila stepped out of the limo, he carried her inside the house. They hugged and kissed with passion then Sheila began feeling a little nervous and Zechariah noticed it.

"Sheila, what is wrong? Baby, I am in no hurry, and we can take this as slow as you want, I promise you that."

It is statements like this and what she felt for this man, caused her to love him so much more.

"Thank you for your patience and I don't mean to bring up the past, but my ex-husband is the only man I have ever been with. He was my first and last."

"I understand where you are coming from and how you feel. We are one now and I am here for you. Can we pray first?"

Once again it was as if he read her thoughts and this alone made her relax a little. They kneeled next to the sofa in the living room and prayed for a while. When they were done you felt the spirit of peace and calmness in the room. Sheila felt much better and was no longer nervous. They walked to separate bedrooms to shower and change.

Sheila looked at herself in the mirror and had to admit she looked good at forty-three and had a tight body from working out in the gym four times a week for many years. It was a stress reliever, especially after her husband was killed and dealing with many family situations. Prayer and fitness carried her a long way. Now she was about to give herself to her husband of the present and for life. She giggled to herself because she began feeling horny and wanted Zechariah to take his time but be himself as well. She wore heels, a matching bra, and high-cut panties with a thin robe.

Zechariah was thinking about how long it has been for him and laughed but he took good care of himself in prison and he was confident of his sexual skills. At forty-four, he looked great. He sat on the edge of the bed wearing silk boxers and the very thought of having Sheila, aroused him.

Sheila walked into their bedroom excited and ready for this man, so she thought. When he stood to greet her and looked at his incredible-looking body and the impression of his erection, made her have second thoughts.

"Do you see anything you like?" She turned around and let her robe fall to the floor to show off her body.

"You are one fine-looking woman," he stepped closer and pulled her into him and pressed his body against hers and put his hands on her hips, and slowly kissed her. "I want you Sheila, I want to make love to you and..."

Sheila put her fingers against his lips.

"Baby I am not going anywhere, and I am all yours." She placed her hand between his legs and felt his penis. She shook her head and thought, *oh my, his dick is so hard and big.* Sheila stepped back, took her bra and panties off while looking at Zechariah.

"Wow Sheila." He pulled his underwear off, moved closer and his hands caressed her hips and butt while his lips caressed hers and his tongue teased her nipples with every lick. He sucked and licked them until they became hard and he continued licking as his hand slid between her legs and felt her wetness.

It has been so long since Sheila had been touched in that way and Zechariah made her body feel like it was on fire. She caressed his penis feeling the heat of it and never took her hand off it or her eyes off his. She lowered herself slowly to her knees and put her mouth on his penis and began sucking it and it was not long before she realized he was close, based on his breathing. Not wanting him to cum just yet, she stood and held his hand and walked to the bed. She laid down and motioned with her eyes for him to do the same.

Zechariah moved to his knees and licked her from her ankles up, until his face was between her legs and allowed his lips and tongue to speak for him.

The sensations Sheila felt were incredible and made her entire body shake and without warning his tongue hit her spot and she screamed with pleasure.

"Ahhhh, Zechariah I am cumming, oh my God I'm cummming baby. Don't stop ohhhhhhh."

He continued licking and enjoyed hearing Shelia's moans and screams of pleasure and then moved his body up, looked into Sheila's eyes, and slid inside her. She was so wet and tight, which caused him to be more aware of her comfort and relaxed state.

The feeling was unbelievable to Sheila especially after so many years of abstinence but when she felt him slide inside, she wrapped her legs around his waist.

"Ohhhh Zechariah, it has been so long, and you feel wonderful baby. Make love to me. Your dick feels so good. Keep going baby, yes that's it, ohhhhhh I am cummming." She wrapped her legs around him tighter.

Not wanting to make her sore, Zechariah continued to make love to Sheila slowly and gently until he could not hold himself back because she was so hot and tight.

"Oh, Sheila you are so good. I am cummming in you baby, ahhhhh." He continued thrusting slowly until they both relaxed.

This night was just the beginning of their lovemaking. Sheila greatly appreciated Zechariah's soft touch and gentleness but now she wanted him to let go and wanted him to know she was all the woman he would ever need. They made love all over the bedroom in various positions until neither of them could take anymore. After showering together, they prayed and laid down to rest.

# CHAPTER NINETEEN

*Leticia's Power*

Leticia Wilson has the full powers of Mr. Bones but was a public figure so she needed to be careful when and how she displayed her powers. She hated the way Victor Augular did his business and the mistakes he made but she understood his vision of total domination. Leticia wanted to become the most feared person in the world and the wealthiest. Therefore, it was necessary for her and the security team to take this trip to India. Through the spirit of Mr. Bones, she found out an undiscovered diamond mine was in a remote area of India. She wanted to have control of the resources coming out of this mine because it was revealed to Leticia this would be the largest producing mining in the world. She needed to move fast before someone discovered its location and word reached the politicians. If that were to happen it would make her take-over deal more complicated. She had her private team of experienced miners in place waiting for her instructions when she arrived because no one knew where this location was but Leticia.

Even with Leticia's private plane it still took nineteen hours to reach India and they arrived early in the morning, sleeping most of the way. They were well rested upon arrival. The moment Leticia and her team walked into the lobby of the *Four Seasons Hotel* in Mumbai, all eyes were on them. They wore white, long dresses that did little to hide their voluptuous figures. The best luxury suites were offered to them, but she made it clear not to disturb her during her stay. They unpacked and changed into tan color fatigues and boots. She had twelve of her team members waiting in front of the hotel in a caravan of trucks with supplies of food, water, large tents, automatic weapons, sniper rifles, and hand grenades. They walked outside and got in the trucks but even in their fatigues, they were sexy. Their first stop was the *Office of Deeds and Records* where Leticia purchased the one-hundred-twenty-five acres of land where the mine was located. When she left, the person in the office laughed at her because they knew she purchased some useless piece of land out in the middle of nowhere. If they only knew. Leticia gave the driver instructions of where to go and the rest followed. It took them four hours to get to the location and Leticia was surprised and angry to see another group was already there. Twenty men dressed in fatigues stood close to tents. These were not your average security guards but well-trained mercenaries who pulled their guns out quickly and aimed them at Leticia and her group the moment they drove up. Leticia and her five bodyguards got out of the trucks, and she motioned for the others to remain. Four distinguished looking businessmen walked out of one of the tents. One of them, who happens to be the best looking, stepped closer to Leticia.

"Good afternoon to you Miss. It is nice to see such an attractive woman in a place like this but unfortunately, you are trespassing." He motioned for his men to lower their weapons.

"Interesting because I was about to tell you the same thing. I own this property and it is you who are trespassing. Who are you?"

It was hard for him to remain focused because Leticia was so attractive.

"My name is Mr. Levin, we represent Mr. Clemente Silva of Silva Management Corporation. The paperwork for ownership of this property is being taken care of as we speak. And you are?"

The moment Mr. Levin said Silva Management Corporation Leticia looked at her bodyguards which put them on high mental alert. They were prepared to start shooting but she rubbed her forehead with her fingers when she looked at them which was a sign for them not to react.

"My name is Miss Leticia Wilson. It seems we have a dilemma Mr. Levin because I had a deed check before I purchased this property and there were no owners. Which means, even though you arrived here before me, you and your men are on my property, and I would appreciate if you leave?"

Mr. Levin knew she was right, and he knew exactly who she was along with the rumors attached to her, but he was under strict orders to get this land at all costs, and that was exactly what he was going to do. He planned to let them set up for tonight and have his men kill them all later. He smiled at her.

"There is a problem, but I am sure we can come to a mutual understanding that would benefit all parties concerned. So, in the meantime, why don't you set up for tonight and we can get a fresh start on business in the morning."

Leticia knew it was a setup, but he had no idea who he was dealing with.

"I could do that." She smiled and brushed her shoulder against him as she walked away. She and her five bodyguards walked back to the caravan of trucks informing the men to set up tents for tonight.

Leticia and her bodyguards talked among themselves while the men set up four tents. They brought three 8-person tents

because she wanted the men to have plenty of space and be comfortable and her luxury tent made to her specifications. Thirty-foot-wide by sixty-feet long with a ten-foot center. There was enough space in the tent, she and each of her bodyguards had their room and it was equipped with running water for a shower. After they all showered, she sent a message to the businessmen to come over and enjoy some wine. Everyone was having a great time talking, laughing, listening to music, and smoking weed. The women flirted with the men until everybody was naked. Leticia was in her room on top of Levin riding him hard and when he called her name from sexual release, she transformed into a wolf. Levin never screamed so loudly, for about five seconds, then the wolf bit him in the throat and ripped it out. Blood squirted everywhere, and his body shook. The wolf's jaws opened wide enough to sink its teeth on both sides of his head, bit it in half and his eyeballs popped out. Growling and foaming at the mouth, it ripped the flesh off his bones and then ate it.

Blood dripped from the wolf's mouth as it walked into each of the girls' rooms and watched them stab the men to death. It walked in and snapped each of the men's bones in two with one bite. You heard the echo of the screams from a mile away. After being repeatedly stabbed one man tried to run out but the wolf leaped on his back and bit his head off. Blood shot up like a fountain as his body stumbled until one of the women kicked it to the ground and the wolf commenced to snapping his bones and eating his body in one minute. Leticia's other guards killed everyone else. The five women stood next to each other naked and bloody and they looked at the wolf when it changed back into Leticia. They showered and had an orgy.

The following morning Leticia had the men drill small holes in the ground two hundred feet deep in a six-hundred-yard circle and plant explosives. She walked around the circle six times mumbling some words and then drove two miles away and she had the men set off the explosives. It sounded like thunder many times over with the ground shaking for miles. It was a large two-hundred-foot hole in the ground six yards wide. Diamonds were scattered on the ground, and you saw thousands of diamonds at the bottom of the hole. All the men laughed and jumped up and down. This was the start of Leticia's growing empire and take over.

# CHAPTER TWENTY
*A Long Journey*

On this wonderful spring Sunday morning, instead of being in church like she always was, Grandma Harris drove to Leticia's Palace to meet and have a talk with Miss Leticia Wilson. God put it heavily upon her heart and spirit to share his word with her with hopes she repented and turned from the wicked journey she chose to walk. She drove up in front of the hotel wearing a long dress and carried a bible and valet parked her truck. Leticia stood in the lobby with her five bodyguards and they all wore heels and black dresses. Grandma Harris prayed with each step. She disliked coming to this place because she felt so many evil spirits but obeying God was far more important than her comfort zone.

"Hello, miss Harris. I was surprised when you called me, but it is a pleasure to meet you." Leticia smiled and extended her hand to her.

They locked eyes as they shook hands and for a few seconds, it was a battle of the spirits. Leticia had to withdraw her hand because the powerful spirit she felt coming from this woman was unlike anything she ever experienced. It scared her, but no one knew.

"Nice to meet you, Miss Wilson." Smiling at her knowing the fear she saw in her eyes was the fear of God. She looked at the other women who stood next to her and felt evil all over them.

"Time will tell. Now if you do not mind, we can go to one of the meeting rooms and talk. Please, follow me."

They all walked to the meeting room. Leticia and Grandma Harris sat down across from one another, but her bodyguards waited in the hallway. Food was brought in and they ate while talking but Leticia was losing her patience with this woman and regretted taking the time from her busy schedule to meet her.

"I thank you for your time and I know you are a busy lady, so I will get directly to the point," she leaned closer to her. "You have been through a lot and lost your sister, someone very dear to you, at the hands of Mr. Victor Augular. He was a very evil man, but he is no longer alive, and as painful as it may be, it would be best if you left the past in the past. Repent of your sins and ask God to come into your life to heal, deliver, and save your soul. This is the message from my Lord Jesus. Please do not turn a deaf ear to his calling in your life."

Leticia wanted to leap across the table and choke this old woman to death but refrained and started laughing.

"You must be joking old woman and I know who you are but this ain't bible study class and I don't need your preaching or your God," she leaned closer as her eyes turned red with anger. "It was very brave of you to come here to talk to me like this. Pray you walk out of here like you walked in, old woman."

"You made a serious mistake and it is not me you turned your back on, but God. You have embraced the God of this earth; the devil and he has deceived you like he has deceived so many others. This is the day of your salvation call," she stood up. "Message delivered and my time is up. Good day to you, Miss Leticia Wilson, and may God have mercy on your soul."

"Where do you think you are going? I did not dismiss you yet." She grabbed Grandma Harris' arm.

"Take your hand off me devil. In the name of Jesus." She stared at her.

Once again Leticia felt power and fear like she has never known, it felt like electricity went through her body. She let her arm go quickly and slid back without ever moving her feet but she would not be intimidated especially by an old woman. Mumbling some words, she began changing into a wolf.

"Oh my Lord Jesus." Grandma Harris stepped back with her hand on her chest because she could not believe what she witnessed. But God gave her courage and strength instantly to stand on his word. She pointed at the wolf. "Isaiah 59:19 *So shall they fear the name of the* LORD *from the west, and his glory from the rising of the sun. When the enemy shall come in like a flood, the Spirit of the* LORD *shall lift a standard against him.* Be gone devil."

Leticia was halfway into her transformation but the power she could not resist stopped her and she changed back to human form and dropped to her knees and screamed. Her bodyguards rushed in with blades in their hands ready to stab Grandma Harris. She turned to them and yelled.

**"Yea though I walk through the valley of the shadow of death I will fear no evil, for thou art with me, thy rod and thy staff they comfort me.** Now bow down before King Jesus."

The bodyguards stopped in their tracks and dropped to their knees. Grandma Harris walked past them praising God and out of the hotel. The valet brought the car to her and she drove away praising the name of the Lord.

She visited Sheila and Zechariah. The moment she walked in the spirit of peace touched her and they hugged and invited her to come in and have dinner. It was a pleasure to be in their company and the food was great. She thought about sharing what happened to her at the hotel but decided against it because they looked so good together and did not want to ruin the mood. After talking for a while, they prayed together and asked her to spend the night. Grandma Harris looked at them with such love and care before she laid down to rest.

In the morning Sheila and Zechariah were in the kitchen laughing and flirting with one another while cooking breakfast. Sheila called out to Grandma Harris to come and eat and wondered what took her so long, so she knocked on the bedroom door and walked in. She was still sleeping so Sheila shook her, but Grandma Harris' journey was over now, she died in her sleep. Sheila fell to the floor crying and screaming. Zechariah ran to the room and saw Sheila on the floor and looked at Grandma Harris who had a very peaceful smile on her face. Zechariah knew she was dead.

"Zechariah, she is gone, Grandma Harris is dead, oh Lord no." The pain hit her so hard she screamed from her soul.

All Zechariah could do was hold and comfort her but could not hold back his tears. He knew Sheila lost her best friend but maybe, just maybe, God allowed them to connect at this time. He looked into his wife's eyes and saw her deep pain.

"Lord, help us all." He whispered.

# CHAPTER TWENTY ONE

*Tears of Love*

The last two weeks were difficult and painful for Sheila and her family. Grandma Harris was well known and loved by so many people in Maryland and other states. The morning she passed away, Sheila called Diana who did not take the news well at all. She dropped the phone and fell to the floor crying and it was a blessing Ron was home to comfort her. Keith and Stacy happened to be there as well. Sheila also called her daughters but after that, she was unable to call any more people, so she asked Zechariah to take over. Which he did, and Pastor Williams assisted him with the funeral arrangements and everything else associated with this great loss.

It was the day of the funeral, and the viewing of the body and service was at church, which was standing room only. Diana, Sheila, Zechariah, Ron, Keith, Stacy, James, Catarina, Rick, Christine, Sandra, Shantai, Cynthia, and Tonya sat on the front rows. Catarina went home but came back to be with James when he told her about Grandma Harris' death. The choir sang some of Grandma Harris' favorite songs. Pastor Williams had to keep his emotions in check the entire day because of the care, love, and friendship they shared was great and he along with so many others were going to miss Grandma Harris greatly. He wore a black and red robe and approached the pulpit.

"I thank God for all of you being here and your much-needed prayers for Miss Harris' family, loved ones, and many friends. There are no words that could be said to express how loving and caring this sister was. She did not just come to church, she lived it. And for all you that know anything about her, we can all agree, this woman was a prayer warrior, seven days a week."

"Amen." The church said.

"Miss Harris or Grandma Harris as everyone called her was eighty-four years old but with so much energy and drive. She was an example of a person living their life and not just existing and walking in the spirit of Christ. I am not going to give a sermon because her life was a sermon, and it would take far too long to share such a great woman's story. She had many testimonies of overcoming and seeing God move in so many other lives around her. Now, you all can come up front to view her and say your final farewells, and may God bless us all to get through this day."

Sheila and immediate family members came up first but when Diana and Ron walked up, Diana became very emotional and leaned over into the casket crying, holding on to Grandma Harris' body. Ron had to comfort and gently pulled her away with Sheila and Zechariah helping him. Over a thousand people viewed her body, and the funeral procession was just as long going to the cemetery. As the Pastor said his final words, you could hear the cries of hundreds of people. This woman was loved. Ron held Diana's hand the entire time as she sat in the chair and stared out in space with a blank look on her face.

The service was over, and everyone was leaving but Diana would not leave, and no one could make her. Ron told everyone to go, and he would sit here with her for as long as it took. Zechariah did not want to leave her, but Sheila said she was in the best of hands, her son. He kissed her and they walked away but not Keith and Stacy. As always, he stood by his friend and had four of the *Young Wolves* with him as well. Three of the

Cemetery grounds keepers responsible for lowering the body in the ground became impatient and wanted them to leave. One of them walked over to Ron.

"Excuse me sir, we are sorry for your loss, but we have a job to do, and we need to lower the body and cover the hole so we can go home and eat."

It took the power of God to keep Diana from leaping out of her chair on this man, but she stared at him with so much anger in her eyes.

"Get away from her, don't you touch her." She yelled at him then looked at Ron. "Ron, please make them go away, don't let them take my grandma yet, please." Her eyes filled with tears as she looked at Ron and held on to him for dear life.

Ron gave him a look that said it all and then looked at Keith, which was all it took. Stacy knew how protective Keith was over Ron, so she held his hand and kissed him.

"Baby, remember who you are in Christ and do not allow the devil to use you, but my heart is breaking because I see so much pain in Diana."

"Yeah, okay I know who I am." He looked at Stacy and he and the *Young Wolves* walked toward the man.

"Sir, I know you all got work to do but I am sure you can understand the situation." He smiled at the man and the other two with him and the *Young Wolves* opened their suit jacket revealing guns in their shoulder holsters while smiling.

"Take all the time you need sir, we are gone." He looked at the guys with the guns and all three walked away, quickly.

An hour later, Diana was finally able to stand with tears in her eyes and little physical strength, but she said her final goodbye to Grandma Harris and held on to Ron as they all walked to the limo and drove away.

The cemetery was close to woods and after everyone left six large wolves appeared at the edge of the woods. One began to change into Leticia Wilson, and she stood there dressed in all black. The other five walked from the woods toward the casket and started growling and biting on the casket. The three grounds keepers saw the wolves and were about to run when lightning came out of nowhere and hit the ground close to the wolves. The wolves ran towards the woods but did not make it. Lightning struck again, hitting them all and their bodies imploded, leaving nothing but ashes. The men saw all this and took off running and yelling.

"Help us Jesus, help us." One of them fell and he started screaming. "Forgive me Lord, I won't cheat on my wife no more, slap her around, and use your name in vain."

The other two stopped running and went back to help him get up. They continued running, repenting of their sins with each step they took.

After Leticia witnessed all this, she now fully understood the confidence of Grandma Harris approaching her the way she did. Even after seeing the lightning strike and the wolves destroyed, her arrogance compelled her to change back into a wolf and slowly walk towards Grandma Harris' casket but only made three steps when it started thundering and lightning. The wolf looked up and howled and ran back into the woods.

# CHAPTER TWENTY TWO
*Positive Distraction or Downfall*

**W**eeks passed and Diana has not been the same since Grandma Harris died. She and Ron have not made love, she does not go out unless she absolutely must, and the only people she talks to was Zechariah and Sheila. Ron fully understood what she was going through and was being very patient with her and treating Diana like a queen. And he dealt with his grief as well, he loved Grandma Harris. He was finally able to convince Diana to ride with him to the club for a while because he needed to be there for an important company meeting. They were casually dressed. Diana wore a dress and Ron wore dress slacks and a shirt. They would go out and eat afterward. As Ron drove he placed his hand on her thigh and Diana knew what he wanted.

"Ron, I thank you for being so patient with me through all this, but I need a little more time."

"Diana, I love you for better or worse and I miss Grandma Harris deeply, always will, which is why it is so important for me to keep mentally busy," he caressed her thigh. "But on the real, and this is to make you laugh but it is the truth. I miss us being physically close. I miss your warm touch tremendously. Yes, I miss you and all your good hot lovin. The other morning when you got out of bed with your T-shirt and panties on, I looked at you shaking your hips and butt, my dick and brain got hard. I thought I was going to pass out." He smiled at her.

Diana was not in the mood to laugh but laughed at what Ron said and she shook her head.

"You know what Ron, you are a man. All it takes to satisfy you all is some good cooking and sex. I love my husband."

"Thank you for your love but I don't want some sex, I want to make love to my wonderful wife and when I do, you better be prayed up sister because it's going to be some furniture moving in our house." He leaned over and kissed her on the cheek.

They arrived at the club and Diana was impressed by all the changes they made to the place concerning decorations, but she still did not like being here. She always felt in her spirit this place would be Ron's downfall but so far, his walk with Christ has not changed. And he treated her with so much respect, so she did not complain to him that often. As they walked to one of the main lounges Keith, Stacy, Zechariah, Shantai, Cynthia, Tonya, the *Young Wolves*, and ten other club employees sat at a long table. All the women wore dress shirts and skirts and the men wore business suits. Zechariah was the first one to stand and hug Diana.

"Hi, Diana it is good to see you sweetie and I am glad you decided to get out of the house. I missed you."

"Thanks dad. I'm not adjusting well with my grandma gone. Every time I think of her not being in my life, and she was my only family. It is heartbreaking." She started crying.

"Your grandmother can never be replaced but you have me and I will love you for life." He hugged her.

"I know and thank you. I love you back, you know that." She hugged him.

Keith, Shantai, Cynthia, and Tonya hugged her as well, and then Stacy whom she has missed the most.

"I missed you Diana," Stacy kissed her on the cheek. "Before this meeting gets started let's walk and talk please." They walked away to another section of the club to have some privacy.

Everyone sat down and the meeting began with Keith talking about the grand opening of the club and how he and Ron wanted things to happen. Zechariah discussed security details and the new changes he made in the exterior and interior of the facility. Ron emphasized keeping a strict dress code and behavior concerning customers along with escorting any customers to their car if requested. The meeting continued with various details of business being discussed but thirty minutes later, Stacy and Diana had not returned so Keith went to look for them.

Stacy and Diana sat at one of the private booths talking when they realized how long they have been away and were missing the meeting.

"Thank you so much Stacy for talking to me, it helped, and I have missed us spending time together, but I know Ron and Keith are going to be upset with us for not being at the meeting."

"Don't concern yourself with Keith and his emotions. My baby loves me, and I love him back. And he can't resist all this *FULL SEVEN* lovin I am giving him. The brother is sprung." She smiled.

Diana waved her hand in Stacy's face.

"Too much information, thank you very much. I know you two love each other deeply. It is such a blessing to see people walk in the spirit of real love and not material things. You know I love Ron so much, but I have not been the same since my grandma died and I have no sex drive. Nevertheless, Ron has been very patient with me, and I love him for it."

"Give it time Diana. Anyway, we need to go." They stood to leave, stared into each other's eyes, and kissed, and Diana put her hands on Stacy's butt and rubbed it.

Keith was close and saw them kissing, which gave him mixed emotions of anger, betrayal, jealousy, and a sexual turn on. He stepped back so they would not see him and made it look like he was just walking towards them.

"Excuse me you two but there is a company meeting going on and your presence would be greatly appreciated. Thank you."

"We are coming baby." Stacy said after they hugged again and walked towards Keith. Stacy tried to kiss him, but Keith played it off by turning his head and caressed her hips playfully.

Stacy knew Keith so well she could detect his change in mental behavior and she noticed his vibe towards her was different. She wondered if he saw them kiss? If so, this would be bad. They walked back to the table and continued with the meeting. After talking for another two hours, it was time for the meeting to end and everyone was laughing at this point and having a good time.

The club doorbell rang and one of the employees answered it. Leticia Wilson stood there wearing heels and a body-hugging dress to her ankles with a long slit on both sides. Her five bodyguards accompanied her wearing white business suits. Leticia walked in like she owned the club with every step, showing her beautiful legs. The employee escorted her to where the meeting took place thinking she was part of it. The moment they saw her, Keith, Ron, Zechariah, and the *Young Wolves* stood and you saw the instant attitude on their faces. The *Young Wolves* pulled their jackets back exposing their guns.

"May we help you miss? You are interrupting our meeting." Zechariah said with a serious attitude.

"Good afternoon everyone and please forgive me for my untimely entrance but I came by with hopes we could discuss a business venture. I also wanted to congratulate you on your forthcoming grand opening, I plan on attending and would like to support you. I can make sure it will be a success by having the right people attend, this would bring your business national attention."

They all looked at each other and then looked at Leticia like she was crazy.

"Well, from one business owner to another we appreciate the kind jester, but we have everything under control and our grand opening has already been planned.  If you would like to make an appointment to discuss business, we will be glad to sit down and hear what is on your mind." Keith said.

Stacy and Diana stood next to each other and gave one another a look they understood because they knew this lady was nothing but trouble. And she did not have good intentions and did not want Ron and Keith dealing with her on any level. Stacy knew a trick when she saw one, regardless of her class and wealth.

"I have a thought. Since I am already here and it looks like your meeting is over, what I have to say, will not take long. So, would you spare me some of your valuable time now?"

Diana and Stacy gave Keith and Ron a look that said, you better say no. Shantai, Cynthia, and Tonya stared at Leticia admiring her beauty. Ron looked at Keith and nodded his head.

"We can make an exception this once since you are already here. Please come to the table and have a seat." Keith said.

The employees who sat at the table left. Leticia walked over and sat across from them purposely exposing more of her legs than necessary. Her bodyguards sat at another table close by and they and the *Young Wolves* watched each other. Everyone felt the sexual seductive spirit Leticia operated in and it made all the women at the table angry and some were also turned on. Stacy could not hold her piece any longer.

"So, what business venture are you here to discuss." She looked at Leticia with a serious attitude.

"Miss Stacy, you are very direct, and I like that." She rolled her eyes at her and looked at Keith, disrespecting Stacy's very presence.

Diana sat next to Ron and pinched his leg underneath the table. Ron knew why she did it and what she wanted but business was important, and a wise person does more listening than talking.

"Miss Wilson, please get to your point. We are busy." Ron said.

Leticia wanted to kill them all right here and now, but she knew it was not the time, so she controlled her rising anger and remained focused by giving Ron a fake smile.

"My business proposal is this, my hotel and casino is a very thriving business attracting customers from around the nation, which will only increase. I know your business will be successful, so why not work together sending customers each other's way, thereby we could lock down the entire DMV area and surrounding states. In time, your business could hit the billion-dollar status as well. So, what do you think?" While she talked she mumbled to herself speaking curses to the club. She knew all the women disliked her being here, so she decided to give them all something to hate her for. Leticia uncrossed her legs slowly knowing they all could see her panties.

For a few seconds, everyone at the table looked between Leticia's legs which were what she wanted. Shantai, Cynthia, and Tonya had the same lustful thoughts at the same time. Ron and Keith were glad they were sitting down to hide their growing erections, but Zechariah was not moved by her and knew she was a wolf in sheep's clothing. He was hoping they would not do business with this woman.

"Miss Wilson, we appreciate your offer, but we are going to have to decline. Keith and I have a plan for our business and future businesses as well and the direction we desire for them to go in. But again, thank you for your offer." Ron said.

"Yes, we thank you for your offer and time. Now, if you will excuse us, we have a meeting to finish." Keith said trying not to show his interest in her, but he found her very captivating in various ways.

"Well, don't say I did not offer, and I wish you the best on your businesses," She moved slowly when uncrossing her legs to stand and kept them open a few seconds longer than necessary. "Have a good day everyone." Leticia walked out as gracefully as she walked in, knowing all eyes were on her again, as she liked. Her bodyguards followed behind her.

Keith and Ron were not thinking when they stood, realizing too late they had erections. Stacy and Diana noticed and became livid because they knew Leticia was the cause of it and not them. The look they gave them could kill. What made matters worse was Cynthia, Shantai, and Tonya noticed their erections as well and this caused Cynthia to desire Keith more than she already did.

Cynthia loved Stacy but felt she was not the same woman, and Keith needed more excitement in his life than what Stacy was giving him. She also began to question her life choices. Did she give her life to God for herself or because she felt like she had to? Anger began to build up in her and she wanted to take it out on Leticia. So, she walked towards the door quickly.

"Cynthia where are you going?" Keith said.

"I will be right back." Never breaking stride as she walked out.

Leticia and her bodyguards were about to get in the limo when Cynthia walked towards them with fire in her eyes. Leticia looked up and saw her coming and motioned for her bodyguards to relax because she saw this as a great opportunity.

"Miss Wilson, I would like to speak with you."

Leticia stepped closer to her.

"Yes, what can I do for you and make it quick because I am in a hurry."

"Not a problem. Why did you come here? All I see is a woman trying to use her looks and money to control people. Don't you have enough money or are you that damn greedy?"

Leticia saw fire in her eyes which she liked but also wanted to reach over and snatch her throat out for talking to her so disrespectfully.

"You are direct. You may see it that way but all I was doing was trying to collaborate with another business owner so we all may prosper. Since you are standing here, do you mind going for a ride with me so we can talk? I know you are working here but I can offer you a lot more. At least give me the benefit of the doubt and hear what I have to say."

RONALD GRAY

109

Cynthia knew this was a bad idea but at the same time, this could be the opportunity she needed to establish her business contacts. She wanted her club and working for Keith and Ron would give her good experience but maybe, just maybe this woman could help her. She heard a voice in her spirit say, *don't go, beware*. She dismissed it.

"There is no harm in listening to what you have to offer but I can't stay long, and you have to bring me back here."

"Not a problem, please get in."

They all got in the limo and it drove away. Cynthia sat across from Leticia and Leticia continued crossing her legs as they talked.

"Let me get directly to my point. What do you want for yourself? Because I see a determined young lady who desires her own business. The question is, how badly do you want it? Or are you so many others who talk and think it is magically supposed to happen? Reality check, life is not like that."

"You got me mixed up with someone else. I will do what is necessary to get what I want, believe that."

Leticia stared at her.

"That is good to hear. Then come work for me and I will give you a starting salary of one-hundred and twenty-thousand dollars a year plus many perks."

"What! You would pay me that? Wow, well it does give me something to think and pray about."

"You do that and think about this as well."

Two women who sat on both sides of Cynthia grabbed her arms and started rubbing and caressing her legs and before Cynthia could react, they pulled her shirt open and snatched her bra off. One was kissing, licking, and sucking her breasts and the other was kissing her lips. Cynthia tried hard to resist and pushed them off, but Leticia lifted her skirt, pulled her panties down, and buried her face between her legs quickly. She mumbled some words and licked her to orgasm with great oral skills.

For the next hour, they had sex with Cynthia in the back of the limo giving her multiple orgasms even when she begged them to stop because she could not take any more. What she was experiencing was evil spirits controlling and corrupting her. She felt as though she had no will of her own and let them do whatever they wanted to her because everything felt incredibly good.

Cynthia was dropped off at home and could not take a shower fast enough. She felt so dirty and repulsed and could not believe something like this could happen to her so quickly. She remembered turning a deaf ear to the voice that warned her not to go. She laid on her bed in a T-shirt after showering and cried for hours, then prayed, asking God to forgive her but she felt nothing and went to sleep thinking God had left her.

Cynthia woke up hours later sexually turned on more than she has ever been in her life and started thinking about Rick and how good he was in bed and how freaky he was. She had to call him.

"Hi Cynthia. It's three o'clock in the morning are you alright?"

"I know it is late Rick and I apologize for calling at this hour, but I need to talk with you. I am dealing with something." She started crying hysterically.

"Cynthia, calm down and pray, I will be there as fast as I can."

"Thank you Rick and please hurry, I feel like I am about to go crazy."

"Just relax, I am on my way." He hung the phone up.

Cynthia stopped crying and started laughing.

"Rick, you have no idea what is coming your way. I am going to fuck you so good and you can have me any way you want. I will be your super freak." She started masturbating.

Rick took a quick shower and got dressed so fast he was out of the door in thirty minutes. He put on tennis shoes, sweatpants, and a T-shirt but he forgot to do the most important thing, pray. If so, God would have revealed to him what spirit Cynthia was operating in. Rick was headed for a meeting of the worst kind.

# CHAPTER TWENTY THREE

*Not Praying*

**R**ick arrived at Cynthia's condo an hour later knocking on her door. She opened it and stood there in a pair of thin shorts and a T-shirt with no underwear or bra on. He could tell she had been crying and she hugged him tightly making sure to press her breasts against his chest.

"Oh Rick, I am so glad to see you. Thank you for coming by, please come in and sit down." She walked across the room shaking her butt and sat on the sofa and crossed her legs. She had it going on and knew it and she and Rick have been together, so she knew exactly what turned him on.

Rick watched her walk across the room. He noticed she had no bra on or underwear underneath those thin shorts she wore. He sat next to her and knew this was a mistake, but he was here now and felt he could handle it.

"So, tell me what is wrong and bothering you so much. You don't seem like the type of woman who would allow much to affect you."

"Damn Rick, you make me sound like a cold heartless woman. Fact is, no matter how strong I may be, I have feelings and needed someone to talk with who would not judge me or tell me the devil is attacking me."

Rick could not help laughing.

"Cynthia, I am not laughing at you it's just the way you said what you said. I am here now so talk to me. What's wrong?"

"I have been having some awfully bad dreams of people chasing me and having some extremely nasty erotic thoughts. I pray and read the bible, but the problem is not going away. I try to live the right life, but all this is affecting me, and I do not know what to do. Rick, I have not been with anyone since you, but I have been masturbating a lot lately. My mind feels like it's going in so many directions at the same time."

Cynthia kept twisting her body while on the sofa talking to Rick, knowing this made her shorts go up in her butt. She leaned over and rested her head on Rick's shoulder and brushed her leg against his. Rick knew she did this on purpose, and it was getting to him, so he was ready to leave.

"Cynthia, I know you are dealing with a lot, but I know prayer is the answer to it all. I am no one's judge because we all have something in our lives to deal with. So keep praying and let God do the rest. Now, I don't want to but it's late and I need some sleep because I have an early rise in a couple of hours."

She was not about to be defeated when she was so close.

"Please don't leave yet Rick. All I want is a friend to lean on so don't turn your back on me now, please." She began to cry, stood up with her shorts between her butt, walked over to the kitchen counter, and leaned over it with her head down.

Rick was about to leave but when Cynthia stood up, all he could focus on was the shorts all up in her butt and her leaning over the counter. He became aroused instantly. Cynthia turned her head to see the print in his pants and this was all she needed. She walked over and sat in his lap grinding on his erection while facing him. Rick was about to get up when Cynthia reached over and grabbed the back of the sofa with both hands so he could not stand and pushed down on him hard. Rick put his arms around her waist and kissed her. She whispered in his ear every nasty and erotic word that came to her mind, sucking and kissing on his neck. That was it for Rick, he snatched off her shirt and sucked on her breasts and nipples. He pulled off his sweatpants, underwear, and her shorts. Cynthia sat on top of him riding his dick fast and hard while holding on to his shoulders. She started cussing and biting his neck then had a powerful orgasm. Rick bent her over the sofa, and it turned him on so much watching his dick slide inside her and feeling her round butt with each stroke. He made Cynthia climax again. They moved to the floor and eventually to her bedroom.

For the last three hours, they had sex and now the sun was coming up and they were still having sex. Cynthia had several orgasms and they took a break to get something to drink and back to sex. Once again Rick licked, sucked, caressed, and tasted her body front and back but this time Cynthia was not going to allow him bragging rights later. So, she showed him more of her skills by sucking his dick very well. Afterward, they were finally exhausted. They looked at each other and laughed then got up to shower and laid down embracing one another until they fell asleep.

# CHAPTER TWENTY FOUR
*Emotional Bridge*

Ever since the meeting at the club, Keith thought about seeing Stacy and Diana kissing, wondering what was going on or maybe he thought too much about it. Well, he was tired of wondering and not having answers, so he decided to confront Stacy. They were the best of friends and no matter what, they could always discuss anything and had each other's back, right or wrong. They were at home in their gym working out together. Stacy wore tennis shoes, a tank top, and shorts that left little to the imagination. Keith had on boots, sweatpants, and a tank top. Keith was doing a set of squats on the squat rack; he finished and changed the weight for Stacy. He stood behind her as she did ten reps and he saw a lot of her butt and rubbed it each time she did a rep.

Stacy turned around and hit him in his chest while drinking some bottled water.

"See, that's why you can't get your workout done, too busy focusing on my butt," she turned to the side and looked at it. "It is very nice and hard to resist." She smiled at him.

"You are absolutely beautiful Stacy, inside and out. Is that why you and Diana were kissing because it was hard to resist."

Diana was drinking water when Keith said that, and she almost spat it out. This caught her completely off guard and she did not know what to say. Should she finally tell him the truth? No! It would destroy what they share and hurt his ego, but she could not lie either because he would see right through her. So, she decided to tell the truth but downplay it.

"Keith, you are talking about seeing us being affectionate at the club. It was not what you might think. Diana is going through a very rough time in her life right now and needed to talk. We hugged and kissed it is no big deal. Women show affection differently than men."

"Yeah, well all that is true, but I saw her hands on your ass, rubbing it when you two were kissing. That is not just being affectionate, and you know it and don't insult me." He pointed his finger at her.

"Baby, you are making far too much out of all this. Okay, let me ask you something, why do men pat each other on the butt when playing football. They keep doing it throughout the entire game. That's a lot of butts being rubbing."

He did not want to admit it, but she made a good point.

"Good point and personally I never understood why they do that. I do not care how cool I am with someone; you will never see me patting him on his butt. Ron is my best friend, but we do not go around patting each other on the butt. We give each other pound but that's it, ain't no butt rubbing." He knew he could never tell Ron about Stacy and Diana kissing. It would ruin what he and Diana shared for sure.

Stacy began to feel she convinced him but hated deceiving him but saw no other way to get out of this situation and keep the tight bond between them.

"That's my point. Besides, you must admit," she stepped closer, turned her back to him, and started rubbing her butt on his crotch while looking back at him. "All this is hard to resist." She laughed and turned around and kissed him.

He placed his hands on her butt.

"I don't have to resist rubbing all this fat ass of yours because it's all mine, you remember that." He started kissing and sucking on her neck and tried to pull her shorts off.

She backed up from him and laughed.

"Baby not now, I am all hot and sweaty. Let's go take shower first and then..."

Keith pulled her into him and slid her shorts and panties down quickly, in one move.

"I like you all hot and sweaty." He kicked his boots off, pulled his sweatpants and underwear off and bent Stacy over the bench and rubbed his dick between her butt until he was fully erect then slid inside her. He was not fully convinced she told him the total truth, but he would deal with that later, right now he wanted to be nasty and started pumping into her while smacking her on the butt.

"Oh Keith, you are so nasty, but I love it. Your dick is so hard baby and so good."

For the next thirty minutes, they tried to sex each other's brains out until satisfied and took a shower together. Afterward, they gave one another full-body massages, got dressed, and went shopping to have some fun. It was a great day as they enjoyed each other's company but Stacy felt a difference in Keith's spirit towards her. She also noticed Keith looked at other women more than he ever has. It made her wonder was he drifting away from her, or has she caused an emotional wall between them? Any two people can have great sex and still not be close where it matters. Her spirit was sad although she smiled on the outside and thought about telling him the entire truth but quickly decided against it. She hoped they would spend more time in prayer and let God work it out, she hoped.

# CHAPTER TWENTY FIVE
*Truth Revealed*

It is Friday night, two weeks after the employee meeting at the club. This was the grand opening of Keith and Ron's club, *New Beginnings*. A lot of marketing and advertising was done to promote this event including radio, flyers, and TV commercials. Everything was in place and going well, except for Diana, she was not in the mood to go. She had no desire to get dressed up and go to some club, grand opening or not. So far, Ron has not been able to convince her, and he has tried everything he knew but was now losing his patience with her. They were in their bedroom, and he was getting dressed while Diana sat on the bed watching TV. Ron picked up the remote and turned the TV off and then snatched the batteries out and threw them in the trash.

Diana looked at him like he lost it.

"Ron, I was watching TV and I can't believe you would be so rude and disrespect me like that. What is wrong with you?"

"Me, what is wrong with me," he looked at her like she was crazy. "Diana, I know you have been on an emotional roller coaster with the death of Grandma Harris, and I have been very understanding of this. However, you are being selfish because it is not all about you. I am your husband; we are a team. We laugh, cry, pray, dance, and do everything together. This is a big night for me and you know it, so can you please get dressed?"

"I know you have been patient with me, and I know this is a big night for you but even if I was not depressed, going to the club is not my thing. We should be in church on Friday night, not a club."

He knew she would eventually go there.

"Diana, you are right and most of the time we are in church on Friday nights. This is the grand opening of the club, this is your husband's business, this is how we provide for ourselves so we can eat. So, stop being selfish and support your husband as you know I would do you, with no question. This seems to be a pattern with you when things get tough in our relationship you don't support me, as you should."

"I can't believe you would say something like that to me Ron when you know all the things, I have dealt with concerning you. Your rebellious ways, prison, more rebellious ways, and lying to me many times, so you can have your way," she walked towards him and put her finger in his face. On top of all that, you deceived me so we could get married. You spent all that money to get me, told me you were no longer involved in the drug life when you were. That is an outright lie. You knew that was the only way you could have your way with me and get me in bed."

Ron looked at her in total disbelief.

"Interesting words Diana and you meant every word you just said. The bible says, *Out of the abundance of the heart, the mouth speaks,* and you spoke your heart. Yes, I made some mistakes, but I have never turned my back on you and if you think I married you at that time, just to have sex, you are delusional Diana. This is a wake-up call sister, I was good-looking and well paid then, I am good-looking and well paid now, only my heart is right. I don't have to pay for sex, you are something else," he lowered his head in sadness then looked at her. "You know what Diana, since you feel that way, you don't have to go with me tonight or any other night for that matter. Fact is, you do not have to be with me at all since I tricked you into marriage as you say. I am going to work and remain focused on the things I must do. You can do whatever it is you desire to do with your life. Know this, I married you because I love you deeply and always have, always will. You pushed me away, remember that. Since you do not want to support me, stand by me, or be with me, then we are done." He stared at his wedding band, took it off and threw it on the bed. He walked away to finish getting dressed.

Diana felt bad now for what she said but at the same time, spiritually she felt as if a weight was lifted from her because she held all that in for so long. When Ron took his wedding band off and threw it on the bed, something in her snapped. It felt as if a part of her was ripped into, the pain was instant and tremendous. She knew for a fact she does not want to lose her husband. She grabbed the ring and walked towards Ron holding her hand out with the ring in it.

"I cannot believe you did that. I know you are upset with me, but you better put this ring back on, you are still my husband, and I am not playing games with you Ron."

"Diana, you made your point very well and for the record, I don't play relationship games. I will not go back and forth with you, wondering if you are going to stand by me this day or the next. That is playing games. So, do whatever you want. I am almost dressed, and you do not have to be bothered with me, I am not coming home tonight. I will be at Keith's." He turned to walk away.

Diana was angry now and wanted him to listen. She grabbed his arm, pulled him back, and got in his face.

"Ronald Emmanuel O'Neil, if you do not put this ring back on and you walk out that door and do not take me with you, it is

RONALD GRAY                                              121

going to be some furniture moving in this room and it will not be because of sex." She looked directly into his eyes and held the ring out to him. "Ron please don't leave me. Can we pray for a while, please?" Tears began to flow from her eyes until it was like a flood gate opened and she fell to her knees crying hysterically.

Everything she just said and seeing her pain touched Ron's heart and spirit. He kneeled next to her and held Diana as she cried. Ron knew it was a great deal more than the club, she was hurting from her loss and all the things she has been through. He could not hold back his tears. After Diana cried herself out, they prayed and called on God to heal and help them remain strong. Ron put his ring back on and carried Diana to bed.

"You don't have to go, and I will be back as soon as everything is over, I promise." He leaned over and kissed her.

She grabbed his arms.

"Ron, please don't go, make love to me. I need my husband, please baby."

How could he resist the woman of his heart and spirit? He got undressed and laid beside her. For the next hour, they hugged, kissed, and made love like it was the last time, so full of passion and emotional desires. Diana cried as she held on to her husband for dear life, and he was so gentle with his every touch to please her and not just physically but emotionally as well. Her tears flowed as she asked God to keep them as one. This was a night neither of them will ever forget. Diana screamed from satisfaction when she climaxed, knowing her husband of many prayers was loving her the way she desired and welcomed his seed inside her.

They held each other and kissed for a while before getting up to shower and got dressed. Diana was no fool, she was going with her man. She was dressed to impress, not the world, but her husband, her friend. She stepped out of her walk-in closet wearing Ivory color heels and a tailor-made ivory color jumpsuit, that hugged her every curve. Yes, she felt a little convicted for wearing such a revealing outfit but tonight would probably be her last night going to this club, so pleasing Ron was important to her. Ron wanted to look like money tonight and have some fun, so he put on a *Ermenegildo Zegna* ten-thousand-dollar suit, three-thousand-dollar *Berluti Rapieces* shoes, and a seventy-thousand-dollar *Rolex Daytona Cosmograph* watch. When he stepped out of the bathroom and saw Diana, he wanted to stay home. He got an immediate erection.

"Wow, you look so fine, and I know you are wearing that outfit for me, and I appreciate it, but you don't have to. Damn, you look good. When I get you home tonight, I am licking your ass and pussy." He smiled at her.

Diana could not help but laugh.

"Ron, you are something else. I like dressing up for you and speaking of dressing. I have never seen that suit and I will not ask how much it cost because it looks expensive. You look so good in it, and you thought I was going to let you walk out of this house by yourself. I don't think so." She hugged and kissed him and felt his erection and desired him all over again.

"Let's get out of here baby before we can't leave, and I have you up against that wall holding your hips."

They laughed and kissed then walked out of the house and into the Bentley.

# CHAPTER TWENTY SIX
## New Beginnings Grand Opening

It was a perfect night for the opening of the club. The temperature was seventy-five degrees outside with a cool breeze. The function of the *New Beginnings* club was set up differently than most nightclubs with various rules and regulations. Through company policy, they instituted a moral code of respect that was highly enforced the moment you set foot inside the facility. There was zero tolerance for the use of profanity, a serious dress code, no use of the *N-word* or the *B*-word. Patrons would receive one warning, the second time they would be asked to leave the premises, subject to being barred forever. The club did not have bouncers, it had security personnel called, *Special Police* and everyone had degrees in criminal justice and was highly trained in this field. The uniform was all black and they wore body armor with *Special Police* written across the back. Company policy mandated all security personnel respect customers to the fullest. Proper attitude and manners were to be used always but the security personnel powers started and stopped at the club.

When Ron and Diana drove up, they saw the long line wrapped around the corner and everyone was dressed nicely. Zechariah was outside with other security personnel talking to the customers and admitting them. He looked great in his *Hickey Freeman* suit. Sheila did not like him working at the club, but she understood how difficult it was for convicted felons to find decent jobs and she was supportive of him. As they drove up in front, Zechariah greeted them with a hug and kissed Diana on the cheek then stared at her.

"You look great Daughter. You know I like saying that."

"Thanks Dad," she hugged him again, stared at him, and had to hold back the tears because she loved him so much and he was her only family now. "You look good in that suit."

"Thank you," he looked at Ron. "Your husband is killing them in his suit. Is this the owner of the entire state?" They all laughed.

Three white Cadillac Escalade ESV's pulled up in front of the club and four young black men stepped out from each vehicle wearing grey boots and grey security uniforms with *Young Wolves* written on the back of the shirts. All were clean-cut and muscular with two shoulder holsters carrying Glock 17's. Keith walked out of the club and saw them. Everyone knew who they were. Keith and Zechariah greeted them, and they all gave Ron a nod out of respect when they walked in. Keith was dressed the same as Ron but had on a different color suit and a different watch.

Four burgundy Cadillac Escalade's ESV's pulled up and had everyone's attention including Zechariah, Ron, Diana, and Keith as they wondered if this was a celebrity. Five large men wearing suits stepped out from each vehicle and then James and Catarina stepped out. They looked so good together with James wearing a tailored-made suit and Catarina wearing a tailored oriental style dress with short slits on both sides. Everyone greeted them with hugs. Ron and Keith wondered what the deal was with all the extra security traveling with him. James said he would talk with them later. Catarina did not want all this attention, but it was ordered by her father because his men went missing in India and he was concerned for her safety. The valet personnel moved all the vehicles.

As Ron, Diana, Keith, and Zechariah were about to walk in the club three white stretch limos and three white Rolls Royce's pulled up. Several attractive women stepped out of the limos wearing sexy outfits. Five women from each Rolls stepped out wearing white dresses and pants and among them was none other than Leticia Wilson with her bodyguards. She did this to make a scene because she loved the attention. Leticia and her bodyguards wore white dresses with long slits on the side. And they walked with such raw eroticism, all eyes were on them. Keith stepped forward to greet her.

"Miss Wilson, you do know how to make an entrance and that dress you are wearing may get you in trouble." Keith smiled but did not like her.

"Good day to you sir. You know I would not miss your grand opening and brought some people with me." She stepped closer to Keith and whispered in his ear. "It's not the dress that causes problems but who is wearing the dress and you know you want to fuck me." She bumped into him, and she and her team walked into the club.

Keith stared at her walking away and had to repent because her warm breath on his ear and the words she used aroused him. He looked around nodding to Zechariah and Ron and walked in. Ron shook his head as he walked in but as he passed Zechariah, he gave him a pound and then Zechariah touched Ron's shoulder.

"Ron, watch out for my baby girl."

"Always my brother, with my life." He walked to catch up with Diana and looked at the way she walked drawing a lot of attention. He put his arm around her waist. Diana always loved the attention he gave her and the queen treatment.

Tonya, Shantai, Cynthia, Catarina, and Stacy wore dresses and skirts. They were tight but not too short. Rick had on dress slacks and a dress shirt, and they all sat in one of the VIP sections with Catarina's security close by and the *Young Wolves*. Ron and Diana walked over, and everyone greeted her. Leticia and her team sat in another VIP section. This was a great time for everybody, talking and laughing and enjoying this wonderful event. Stacy gave Cynthia mean looks for having Rick here. She did not dislike him, but she felt it was only a matter of time before something happened between them, that should not. If she only knew.

Keith walked over and Stacy hugged him like they have not seen each other in weeks. They kissed then sat down and joined the conversation. Cynthia tried not to be obvious concerning her attraction to Rick, but he sat next to her, smelled, and looked so good. For an older man, he was well put together. Everyone saw they were attracted to each other. Derrick, one of the *Young Wolves* who Tonya was attracted to, desired to talk with her but now was not the time, although he would come and check on them from time to time mainly to see her. This made Tonya feel special and she planned to talk with him later.

The club was full, and the music was great with people dancing and having fun. Leticia saw them from where she sat and was getting bored, so she decided to do what was in her nature, flirt and cause trouble. She walked over to them and asked Rick if he wanted to dance. The look Cynthia gave Rick and Leticia said it all which motivated Leticia to do more than what she had planned, to cause more problems. Rick thought this was a good idea to keep Cynthia on her toes, besides this woman was gorgeous.

"I don't mind if I do," he stood up. "I need to stretch my legs anyway. Lead the way."

Cynthia was so angry she could spit fire because she knew what this heifer was about, but she had to calm down because she did not want her feelings for Rick to show.

Leticia held Rick's hand as they walked to the dance floor and he looked at this woman up and down, lusting hard but tried not to. As soon as they stepped on the dance floor Leticia started grinding her body on him and she could dance very well, and so could Rick. Cynthia, along with everyone else saw them bumping and grinding while dancing.

Catarina had enough of watching others have fun so she and James got on the dance floor. The others followed, except Ron and Diana who were talking and kissing.

"Ron, you know I am enjoying all this attention you are giving me, but I know you want to dance as well."

"I am good baby, having you next to me is all good." He kissed her.

Diana stood and held her hand out to Ron.

"Come on Ron, dance with me."

"Baby I told you I am good."

"Well, I am not, and I am tired of sitting here, so come on."

"Since you insist, let's do it." They walked to the dance floor, and it was like old times with them as they danced. Diana began feeling convicted of being here and seeing all the people dancing and grinding on each other. Some looked like they were almost having sex on the dance floor, especially the way Leticia was grinding her body all over Rick and she saw the heated look in Cynthia's eyes. But she was here now and wanted to make the best of it.

Two hours later Leticia and her team left then James and Catarina said goodbye to everyone and they left as well. Rick stayed to relax and talk with Cynthia but she gave him the cold shoulder, using work as a reason to walk away from him. He laughed to himself knowing she was upset with him, but he does not play games and would not pursue her in this place. Nonetheless, he stayed to talk with her later.

Tonya and Derrick talked for a while, and he asked her out and she was flattered and said yes but invited him to church and then they would see where things go from there. He smiled and hugged her.

"That woman is fine and got a body." He spoke softly.

Tonya turned around walked towards him.

"I heard what you said." She kissed him on the lips and walked away smiling.

It was three o'clock and time for the club to close, but the place was still packed. The DJ made the announcement its closing time and everyone started leaving. The staff started cleaning the club and it was time for the night's meeting to discuss how everything went. Tonya, Shantai, Cynthia, Diana, and Stacy sat at the meeting room table. Ron, Zechariah, and Keith walked in and sat down.

"I am happy with the way things turned out tonight, a great grand opening. I have no complaints," he looked at Ron. "What about you my brother?"

"It was a good night, despite Leticia Wilson showing up basically to be nosey and be seen."

Rick walked close by and leaned on a railing and looked at Cynthia. Ron noticed him and wanted to have some fun with Cynthia.

"Cynthia, your old man is waiting for you." He started laughing then he, Zechariah, and Keith gave each other some dap and laughed.

Cynthia gave them a mean look and rolled her eyes then stood up.

"He is not my man Ron, and you know that. You three need to mind your own business. Zechariah, don't pick up bad habits being around these two." She walked towards Rick.

"Cynthia do not pay them any attention," Stacy said then gave Keith and Ron a mean look. "You two leave her alone and mind your business." Although she was concerned. "Keith, are you ready to go baby?"

"Yes, let's ride. Ron are you ready? Zechariah the rest is all yours my brother."

"No problem, it was a good night we will talk later." He, Ron, and Keith gave each other dap and he walked away with some of the other security personnel.

Diana looked at him like he lost his mind.

"Zechariah, come back here, you forgot something." She yelled.

He walked back and hugged her.

"I could never forget about you."

"I can't tell." She hugged him again and kissed him on the cheek. Then he walked away.

Shantai and Tonya hugged Keith and Ron and they left. Cynthia was talking to Rick and they walked out together. Ron, Diana, Stacy, and Keith left as well with the girls walking in front and Ron and Keith staring at them. They looked at each other and smiled.

"It's like old times partner, only it is much better not living a crazy criminal life and living in Christ." Keith said.

"Amen my brother and look what is in front of us?" He pointed to Diana and Stacy. They ran and picked them up playfully kissing them on the cheeks and lips.

# CHAPTER TWENTY SEVEN
*Brazil meets Maryland*

James was at a point in his life where he knew exactly what he wanted and he wanted Catarina, but her dad was a hard man and was very protective of his daughter in every way. He was determined not to allow this to stop him. Two months after she came to the club's grand opening she and James became much closer. Catarina was back in Rio working but was sick of the dirty aspect of her dad's business, all the prostitution and everything attached to it. She wanted to be with James but was torn between him and leaving her dad. All they had were each other. Her Mom was killed in a car accident when she was very young, so she was told but always wondered if the rumors of her dad having her killed were true. The rumor was she caught her dad cheating and was going to divorce him and take half of his wealth. A week later she died in a car accident because of failed brakes. Yet, she loved her dad and resented him at the same time. She prayed daily asking God to guide her steps and give her wisdom.

Catarina was at the *Galeao International Airport* in Rio waiting for James and of course, her bodyguards were nearby, at her father's orders. Seeing him always made her a little nervous like a teenager. He walked towards her carrying one bag wearing a short-sleeved shirt, dress slacks, and sandals. He looked good with his tight muscular body and always dressed nicely. She wore heels and appropriate shorts and a blouse.

It was Catarina's loving heart and spiritual maturity James was so drawn to and yes, she was physically breathtakingly beautiful. When James hugged Catarina, he picked her off her feet making her laugh.

"James Reed, you better put me down I do have on shorts, business attire shorts but still shorts."

"You look good in your shorts and everything else you wear." He put her down and they kissed passionately.

She allowed herself to get lost in this moment not caring about her surroundings or who was looking as James' tongue explored her mouth. She felt his hands slide down her hips and fingers touch her butt which made her jump.

"James, behave yourself and let's go before we get in trouble," She looked around and saw her bodyguards looking at them and whispered in his ear. "The bodyguards were looking at us and I know the word will get back to my dad, oh well. I missed you, so let's go."

"No problem," he picked his bag up and pointed to her. "I will follow you and watch." He looked at her up and down.

"Okay, so while you are watching me walk my brother, will your mind be on God or my body?" Smiling at him.

"Well since you put it that way, the truth shall set you free. I will be watching you from the top of your head to your feet, including your nice hips." He started laughing.

Usually, she would find this very offensive, but she had to laugh and grabbed his hand.

"You are something, now come on and we can walk side by side."

They walked out of the airport with her bodyguards and the limo was parked close. They drove back to Belmond Copacabana Palace where Catarina reserved a suite for him. They walked to his suite and the moment the door closed James stepped closer to her, but Catarina held her hand out to him.

"James Reed, stop walking towards me and remove any thoughts from your mind you may be having right now. I only walked with you to your room to be hospitable so..."

James pulled her into him and kissed her passionately while caressing her hips. Catarina's instant reaction was to slap him but found herself jumping up and wrapping her legs around his waist kissing him back just as passionately. The truth was she wanted to make love to him but James did something that surprised her. He put her down and stepped back from her.

"Catarina, I love you and don't want to disrespect you ever so please forgive me." He got down on his knee.

"James, I forgive you baby, you don't have to get on your knees to beg me forgiveness, so please stand up."

"I am not begging you," he reached into his pocket and pulled out a ring. "Catarina Silva, I love you deeply and want us to spend all our days together as husband and wife. Will you marry me?"

Catarina stumbled and almost fell to the floor because of what James just said and did. She was incredibly surprised and could not help but cry.

"James, you have, you have blown me away. Oh my God, you truly have, I don't know what to say."

"Well, if it is truly your heart as it is mine, you can say yes before I get a cramp in my leg."

She stared at James in disbelief and so many things were going through her mind at this very moment but in her heart, she already knew.

"Yes, Mr. James Reed, I will marry you. Oh God, I love you from my spirit and heart." She stepped closer to him.

James put the ring on her finger and kissed her hand.

"You can stand up now my love and hug your fiancé."

He hugged and kissed her with a great desire to have her for life.

"Your lips are always so soft and warm. I could kiss you for many years to come, I want you." He moved behind Catarina and wrapped his arms around her and pressed his body into hers, kissing and sucking on her neck while caressing her hips. His erection was pressed against her butt as his hands moved up to her breasts and caressed them.

Every fiber in Catarina's body wanted him to make love to her and feeling his penis against her was turning her on greatly. She was fighting feelings long suppressed deep within her, but James brought them all to the surface.

"James don't do this to me, you know how badly I want you."

He moved in front of her, got on his knees, and began kissing her stomach while unbuttoning her shorts so he could kiss and suck on her panties and slid his tongue closer to her wetness.

Catarina was so close to climax from James doing this and was going to let him do much more but she could not.

"No James, stop. We can't do this, we just can't." She fixed her clothes and sat on a chair motioning for James to do the same. "Baby please sit down so we can talk."

He looked at her trying to hide his irritation and frustration as he sat on the edge of the bed and pointed his finger at her.

"You are trying to send me to the hospital," he smiled and laughed. "You are a tease, Miss Catarina."

This made her angry because she was called that by many men because she would not have sex with them. She was not able to hide her anger and emotionally snapped.

"Do not call me that. I am not a tease because I don't drop to my knees and start sucking your dick like some slut you met at a club."

James stated laughing and this made Catarina more upset. She stood up to leave when he stood in her way.

"Relax woman, I am laughing because you are so sexy when you get angry, and it only makes me want you more. I have a good job and good credit. Can we get married soon?"

"That's because you are sick, and I am glad you have a job and good credit." His attitude made her smile.

"You have a beautiful smile. Anyway, how do I know you are any good in bed? You might be one of those who lay there. Are your oral skills any good? Basically, how is your head game, you know, can you work your jaw muscles and tongue?" He burst out laughing.

Catarina knew he wanted her to become more upset, but she would not give him the satisfaction.

"I should be asking you that. How are your oral skills, brother?" She leaned towards him making a face then stood holding her arms out. "James let's stop this before a line gets crossed. Hug me, and don't grab my hips or butt." Smiling at him.

He hugged and kissed her, and they walked out of his room holding hands on the way to see her dad.

What Catarina did not know was James had a surprise for her. He was confident Catarina would say yes, so he asked his closest friends to come to Rio and share in his moment. The plane landed in Rio with Zechariah, Sheila, Ron, Diana, Keith, Stacy, Rick, Christine, Sandra, Tonya, Cynthia, Shantai, and ten of the *Young Wolves* walked through the airport. They got in the limos parked outside to carry them to the hotel where James had secretly arranged suites for everyone.

Leticia Wilson was a step ahead of them all. She knew where they were going and what rooms they would all be in. Through out-of-body experience, Leticia transformed her spiritual body to Rio and in each of their rooms, she spoke curses and demonic evil spirits throughout the room. They should have prayed as soon as they walked into their rooms but did not.

They wanted to be here to support James and Catarina but some of them had other motives as well. This is Rio where there are no sexual inhibitions like back in the States. Tonya, Cynthia, and Shantai wanted to walk the beach and show off their bodies especially after they worked out so hard to remain in good shape. Each had the same type of swimwear selected but in different colors, two-piece bathing suits with thongs and a sarong wrapped around their waist. They left their rooms and walked to the beach. Rick had his suite as well and was going to make the best of being in Rio by doing as much site seeing as time would allow and was thankful to have received the call from James. He and James grew closer over the years. Rick tried to talk with and spend time with Cynthia, but she wanted them to keep a low profile. This irritated him but he was in Rio, so he changed and went to the beach to see and be seen. He saw Cynthia with her friends, and she looked incredibly good in her bathing suit. She stopped to talk and flirt with him for a few minutes to be playful and then kept it moving. Zechariah and Sheila prayed in their rooms and then made love. Christine and Sandra wore conservative one-piece bathing suits before going to the beach. The *Young Wolves* were instructed to relax and go to the beach for today. Ron, Diana, Keith, and Stacy shared a large suite and got ready to leave for the beach as well.

"Ron, hurry up so we can go swimming before it gets dark."

"I am ready, let's roll."

Diana and Stacy gave them nasty looks because they knew it was not swimming they were so interested in but going to the beach and watching women. Christian or not, all flesh is the same.

"Ron, you and Keith must think Stacy and I are stupid. We know you only want to go to the beach to see all those nasty girls walking the beach with breasts and butts exposed. They walk around almost naked."

Ron walked over to Diana and kissed her on the lips,

"Diana relax, you are my wife and I only have eyes for you baby. Besides, you are who I desire to come home to every night."

Stacy pointed her finger at Diana.

"Diana don't go for that sweet talk we know what time it is, furthermore, we are going to the beach with you. Believe that!"

"Stacy, you are my wife for life, my ride-or-die but you know how it goes, you don't bring sand to the beach baby." He and Ron started laughing.

"Okay Keith, you and Ron got jokes, no problem. Diana let's go to the other section of the room and get dressed. Keith, you and Ron better not walk out of this room without us."

She and Diana walked to the other side of the room and pulled the divider and changed clothes. When they walked over to them, they wore the smallest tops barely covering their breasts and thongs with a sarong wrapped around their waist. Keith and Ron stared at them then looked at each other and Ron saw anger in Keith's eyes he has not seen since he gave his life to Christ.

"Stacy, I don't know what you are trying to prove but you are not going out in public with your breasts and ass hanging out. Christian or not, don't try me." His anger was building by the second as he looked at her, he exhaled to relax and prayed silently.

"Diana, you think this is funny, go change."

Diana looked at Ron and Keith and then at Stacy. She and Stacy started laughing and walked over to the other side of the room and changed into a conservative one-piece bathing suit and walked over to Ron and Keith.

"So, what was all that about?" Keith said.

"It's about having fun in life but not forgetting who you are. Your joke about not bringing sand to the beach. If you want respect, then give it Keith," she turned to look at Diana. "Diana forgive me for what I am about to say," she looked at Keith. "Keith, you and Ron can try and be sneaky looking at half naked women all you want but if I see your dick hard, when we get back in this room, we are going to have a problem. Believe that."

"Baby how are you going to talk to me like that in front of Ron and his wife. You know that's foul." Trying to keep from laughing.

"Don't play with me Keith Washington I am not in the mood. Let's go Diana." They walked out of the room and down the hallway.

Ron and Keith look at them and laughed.

"Keith, those two are something and I don't feel like going to the beach now. Fact is, I want Diana badly for some reason. I am talking straight freaky type sex."

"I thought it was just me, but I want to snatch Stacy's clothes off and get buck wild with her."

They dapped and walked out.

As Diana and Stacy walked down the hallway Diana could not help but look at Stacy like she used to and was sexually aroused.

"Diana, for some reason and more so than usual I am so horny and want Keith badly."

"Wow, I thought it was just me because I am super horny and dealing with some serious erotic thoughts right now. I don't know why."

"Erotic thoughts, how erotic are those thoughts of yours." She smacked her on the butt.

"Stop Stacy, I know who I am and so do you. So keep your dirty filthy thoughts to yourself, and pray sister, pray."

They got on the elevator laughing at each other.

The limo pulled into the driveway of Mr. Clemente Silva's forty-thousand-foot mansion with a ten-foot wall around the property. It boasted 15 bedrooms, 20 bathrooms and every amenity one could think of including a private indoor pool underneath his 2,000-square feet master bedroom. His bedroom had a door leading to steps to the pool. Mr. Clemente is 56 years old, six-foot-three, two-hundred- forty pounds, brown skin complexion, salt and pepper hair, and handsome with a good physique from daily workouts. His only real love is his daughter

Catarina who he would do anything to protect, at all costs. Due to his mass wealth, armed security guards walked around outside and indoors as well. His staff of ten people catered to his every need twenty-four hours a day.

As James and Catarina got out of the limo he shook his head at the size of this place. Mr. Clemente opened the front door and walked out to greet them. His eyes always lit up whenever he saw his daughter. He hugged and kissed her on both cheeks, which always made her smile and feel like a little girl.

"Daddy, have you missed me as much as I have missed you?"

"I have missed you more," he hugged her again then looked at James with a scowl expression on his face but extended his hand to him. "Mr. James Reed I hope you are taking excellent care of my daughter."

He shook his hand with a firm grip overlooking his scowl look.

"No question sir, she is the love of my life, and it is good to see you again."

"If you say so but I know it's my daughter you want, so many do."

Catarina pinched her dad.

"Daddy please don't start and don't be mean to your future son-in-law." She extended her hand out to him revealing the ring on her finger.

He held her hand and gave her a fake smile as he looked at the ring because he knew someday this would happen but for him, no man was good enough for his daughter. James, who he had a complete background check done, was no exception. Nothing negative came back which he was impressed with because something negative always shows up. He respected

James and his clean life but he did not like him that much. He trusted him because of his strong Christian convictions.

"Wow, that is a beautiful ring and I guess congratulations are in order. Let's go in so we can talk over a lovely seafood meal that has been prepared." He kissed Catarina's cheek and put his arm around her waist as they walked in. James and the security guards followed.

As he walked in, James looked around and was impressed with the ambiance and the size of the place and everything in it was incredible. One could easily get lost walking around without an escort but Catarina was his eyes' primary focus.

"Mr. Silva your house is amazing sir. Incredible, truly incredible. An army of people could live in this place."

"No, they could not, my daughter and I are enough and the necessary staff of course." He looked at James and laughed.

"Dad, be nice please, for me. Remember I am getting married."

They reached one of the dining rooms with a large table in the center that could seat sixteen people and it was decorated immaculately.

"Please sit down so we can talk."
Catarina and James sat next to each other, and Mr. Clemente sat across from them. For the next four hours, they talked and ate while listening to jazz music, requested from Catarina of course. Mr. Clemente wanted to test James by putting him on the spot mentioning if he loved his daughter so much, why have such a long engagement period Americans are famous for. James smiled knowing what he was doing but it fit his plan perfectly and thank God. He asked Catarina would she like to get married in three days. She jumped up and hugged James and kissed him and said

yes. The look her dad gave her was all anger but she dismissed it knowing he did not want them married so soon but he would do whatever made her happy. So, she hugged him too.

# CHAPTER TWENTY EIGHT

*A Day to Remember*

Three days later everything was in place for James and Catarina's wedding. It would take place in the backyard of her home and was beautifully decorated. White and Red roses were everywhere, and one hundred white doves were to be released at the proper time. James had Pastor Williams flown in to assist in performing his wedding along with Pastor Connors of Catarina's church. She wanted the wedding to be simple with close family and friends, but her dad invited his closest business associates. All this attention made her feel a little nervous, but James asked Catarina to relax because all this would be over in a short time. A thousand people attended her wedding including plenty of media coverage.

It was one o'clock in the afternoon and the wedding started on time, Mr. Clemente would have nothing less. Zechariah, Sheila, Ron, Diana, Keith, Stacy, Rick, Christine, Sandra, Tonya, Cynthia, Shantai, and ten *Young Wolves* sat up front. Everyone was dressed well. Catarina's Pastor, Pastor Williams, Mr. Clemente, and James stood up front waiting for Catarina to walk down the aisle. There were five hundred and ten white chairs on both sides. James wore a Grey eight-thousand-dollar *Brioni* suit with shoes and everything to match. The moment had come and *"If This World Was Mine"* by *Luther Vandross & Cheryl Lynn* began playing. Mr. Clemente motioned for everyone to stand as Catarina began walking towards the front wearing a four-hundred-thousand-dollar white wedding gown by *Sarah Burton*, it had a full veil and a twelve-foot train.

Catarina was determined not to cry and walked very carefully to make sure she did not fall. As she reached the front, she saw the look of unconditional love in her dad's eyes and sadness at the same time. She knew he felt like he was losing his only child which made her spirit sad but seeing the excitement and sparkle in James' eyes kept her focused on him and their moment. Mr. Clemente gave his daughter away and sat down hiding his deep sadness. James gave each Pastor one of the rings and a prayer was spoken and then gave each ring to Catarina and James waiting for them to say their wedding vows.

James put the ring on Catarina's finger.

"Miss Catarina Silva, the love I have for you cannot be put into words, and saying, I love you will never be enough. Only by my actions will you fully know. God is the glue to our marriage and if we put him first, we can make it. I promise to be your friend, confidant, and husband God desires me to be."

As the wedding vows were being said Tonya looked at Derrick and they winked at each other.

Catarina put the ring on James's finger.

"Mr. James Reed, only by the hand of God are we standing here today by his grace, mercy, and love. What God has brought together, let no man or anything separate. I will be your help mate for life and love you according to the word of God. You are my rib giver, and I am your rib receiver, and this makes us bone of bone and flesh of flesh. Walking in prayer and love will always be our power."

"By the powers invested in me." Pastor Connors said.

"By the powers invested in me." Pastor Williams said.

"We now pronounce you husband and wife. You may kiss the bride." They said simultaneously.

James lifted her veil and they kissed. The white doves were released, and it was a beautiful sight to see them fly away. Mr. Clemente hugged and kissed his daughter and looked deep into her eyes and saw her overwhelming happiness which made him feel better. He walked over to James and they walked a few feet away from others so their conversation could not be heard.

"James, I have no doubt you love my daughter, and she is a great judge of character. My only desire is you treat her with respect and love and never betray her trust for you," he moved closer to James and stared into his eyes. "Don't break my daughter's heart sir. Or I will break you and everyone close to you." He stared at James with intimidation.

James did not like being threatened but realized who he was dealing with and as a dad, where this man was coming from.

"Relax Mr. Clemente, your daughter is my number two priority, God is number one and I would give my life to protect her."

He looked at James and smiled.

"Good, very good sir. Come, it is your wedding day, time to cut the cake."

James and Catarina cut the seven-tier cake together. Everyone began talking and congratulating them. Music played and the dancing started with James and Catarina having the first dance, then everyone else joined in. Cynthia danced with Rick, and it was emotionally difficult because this man did things to her like no other and she did not want to draw any unnecessary attention to them. Derrick and Tonya danced but as attracted as she was to Derrick, it was more than physical. She had serious feelings for him and the feelings were mutual from Derrick. A slow song came on and they looked great together, but their hormones began to get the best of them, and Tonya whispered in Derrick's ear.

"You know I can feel your penis pressed against me Derrick, so this is our last dance together."

"Not a problem, all in good time." He kissed her on the lips and they continued to dance.

A twenty-one-piece band played various songs and everyone danced and had a great time. Hours later James and Catarina wanted to leave and were saying goodbye to everyone. Mr. Clemente hugged and kissed his daughter and handed James an envelope that contained a check for one-hundred-million dollars, his wedding present to him. He shook James's hand and walked off with a lovely young lady on his arm and they got in a limo, and it drove away with security in front and back. The young lady was talking to Clemente and kissing on his neck trying to seduce him, but his thoughts were on his daughter and Leticia Wilson. She has no idea he planned to take everything she has and destroy her, by any means necessary.

Everyone at the wedding was either dancing or sitting down at the tables talking while the band still played. They were oblivious to what was about to transpire in their life.

# CHAPTER TWENTY NINE

*To The Point*

Catarina and James decided to remain at the house for their honeymoon since her dad was not going to be home. This was the first time James had ever been in Catarina's bedroom and it was huge, twice the size of his. They showered separately. The song, *Between the Sheets* by the *Isley Brothers* played when they walked out with robes on. They stared at one another and started dancing slowly until they dropped their robes at the same time with nothing on underneath. These two never left the house for two days. Their lovemaking was what so many songs were written about, they shared passions and their love was more than explosive. Catarina and James ran around the house like kids chasing each other laughing and having fun. The staff was given specific instructions to serve them but not be seen any other time. They went swimming in the outdoor pool naked and made love at night with the moon and stars in the sky as their light. James has never been happier and at peace in every way with the love of his life by his side. Their every touch of each other's skin seemed to penetrate to the heart and Catarina cried many tears for the right reasons. James made love to her like no other, no one she has ever been with was his equal in touch, chemistry, and spiritual bond. Yes, the sex between these two was fantastic because they walked in the same spirit. They had no inhibitions and desired to give themselves to each other in mind, body, spirit, and soul. When James entered Catarina, she gripped his body and knew this was the man for her life, all her life.

# CHAPTER THIRTY
*Say What*

Cynthia tried so hard to resist Rick and not spend too much time with him while in Rio but the more she stayed away from him, the more her emotions and body wanted his touch. It was spiritually creepy in a way. It was two o'clock in the morning when she walked down the hotel hallway in shorts and a top to see him but the moment she was about to knock on his door, she suddenly changed her mind and walked away. She thanked God for giving her strength. At that exact moment, Leticia Wilson's demonic mist laid on Rick's body causing him to have a very explicit sexual dream. He wore boxer briefs and sat up in bed saying Cynthia's name. With a compelling force, he moved with grace and speed getting off the bed and opened his hotel room door, and saw Cynthia walking away. He stepped closer to her.

"Cynthia, where are you going?"

His voice made her jump because she never heard his door open. She turned around and the sight of him in his boxers with a full erection made all her sexual desires for him awaken.

"Rick, you scared me and what are you doing out here in the hallway in your boxers, and you got a hard-on. Are you crazy? Go back inside Rick, me coming here was a big mistake." She turned around to walk away.

Rick grabbed Cynthia's arm and pushed her body against the wall and pressed himself into her and kissed her lips. She slapped him and tried to push him away.

"Stop Rick, we can't do this anymore, stop it." Her mouth said one thing but deep inside she wanted him. She slapped him again and tried to push him off by banging her butt on the hallway wall for leverage.

They were close to Stacy and Keith's room and the bumping sound on the wall woke Stacy, she got up, put a robe on because she was naked. She opened the door and was shocked to see Cynthia and Rick. Cynthia was against the wall and had her legs wrapped around his waist, arms around his neck, kissing him. She stepped out into the hallway.

"Are you two crazy? At least go in the room. I knew it was only a matter of time before you two crossed that line. Now get out of this hallway before security comes and arrests you."

Rick put Cynthia down and looked at Stacy with animal lust and wanted to see what she looked like under her rob. As if Cynthia read his thoughts, she walked over to Stacy and snatched her robe open revealing her breasts, and kissed her hard on the lips. Her first reaction was to give in but no, not this time. She slapped Cynthia and ran back into her room while she had the strength to resist. Stacy woke Keith by sucking on him and then got on top riding his dick fast bringing herself to a quick intense orgasm. She showered then prayed and went back to sleep.

Rick and Cynthia were in his room having the time of their life satisfying each other sexually like dogs in heat. They fucked each other all over his room, in various positions. Two hours later they showered together and laid on the bed next to each other. Suddenly, everything hit Cynthia hard, and she started crying.

"Rick this was so wrong what we did. This is not how I want to live my life. A hypocrite in Christ, I detest how I am feeling right now. I do care for you Rick, but I feel so dirty."

He thought about his life for a while and was in a very comfortable position financially, but he wanted someone stable in his life, not just a sex partner and he likes Cynthia a lot.

"Cynthia, I understand how you feel, and I thought about my life," he leaned over and kissed her lips. "My life is not what it should be, but I know how to change that," Rick kissed her again and looked into her eyes. "I love you Cynthia and want you in my life."

Cynthia leaned away from Rick and looked at him in total shock.

"Say what? You love me! Rick that is not something you just say to a woman. Don't play with me because you want to keep getting all this good hot lovin. If you love me so much, then marry me." Knowing that would shut him up.

Rick walked over to the desk, pulled out a ring box, and got on his knees.

"Cynthia, will you marry me?" He opened the box revealing a diamond ring.

Cynthia's mouth dropped open as she sat up in bed speechless, trying to gather her thoughts. Yes, there is an age difference between them, but she was tired of younger guys and the stupid games they played. Yes, older men played games also, but many were passed that stage in their lives and knew what they wanted. Besides, she had fallen in love with Rick but was never going to tell him.

"I don't know what to say Rick. You have shocked me. I mean one minute we were in bed getting buck wild and the next minute, you tell me you love me and asked to marry me."

"Well, for the record, it lasted a lot longer than a minute." He laughed. "I am still waiting for your answer. I can't stay on my knees all day."

"First, don't be funny. Yes, it was longer than a minute," She stared at him. "Yes Rick, I will marry you." Cynthia got on the floor with Rick and kissed him. "A real ride-or-die woman will meet a man where he is. You are on your knees; I am on mine."

Rick put the ring on her finger then hugged and kissed her. He began caressing her body until Cynthia pushed him away.

"No Rick, I don't want us to make love anymore until we are husband and wife. So, do not push up on me, grab my hips and butt or say nasty things to me trying to turn me on so you can have your way. Although I desire you just as much and you know it. So, let's do this the right way so we can be blessed. We pray and ask God for forgiveness and then we will get married and come together as husband and wife in the sight of God. Then my brother, I will ride your good dick regularly. Know that."

He had no choice but to laugh as he helped her get up, kissed her again, and watched her walk out.

When Cynthia walked down the hallway she thought, *I cannot believe this happened to me. Wow, look at God.* She held the ring up and smiled as she continued to walk down the hallway back to her room.

# CHAPTER THIRTY ONE
*The Ride Home*

$M$r. Clemente and Catarina spent time together before she left expressing how much they were going to miss each other. Catarina would never tell her dad she was not going to miss being the manager of his hotel or the business anymore. He gave her five-hundred-million dollars for a wedding present. His private plane took them home. The plane was extremely luxurious and very spacious on the inside. A seating capacity for fifty people and the seats could be turned into beds and curtains for privacy and the plane had a large master bedroom. The women sat together in one area and the men in the other. Cynthia showed everyone her ring and they were happy for her but Tonya was jealous and felt Cynthia used sex to get Rick.

"Girl you must have put it on that man. They say you work hips, lips, fingertips and shaking butt." She laughed but was the only one. Everyone looked at her in disbelief she would make such an ugly statement. Sheila was embarrassed for Cynthia.

Diana saw the anger in Cynthia's eyes and knew she had to say or do something quickly before this scene turned bad.

"This is 2015 and no real man would ask a woman to marry him just for sex. We live in a time when a man or woman can get that anywhere. Rick asked you to marry him because he loves you and God can do anything." She smiled at Cynthia to bring peace to her spirit.

Everyone said, Amen except Tonya.

"I apologize Cynthia for what I said, and I am very happy for you." She hugged her.

The men teased Rick because of the age difference between him and Cynthia, and he would need Viagra to keep up with her. Pastor Williams laughed but then he got serious and told Rick if God brought you two together then that same God will bless you to remain together, satisfied. Then he smiled and laughed.

Derrick walked over to Tonya and asked to speak with her. All the women smiled as they walked away, and they sat in another section of the plane.

"I wanted to say I am feeling you and want us to spend more time together when we get back. No pressure, just getting to know each other better."

"You surprised me. That would be nice but are you saying you want us to date exclusively."

"Yes, that's exactly what I am saying. We are not children and we know what time it is. So yes, I would like for you to be my lady and we will see where things go. Oh, and don't worry I won't push up on you too hard and turn you out." He smiled.

Tonya wanted to say something mean to him about his statement but thought, *if this brother only knew who I am and what I can do to him.* She looked at him.

"You talk a good game but what makes you think you are the only one who has skills, my brother."

They looked at each other and started laughing.

Everyone talked about how much fun they had in Rio and would like to go back one day. Eventually, everyone went to sleep, and the rest of the ride home was peaceful. None of them knew the spirit of hell was coming their way.

# CHAPTER THIRTY TWO

*Changing Times*

It had been four months since the Rio trip, and everything was going well and peaceful in everyone's life. Sheila and Zechariah grew closer day by day through prayer and lovemaking.

James and Catarina were enjoying being married and she liked being in James' home, which is now their home. Getting away from Rio and her dad's business made her feel a weight was lifted from her spirit. Having a fresh start in life with the right man, was an answered prayer.

Rick and Cynthia were doing well especially after they prayed and asked God to forgive their transgressions and talked to the pastor concerning their wedding date, which would be soon.

Tonya and Derrick were dating and devoted their lives to God becoming closer to him and each other. Derrick asked Tonya to marry him, but she felt it was too soon, but Derrick said it was only too soon for people who do not know what they want or are playing games. He asked again and she kissed him and said yes.

The club was doing great, and it was full every night it opened and made a lot of money. Each night more people would come, and the word spread fast about how nice the club was and how the staff treated you like kings and queens.

Diana was sick lately and found out why after she visited the doctor, she told Ron she was pregnant. He was incredibly happy and for some reason, this increased his sexual desire for her, and he could not understand why. All he knew was, he could not keep his hands off her. In the morning and at night they made love like they just got married and Diana enjoyed all his attention.

Christine and Sandra were drawn to two of the *Young Wolves* and were dating them. Sheila questioned this and wondered if this was a good idea for her daughters and if this was of God or a trick of the adversary to draw them away from Christ. So far, she was impressed with the way the two men walked in Christ and how they treated her daughters. Also, Zechariah noticed how dedicated they were in everything they did, and admired their discipline.

Shantai enjoyed her job at the club and the peace she has walking with God is very comforting, but her spirit was lonely, and she tried hard to live right and not give in to her desires. It was not just sex but the desire to have that special person to share her life with. She also noticed Keith and Stacy were not the same. There seemed to be some distance building between them which made her sad because she liked Stacy a lot and they were good friends. At the same time, her attraction to Keith was increasing which made it hard for her. Keith was playful at times during work, flirting with her but it made Shantai wonder if he was flirting or interested in her on another level. Truth be told, she wanted Keith and always had so she flirted with him as well. One night after the club closed Keith told Shantai she was doing a great job and hugged her then kissed her on the cheek. It took everything Shantai had not to grab him and kiss him on the lips before he walked away.

Keith and Stacy always had a powerful connection in and out of the bedroom but lately, they began to disagree about simple things, and she could not understand it. Keith called her one day on the cell phone and she did not answer his call because she and Diana were having a good time shopping and she forgot. When she came home, Keith was downstairs wearing sweats and no shirt, working out trying to release some frustration. Stacy hugged and tried to kiss him, but he turned his head and went back to lifting weights.

"Keith, what is wrong with you? You act as if you don't desire me like you use to anymore, what's up with that? Are you cheating on me Keith?"

He walked closer and stood there looking at her.

"There is no one else in my life but you and never has been. No, I am not cheating but I should be asking you that. You and Diana were together and when I called you did not answer, I wondered why? Were you two in some sleazy hotel kissing again or maybe you had her spread out on the bed with your face buried between her legs." He stared at her with contempt.

It was not what Keith said, but the look in his eyes when he said it and how he looked at her that Stacy knew without prayer and forgiveness, their marriage would never be the same. She knew he did not trust her anymore and without trust, there was no real relationship.

"Keith, can't you leave that incident in the past and stop bringing it up every time you get upset with me. You know I was doing no such thing. Either you trust me, or you don't."

He stepped closer and put his hands on her butt.

"Look me in the eye Stacy and tell me since we have been married no one has caressed this ass, tasted you, touched you, or put dick or tongue in you except me. Look me in my eye right now and tell me that and I will believe you."

RONALD GRAY                                                            157

For the first time, Stacy felt trapped and did not know what to do. If she lied and he found out later their marriage would be over. If she told him the truth their marriage would be over. So, her only option was avoidance. She removed his hands from her butt.

"Stop it Keith, stop treating me like I am a piece of meat. Yes, a woman loves attention from her man, but we are not just ass. After a while, it gets old Keith. Baby, you got a fat ass, baby your hips are sexy, sexy remark after sexy remark. Stop treating me like I am your OCB contract. On call booty." She pointed her finger in his face. "And don't you dare laugh at me because you know I am serious. I would rather you come home and kiss me sometimes instead of coming home and grabbing my ass telling me how fat it is. Or how you want to put all kinds of dick in me. Please, get real with the, all kinds of dick. You have one dick."

He thought about everything she said and had to admit there was some truth in her words, but the fact remains, she never answered his question which told him all he needed to know. Yet, he still loved Stacy deeply and did not want to lose her ever, but the trust factor would not be the same.

"You are right, and your point was well made." He kissed her and was about to walk away when Stacy grabbed his arm.

"That's it, you are going to kiss me and walk away when you look so good pumped up from working out. No baby, you ain't going anywhere until we make up the right way." She rubbed his chest with her hand and kissed him.

Keith was not in the mood to have sex but turning her down now would only make matters worse. So he allowed Stacy to have her way, for now.

# CHAPTER THIRTY THREE

*Bad Choice*

Leticia's diamond mine brought her greater wealth as she knew it would. She had houses built on the property for the workers and a large house built for her and the bodyguards. The size and quality of the diamonds found in this mine were unlike anything else on the market. The diamond experts who examined the diamonds coming out of her mine were blown away at such rare quality. She had the best security money could buy and a small army working at the mine. After each shift, every employee had to walk directly from the mine through this long hallway and get naked for a body search. Any man caught with any size diamond was instantly killed in a gruesome way to serve as an example to the others. She was on her way to becoming one of the wealthiest people in the world if not the wealthiest.

Mr. Clemente missed Catarina very much but was happy for her and the life she lived with James. Each day his anger was building because Leticia took the diamond mine away from him before he had time to capitalize on it. The disappearance of his men she killed bothered him greatly. He did not become rich by allowing people to take things from him. So, he put together an elite army of two hundred men to go and take over the mine that was rightfully his, to begin with, at least in his mind. These men were the best in the jungle and tactical warfare. They trained all year to take the enemy on any type of territory. He wanted to personally see Leticia killed.

On Thursday night two large cargo planes flew close to the diamond mine carrying Mr. Clemente and his army and four squads of ten men each. They parachuted from the plane dressed in all black. The plane landed close to the site and Mr. Clemente and the rest of the army also dressed in all black, marched through the woods heavily armed.

Leticia and her bodyguards were sleeping when Leticia woke up and transformed quickly into a wolf and ran off into the woods. The wolf saw the men in black walking through the woods getting closer to the diamond mine site. It ran back to the house and transformed back into Leticia and she woke her bodyguards telling them to get ready for war. They dressed quickly and stood outside their house prepared to kill at will.

Leticia was not aware of the size of the army coming against her. Her men were getting slaughtered quickly. An hour later the only people left were Leticia and her bodyguards who stood in front of Mr. Clemente and one-hundred and fifty of his men. Mr. Clemente stepped closer to Leticia and admired her raw beauty.

"It's a shame to destroy someone as lovely as you are, on the outside that is. Your heart is corrupt and evil. Do you have anything to say before you die like the rest of your men?"

Leticia started laughing.

"Look who is talking. You came here and forced yourself on my property, my place of business to take what is not yours to have. I legally own this land, but you want it and could not acquire it through legal means, so you had to use violence and death. You killed all my personnel. So, Mr. Clemente, who is the evil one?

"Point made but enough of all this talking. Do you have any last request before I cut your head off?"

"Well, since you put it that way, yes I do. There are only six of us and many of you, my female associates, and I would like to experience one last night of sexual bliss. You are going to kill us anyway, so we may as well have some fun before we die. I am talking one on one and then a mass orgy. This ain't no love connection, we are fucking like dogs. In the ass, pussy, sucking dick, shaking ass and hips, and sliding dick on wet fingertips." She did not want to give him any time to think, so Leticia and her bodyguards removed their camouflage jumpsuits revealing flawless bodies with incredible figures any man or woman would desire to see and have.

They began caressing themselves and kissed and caressed one another. Leticia spoke to them in a whisper.

"Do not fear, trust me and follow my lead and I promise we will walk out of here alive." They continued to caress one another.

Mr. Clemente has seen beautiful women all over the world and had many but what he saw now was incredible and was not about to turn down such an opportunity. He would kill them later rather than now. He walked over to Leticia, kissed her and she took his hand and walked to her house and five other men did the same with her bodyguards. All were in separate bedrooms in the house having wild perverted sex. Her bodyguards were doing the same thing at the same time to the men, riding their dick. Then, each woman pulled out an ice pick from her hair and stabbed the men in their eyes while covering their mouth with the other hand so their screams could not be heard. They stabbed them repeatedly over their bodies.

The women walked to Leticia's room covered in blood and saw Mr. Clemente sitting in a chair naked with tape over his mouth and hands cuffed behind his back. Leticia stood in front of him naked holding a knife when a rat ran in front of her. She snatched the rat off the ground and cut its head off allowing the blood to drip over Mr. Clemente. She used the blood to draw a footprint of the devil, a pentagram on the ground. Mr. Clemente was trembling and tried to talk. One of the bodyguards slapped him and laughed. Leticia told her bodyguards to stand back as she put the dead rat on the pentagram and started mumbling some words. A few minutes later the ground shook and a rumbling sound was heard, and it got closer. They rinsed the blood off their bodies and walked outside where the men stood, waiting for their turn to have sex.

This would never happen because out of the woods came the largest pack of rats, they ever saw. These rats were two feet long, had large teeth and weighed twenty pounds, and could leap twelve feet in the air. The soldiers began shooting the rats as they came closer, killing them easily but it was too many of them and they moved very quickly. This scene was something out of a horror movie as Leticia and her bodyguards watched the rats leap on the men biting off their limbs. Their arms, legs, and heads were scattered all over the ground. Everywhere you looked rats leaped through the air biting off a body part of one of the soldiers. The soldiers were running and shooting at the same time trying to get away, but their efforts were meaningless, the rats were too fast. A few sniper soldiers climbed tall trees and began shooting the rats. This was a bad choice because now they had nowhere to go. The rats climbed the trees biting off the men's legs until they hit the ground screaming in pain. Rats leaped on their bodies snapping off their body parts in seconds. One man ran as fast as he could but five rats leaped on him biting his legs, arms, and head off at the same time, his screams were never heard because death came instantly. The shooting and killing lasted for a while until all the men were dead, dismembered by the rats.

Leticia and her bodyguards dragged Mr. Clemente in the chair outside so he could see what took place. What he saw almost gave him a heart attack and this would have been a better way for him to die. Every one of his men was dead, blood and body parts covered the ground. The rats lined up behind one another in packs. Leticia took the tape off Clemente's mouth and he pleaded for his life instantly.

"Oh my God. Please do not do this. What in the hell are you anyway?" His eyes looked like they would pop out of his head.

"Now you want to call on God. You have sinned all your life and now you want mercy," Leticia slapped his face hard, rubbed her breasts across his face, and leaned in front of him. "Do you still want some sex? You sorry no-good bastard, there is no mercy for you. Now, who is going to die?"

Mr. Clemente spat in Leticia's face.

"I don't care who or what you are. I hope you rot in hell."

One of her bodyguards took his handcuffs off.

"You first," Leticia stood and pointed to the rats and then pointed to Mr. Clemente. "Get him."

Mr. Clemente started running and yelling at the same time trying to make it to a tree. He leaped onto a tree and a rat leaped in front of him with its mouth opened wide showing razor-sharp teeth, it bit his penis off. He screamed as blood poured and he turned around and saw the mouth and teeth of another rat, it bit his head off. His body hit the ground shaking and other rats ran over and bit his arms and legs off. Leticia mumbled some words and pointed to the rats and they began eating all the dead bodies on the ground until nothing was left, not even blood. Several rats ran into her house and ate the five men Leticia's bodyguards stabbed and licked all the blood off the floor. They ran back to join the rest. One man was alive and leaned on a tree with a leg and arm missing. Leticia was going to have the rats finish him off but decided to let him live so he could tell everyone what happened so she would be feared even more. No one would believe him of course but rumors could be powerful. He leaped away looking back from time to time praying the rats would not get him. All the rats looked at her when she pointed to the woods.

"Another time my friends, another time." She stomped on the ground four times while the rats looked at her.

The rats ran into the woods. The bodyguards looked at Leticia in amazement knowing she was evil, but they never saw it on this level. They realized now she was the devil incarnate. All six women walked back into the house, showered, and put on strap-on dildos. They took turns having sex with each other and together. Leticia was possessed with sex demons and loved sex any way she could get it. In her ass, pussy, and loved sucking dick and pleasing women orally was her specialty. Every one of her bodyguards had sex with her with the strap-on repeatedly, giving her more orgasms than she could remember. She stood in front of them and screamed for more.

# CHAPTER THIRTY FOUR

*From the Dad to the Daughter*

Word of Mr. Clemente's death spread fast, but Catarina heard the news first, Saturday night when she and James were home watching a movie. She thought it was a sick joke but found out it was the truth when talking on the phone to a reliable source. She dropped the phone and screamed.

"Daddy, Noooo! You can't be dead, oh God no."

James held her and prayed.

Catarina talked to her dad the day before he died and told her he was going to India on business checking on a land deal, and now he was dead. This affected her so much she remained in a state of shock. She spent most of her time in bed crying and praying, asking God why. She knew her dad was no angel, but he was all she had. James's heart ached to see his wife in such pain and prepared her for the trip back to Rio for the memorial service. He was concerned about her safety so the first person he called was Ron because he and Keith had the *Young Wolves* for security, and he trusted them. After Ron talked with James, he was sad for him because they were so close and great friends. He owed his freedom to God but also to James for helping him get out of prison. He told Diana the horrible news and she cried hard because she imagined how she would feel if she lost Ron. She wanted to go and be with Catarina, but Ron asked her to stay home so she would not get to upset and cause her to have pregnancy complications. Diana gave Ron her look and that was it, she was going to comfort Catarina. Ron called Pastor Williams letting him know and then Sheila who told Zechariah. Diana, Stacy, and Sheila visited Catarina to comfort her.

Ron and Keith met James in his office to discuss details for his trip and he told them something his wife does not know yet. Rumor has it Leticia Wilson was responsible for her dad's death and a pack of rats attacked and killed him and the entire army with him. This story was told by the man with the missing arm and leg who was there. Ron and Keith looked at each other and shook their heads.

"Not again, this cannot be happening again. First, we get attacked by the two crazy men at my house but thought everything was over concerning that and now a pack of rats attacked and killed people. Only one spirit operates like that and it ain't God." Keith said.

"All this is just too déjà vu for me. When does it ever end oh God?" Ron shook his head.

"I don't know my brother, but Catarina is my wife and I know what I am about to say is very wrong in the eyesight of God and pray he forgives me," he looked down then looked at them. "I will protect myself and my wife at all costs and if it comes down to me putting a bullet in Leticia's Wilson head, then so be it. So, I could use your help on this one."

"You don't have to ask my brother we got you," he looked at Keith who nodded his head. "What do you need and when?"

"Thanks a lot, both of you. Catarina's Dad has a net worth of twenty-six-billion dollars, and she is his only living heir but his will determines how much she receives."

Keith and Ron looked at each other.

"Wow, now that is money." Ron said.

"Bling, bling to the max." Keith said.

"No question but with that type of money comes all kinds of problems because you don't know who to trust. She has been so upset over his death we have not talked about what she wants to do. But Catarina shared many things with me concerning her dad, good and bad and I know she does not want anything to do with his business. So, I plan to fly back to Rio and have the memorial service, sign some papers, and leave as quickly as possible. Without becoming a so call, accident."

"James, you don't have to worry about that, we got you and you can trust us with your life my brother. I do not live that street life anymore and don't want to, but my connections are still good and along with the *Young Wolves* there will be other security in place, seen and not seen. Hold on, let me make a call." He called a member of the *Young Wolves* and spoke in code. "It's done, whenever you are ready James." He nodded his head at Ron.

"We are on the same page Keith, and I know who else to call to help us with this and he will be glad to." Ron, Keith, and James looked at each other and spoke at the same time.

"Rick." All three laughed.

James called Rick and explained a little to him on the phone and Rick said he would be there in twenty minutes. They talked until Rick arrived and James told him the entire story. His heart was heavy as well for his friend, but this news also made him angry because he remembered the details with Victor Augular and Mr. Bones.

"I am sad for your loss my brother and I am glad you called me. I know exactly what you need to be done and I can get it done but it will cost a little more money than what I have." Rick said.

"Thanks Rick and I greatly appreciate your help in this matter. Money is not the issue, whatever it takes to get us all to Rio safely and back. You have a blank check."

Rick nodded his head at James, and he made a phone call to a friend of his in the CIA. They talked briefly in code as well.

"Everything is in motion. There is a SOF (Special Operations Force) on standby to meet us at BWI airport when we are ready to leave, and we will be traveling on a private plane equipped as well as the President's plane. We all go to Rio together, stay together and come back together. While we are in Rio and anywhere else you need to go, they go with us," he turned to look at Keith and Ron. "Keith, I know you and Ron's business associates, the *Young Wolves* have high-security clearance to travel anywhere in the world with whatever weapons they need to bring. I don't know how you were able to do this long ago and do not want to know, but job well done my brothers." He shook their hands.

"You know how it goes Rick, if you put a million dollars in the right person's hand you can get a whole lot of things done." Keith said smiling.

"You are right about that. James, is there anything else you need my brother?"

"Not that I can think of," he looked around his office. "All I ever wanted to do is become an attorney and make a difference and live a simple life. Now it seems like my life is about to become anything but simple. I mean don't get me wrong, God knows how much I love my wife and would not trade her for any woman in the world but when you step into big money status, your life does change."

"I read about her dad in Forbes magazine some time ago. Said he was worth twenty-six-billion dollars. My brother, that is a whole lot more than big money status." Rick said

"Yeah, I know it is. I also know I need a big upgrade in the security system in my home."

"Let me take care of that for you as well. You need the best; I know people who work for the White House, in security."

"Thanks again Rick for everything. We leave for Rio first thing Monday morning and hope to leave no later than Wednesday if all goes well with the paperwork. Now, if you gentlemen do not mind locking up when you leave, I need to get back to my wife." He hugged them and shook their hands then walked out of the office.

They continued to discuss the details of the trip and other things they knew would help James.

Four o'clock Monday morning seven armor-plated SUV Limousines pulled into BWI airport with James, Catarina, Rick, Ron, Keith, Stacy, twenty *Young Wolves,* and SOF's members. Keith told Stacy to stay home but she said no, where you go, I go. Awaiting them was a very large grey nondescript cargo plane, two helicopters, seven limos, and the entire crew was escorted inside the plane. They reached Rio in twelve hours, and one would think the President of the United States landed when seeing all the security coming off the plane. The *Young Wolves* and SOFs members were instructed to neutralize any immediate threat. The limos and helicopters were unloaded from the plane. The entire crew got in the limos and traveled to Catarina's house with the helicopters flying nearby. When they reached the house, helicopters landed in the backyard, and security team members searched the grounds and the house immediately and the *Young Wolves* stayed with James and Catarina. The entire house staff was replaced before they arrived. When James and Catarina walked into the house Catarina felt the spirit of sadness because this was her home for many years. A home her dad built but now he was gone, nothing felt the same and she couldn't wait to leave as soon as possible.

During the plane ride to Rio, Catarina had plenty of time to think of what she wanted and needed to do for herself and the thousands of employees under her dad's company, she wanted to be fair. There would be a formal reading of his will, but she knew he left everything to her. So, after listening to James and his legal advice she decided to sell her shares of the company and be done with it. She was the majority shareholder which made her shares worth billions of dollars.

Everyone settled in the house, changed clothes, and went with Catarina and James, traveling by limos to the Attorney's office for the official reading of the will and discuss her desires for the Company. James, Catarina, and the Attorneys were the only ones in the office for this reading. After all the reading and legal terminology, Catarina signed papers to sell her shares of the company. She was now worth fourteen billion dollars. The money was transferred to her bank account and the other details she and James would deal with when they got back home.

They left the Attorney's office and went to church for the memorial service. The church was packed because so many people wanted to pay their respects to her Dad, but security was on point everywhere. Security personnel blended in with the crowd in suits but had automatic weapons and grenades underneath their jackets. James, Catarina, Rick, Ron, Keith,

Stacy, a few *Young Wolves,* and some of the SOFs members sat on the front row in the church while the Pastor gave his remarks. A large picture of Mr. Clemente was posted in front and service lasted two hours. When they arrived at the cemetery, there was a large headstone in place for her dad. The Pastor spoke more words and it was time to leave. An odd feeling came over James that made the hairs stand up on the back of his neck and Catarina felt the same thing. James approached Ron and Keith.

"I can't explain it, but I have a feeling something really bad is about to happen."

"Yeah James, I was just talking to Keith, Rick, and Stacy about the same thing."

"I am not taking any chances, let's hurry and get everyone back to the limos and get out of here." James said.

About fifty yards away a large wolf appeared foaming at the mouth, it howled and looked at them. They all saw it and security was on high alert. The service was over for her dad and people began walking back to their vehicles. The security force was briefed before they left and informed they may encounter some things that seem unreal but take them very seriously. The team heard rumors about Leticia Wilson using voodoo, but they did not believe it. They were soldiers and believed and fought like soldiers but we're prepared for anything.

James, Catarina, Rick, Ron, Stacy, and Keith were escorted back to the limo by the *Young Wolves* while the Special Forces members stood by watching. The wolf walked closer to them and stopped and began howling loudly. Everyone turned around and saw Leticia Wilson dressed in all black standing next to the wolf with one hand on his head and the other hand holding an old brown cane. She mumbled some words and hit a headstone six times with the cane.

"Time to die, rodents come forth." She yelled and then kneeled behind a large headstone and disappeared in smoke.

Suddenly, the ground started shaking, headstones were cracking and falling over and large rats by the thousands began coming out of the ground. James, Rick, Catarina, Keith, Stacy, and Ron ran to the limo and made it just in time when a rat leaped into the car window smashing its head. Thankfully, the windows were bulletproof. Everyone began screaming and running away trying to make it to their cars, but the rats were too fast and were leaping on them, biting off their arms and legs. People were in panic mode and trampled over one another which made it easier for the rats to get them on the ground. The *Young Wolves* and SOF's members pulled out their automatic weapons and were killing the rats by the hundreds. The more they killed, the more would come. One rat leaped twelve feet over another rat and bit off the hand of a SOF member. When the rat hit the ground, he had the hand in its mouth still holding the gun and ran across the cemetery. The man looked at his missing hand and was in shock and started screaming. Another rat jumped on his back and bit the top of his skull off. None of the guards had ever seen anything like this but Keith was prepared after seeing Mr. Bones in action. He pushed a button on his cell phone and three large trucks drove into the cemetery quickly, the back doors of these trucks opened, and more soldiers jumped out with flame throwers on their backs. They began walking forward burning the rats and all you heard were loud screeching sounds as the rats lay on the ground burning, but they kept coming. The rats killed people with one bite of their powerful jaws and teeth. One man fell and was crawling on the ground when a rat bit his foot off and he screamed in agony and another rat bit off his entire mouth and ran away before a guard shot him in the head.

Catarina and Stacy were crying and screaming while in the armored limo because they never saw anything so horrible in their life and were terrified. They felt bad for the people getting killed so violently. The *Young Wolves* had the limo surrounded and were firing their automatic weapons in unison, blocking the rats from getting to the limo. Ron was getting angrier by the second until he heard the voice from God say, *if God be for you, then who can be against you.* That was all he needed to hear. He opened the door and ran out.

"Ron, Noooooo!" Stacy screamed.

Keith, Rick, and James felt compelled to follow him, so they did. Catarina screamed for James to come back but it was too late. Ron stood there with his arms held out to his side as he began to pray. Keith, James, and Rick stood directly behind him with each man putting a hand on the other's shoulder. The rats stopped what they were doing and ran towards Ron, but he had no fear and pointed at the rats.

"*I can do all things through Christ that strengthens me*, fight this battle oh Lord, in the name of Jesus."

The wind began to blow very hard, and a thunderstorm started, sending golf ball size hailstones hitting the rats, exploding their bodies in fire instantly. The hailstones were hitting the rats only. Those that made it began running back into the ground. Six rats ran towards Ron, and they were about twelve feet away from him when they leaped in the air at the same time. He smiled.

*"Submit yourselves therefore to God. Resist the devil, and he will flee from you,* in the name of Jesus."

Lightning hit all six rats killing them in midair. The *Young Wolves*, the SOFs, and the rest of the people watched this taking place and could not believe what their eyes saw, they were amazed. Everyone knew Ron was someone very special.

Ron, Keith, Rick, and James looked around and saw the horrible sight of so many body parts, dead people, and the injured and they wanted to help but security made them get back in the limo and they went back to Catarina's house.

Everyone was in their rooms relaxing after such a horrible day. Rick was on the phone talking to Cynthia. Ron was on the phone talking to Diana but did not tell her all the details because he did not want to upset her. Keith and Stacy talked, and he told her he would never tell Ron about seeing her and Diana kiss. Stacy wanted to pour her heart out to Keith and tell him everything she was dealing with in her life, but the risk was too great of losing him. But today's event brought them closer after seeing how a person's life can change so quickly. It has been a while since they prayed together but tonight was exactly what they did. They got on their knees, held hands, and prayed until tears ran down their face, weeping in the spirit of God. James and Catarina talked about many things and she told him she never wanted to come back to this house again after they left. The house was paid for, so she was going to give it to the servants who lived there and took care of her and her dad for so many years. She and James talked until the sun came up and they prayed and then made love.

Hours later everyone sat at the dining room table eating individually cooked breakfast. Each person had their favorite food cooked for them. After they finished and left, the *Young Wolves* and Special Forces members rotated shifts and ate breakfast as well until everyone had eaten. Safety was still a major concern especially after what happened yesterday, so security was not taking any chances. The staff was escorted out of the house when they left, security guards were posted in every room of the mansion and spread out on the grounds holding automatic weapons. They were all traveling from the house to the airport by the helicopters in the backyard.

James talked with the captain of the Special Forces team and gave him his sincere regrets concerning the loss of some of his men during yesterday's battle. The captain fought in various battles across the globe but never saw anything remotely like what he saw yesterday.

"I saw it and still don't believe it. Big damn rats coming out of the ground killing people, unbelievable. And your friend Ron. What is he, a Moses chosen type of guy?"

James laughed.

"Something like that captain. He is special."

"Yeah, I saw that. Anyway, whenever you are ready to leave let me know."

"Thanks captain for everything." He extended his hand to him.

He shook James's hand.

"Well, it is not over yet." He shook his head and walked away.

Hours later everyone was packed, and their bags were loaded in the limos, and they were escorted to the helicopters. The limos left first and then the Special Forces members got in the helicopter. One took off following the limos and the other was just taking off when the ground exploded leaving a hole underneath the helicopter. Rats twice the size of the ones that attacked people in the cemetery leaped out of the hole and gripped both sides of the frame under the helicopter. Other rats leaped out of the hole using the others as a ladder and jumped into the helicopter. The men reached for their weapons, but it was too late, all this happened so fast it caught the men off guard. The rats separated their arms, feet, legs, and heads from their bodies with one bite of their powerful jaws. The operator of the helicopter was trying to fly with one arm bitten off and he turned his head to see what was going on in the back. A rat bit his head off and the helicopter crashed into the house exploding. The entire house burned to the ground and Leticia Wilson stood close by laughing and surrounded by rats.

"You can run but you can't hide from me. The spirit of hell is unleashed. There is no prayer in schools and very little in homes and weak churches, this makes my job so much easier. People do not have faith anymore in what they cannot see or hear which I love. Love is a joke to so many people and marriages are crumbling thanks to my spirit of divide and conquer. I am taking so many people to hell with me, there need to be two hells." She held her arms up and continued laughing.

# CHAPTER THIRTY FIVE

*Pastor Williams*

Ron informed Pastor Williams concerning everything that happened in Rio, and he was surprised but not shocked. The pastor was concerned about Ron, his family, and everyone close to him. So, he asked to meet all of them at one time in the church. It was Thursday afternoon and Ron, Diana, Keith, Stacy, Zechariah, Sheila, James, Catarina, Rick, Christine, Sandra, Cynthia, Shantai, Tonya, and ten of the *Young Wolves* sat in the Sanctuary of the church and Pastor Williams sat in a chair in front of them.

"I thank all of you for coming here today and I will be as brief as possible. Before we begin, let's have a word of prayer.

Everyone bowed their heads.

"Lord, we thank you for another day of your grace, love, and mercy. We pray you continue to protect, guide, and give us the wisdom to make the choices pleasing to your eye. We give you all the glory and praise, in Jesus name Amen."

Everyone said "Amen."

"Okay, let me get directly to the point. The times we are living in are truly the last days. Look around and see the continued moral decline in this world. Doing wrong is the new right, the spirit of selfishness in people is increasing tremendously, committing as much evil and mayhem as possible is a good thing. And those who choose to live for King Jesus are considered blind and tricked."

"Speak on it Pastor." Zechariah said.

"Ron, God has chosen you to do great things and your calling is not over. The forces of darkness are and will continue to attack you and everyone close to you. This means all of you sitting here right now. So, because of this, all of you need to be very careful of how you live your lives and the choices you make. What may look good may not be good for you or your future. In the book of Isaiah 59:19 the word says, So shall they fear the name of the LORD from the west, and his glory from the rising of the sun. When the enemy shall come in like a flood, the Spirit of the LORD shall lift up a standard against him. It may seem like the devil is winning but you all can rest assured the power of God has and will prevail, and he will get the glory. Ron informed me of everything he has recently dealt with and all of you as well. My heart and prayers are with you all daily. Please keep in mind the greater the calling in your life from God, the greater the attacks. The devil only attacks those he does not already have. Fasting and prayer are two powerful tools in warfare against the forces of evil."

Derrick sat next to Tonya and whispered in her ear.

"You know how much I care about you Tonya."

"Be quiet, we can talk about all that later Derrick." She rolled her eyes at him and frowned.

"Pastor I have something very important to tell you. Can I come to the front and mention it to you?"

"Absolutely Brother Derrick."

Derrick walked to the front and spoke softly to the Pastor and he smiled and looked at Derrick.

"Are you absolutely sure?"

"One hundred percent Pastor." He stood there with his hands in his pockets.

The Pastor stood and asked everyone to stand.

"Brother Derrick has something he would like to share."

"Thank you Pastor. I am no public speaker, and I am a little nervous, but my heart is true," he looked around and sighed heavily. "Wow, this is harder than I thought. Tonya, you are a great friend to me but that is not enough. I love you and I would like to, hold on…" he pulled out a ring from his pants pocket and got on one knee, and held it up. "Would you marry me?" "What I offer you is the best I have. My friendship, honor, and my walk with God, day by day."

Tonya was flabbergasted and tried hard not to cry but she started crying and shook her hands by her side.

"Oh my God Derrick, you can't ask me in front of everyone like this, oh my God."

"Sister Tonya, he just did." The Pastor said.

"Oh my God this can't be happening to me but yes Derrick, I will marry you. I want us to be the best of buddies for life."

"Tonya, you are still standing here, and he is up there. Go get him." Diana said smiling.

"Yes, oh yes, I am coming baby." She almost ran to the front.

Everyone began clapping their hands and laughing. Tonya held her hand out and Derrick put the ring on her finger and then stood up and kissed her on the lips. Pastor hit Derrick lightly on his arm.

"This is the church and not the hotel my brother. There will be plenty of time for all that after you say, I do."

Derrick lowered his head and smiled then looked at the Pastor.

"You are right Pastor. Forgive me, I got carried away."

"No problem my brother. I think we need to get you two married," he looked at everyone. "This is truly a blessing from the Lord. With that being said is there anything else anyone has to say?"

Rick raised his hand.

"Pastor I just had a thought. Brother Derrick, if you want, we can have a double wedding. You, Tonya, Cynthia, and myself. So, what do you think my brother?"

Cynthia looked at him smiling.

"I don't mind at all."

Derrick looked at Tonya and she nodded her head at him smiling and put her arm around his waist.

"Rick, I think it's a great idea. Let's do it my brother," he looked at Tonya and laughed. "Quickly please." He kissed her on the cheek.

"Once again God is doing his thing and I think it is a great idea. Can I get an Amen?" Pastor said.

Everyone said, "Amen."

"When you four set a date please let me know and I will be glad to marry you. Now before we all leave, let's end this wonderful, surprising evening in prayer. Bow your heads please. Lord, we thank you for what you have done and will do. We thank you for once again bringing your saints together to share their lives as one in you. I plead the blood of Jesus over all of us for spiritual and physical protection and remember our family, friends, and loved ones, oh Lord. We thank you and praise you, Amen."

They all walked up front and shook the Pastor's hand and hugged Tonya and Derrick congratulating them.

Leticia Wilson wore all black as she stood across the street of the church next to a wolf. The wolf walked in front of the church and stood on the sidewalk and stared at it. It walked up the steps growling, and lighting struck its leg knocking it down. It yelped and ran back to Leticia looking at her shaking its head and ran away yelping. She looked at the wolf.

"Stupid wolf," she looked at the church. "I hate you Christians and all Godly people. No matter, because the way the world is now, it's easy to deceive people and blind them. All the rules and laws have omitted prayer in so many places, which makes my job easy. Now the parents cannot discipline the children like they need to. The stupid fools do not read the bible. It says, if you spare the rod, you spoil the child. Damn, I love it when children talk back and curse out their parents." She began shouting and dancing in place and lightning struck the ground close to her, she jumped and disappeared in a cloud of smoke.

# CHAPTER THIRTY SIX

*Crossing the Line*

It was Saturday night and the club was full, and more people waited to get in. This is celebration time for Tonya, Derrick, Cynthia, and Rick concerning their soon-to-be double wedding. Ron, Keith, Stacy, Cynthia, Rick, Shantai, Tonya, Derrick were in the VIP section drinking glasses of expensive wine, laughing, and having fun. They were dressed nicely. Twenty minutes later Diana walked up to the VIP section wearing a dress and she looked radiant. Some would say it is the pregnancy glow. Ron and everyone else were surprised to see her because they all knew she did not like coming to the club. And was four months pregnant but she looked great and not showing much. Sandra and Christine chose to stay away from the club because of bad memories. As Diana stood there smiling, a tall muscular guy walked by and bumped into her causing her to almost fall and he kept walking. Ron and Keith jumped up quickly.

"Fool, watch where you are walking you almost knocked my wife down." Ron yelled.

The guy turned his head to look at Ron then waved his hand at him and kept walking. Ron and Keith walked towards him, but he walked directly into Zechariah and two of the *Young Wolves*. Zechariah saw the look of despair on Diana's face and snapped. He grabbed the guy by his belt with one hand and his neck with the other then slammed him on the floor and put his knee in his chest.

"Look at me. Don't you ever come in this club again and if you so much as breath in her direction, it will be your last breath." He looked at the guy with hate while squeezing his throat.

Ron and Keith saw a look in Zechariah's eyes they had never seen. Ron hit him on the shoulder, but he kept choking the guy, so he hit him harder, and Zechariah let him go.

"Zechariah, he is not worth it. Let him up my brother."

He lifted him roughly on his feet. The guy was coughing trying to breathe and he pissed on himself. Zechariah stared at the guy, looked at Ron, and walked away. The two *Young Wolves* escorted the guy out. Ron and Keith walked back to the VIP section and Keith tapped Ron on his arm.

"Partner did you see the look on Zechariah's face. I think he would have killed the guy with one hand. That brother is a beast."

"No, he is not. Fact is, never mess with a man's daughter."

"Amen to that my brother." He looked at Ron and laughed.

Ron hugged and kissed Diana asking was she alright. Keith hugged her and they all sat down. Stacy hugged and kissed her on the cheek. Ron told Diana how great she looked and the wonderful glow she had on her face. Diana put her arms around his neck and kissed him slowly, feeling his tongue in her mouth. It made her horny instantly. She would have straddled him on the spot if she could get away with it. Rick and Cynthia held hands while kissing and being very affectionate while Tonya and Derrick did the same. The couples were trying to conduct themselves respectfully, but the flesh was calling them. Keith and Stacy were being their usual selves, hugging and kissing all over each other. This was a great night for everyone except

Shantai because she felt left out and lonely. She was happy for everyone but did not have anyone special in her life and seeing Keith all over Stacy made her very jealous. She was very attracted to Keith and knew it was wrong and felt bad for having those thoughts of him. She had a few glasses of wine and was drinking more, knowing it was too much but it did not matter now.

One of the *Young Wolves* approached Keith and whispered to him. He kissed Stacy and they walked away to the stock room. Shantai watching Keith's every step. Minutes later, Shantai excused herself and went to the stock room to make sure everything was okay since she was the hostess. They were still talking when she walked in, and the guy left.

"Keith is everything alright?"

"No, but it will be. I was informed someone is stealing some of the inventory, but we don't know how yet. When I find out who is doing it, that person will have a bad day."

Shantai walked closer and put her hand on his shoulder.

"Keith please let security handle this problem. I know it is your club, but you are not that person anymore and you must keep your hands clean. That means keeping the right attitude, okay?" She smiled and kissed him on the cheek and stepped back.

Keith looked at her with appreciation realizing he made a good choice in hiring her.

"Thank you, I appreciate your concern, good looking out you are an asset to the club."

Shantai looked at him and could not help lusting. With each passing moment, she got lost in his presence and thought, *if he only knew how much of an asset I can be.*

"Thank you for the compliment." She hugged him and looked in his eyes and moved her lips closer to his. Their lips touched and Keith welcomed her tongue in his mouth while his hands rubbed her butt.

Stacy walked in and saw them kissing and his hands on Shantai's butt.

"Keith!" she yelled. "What in the hell! Shantai, you sorry no good slut!" Stacy moved so quickly it caught Keith off guard. She punched him hard in his mouth and blood poured from his lips. She backhanded Shantai in the jaw knocking her down, leaped on her and began hitting her with left and right jabs in the face. As Keith pulled Stacy off her, Shantai kicked Stacy in the chest sending her and Keith falling backward. Shantai ran out of the room and through the club with Stacy running after her. Keith ran and caught Stacy by the arm and pulled her back and she swung at him but missed because he ducked. He picked Stacy up and put her on his shoulder and carried her back to the stock room and closed the door.

Ron and everyone else saw Shantai running through the club and Keith carrying Stacy. Zechariah stopped Shantai and asked what was going on and she started crying and they walked to a private booth to talk. Ron, Diana, Tonya, and Cynthia walked to the stock room and Ron knocked on the door.

"I got this, go away." Keith yelled.

They all walked away with a few of the *Young Wolves* with them and they went back to the VIP section and sat down. They were talking and wondering what was going on and Diana was worried about Stacy.

Stacy walked around the stock room looking at Keith with mixed feelings, wondering if she was angrier at him or hurt. She tried to keep it all together but the image of those two kissing made her emotionally snap. She started swinging at Keith like a wild woman and tried to hurt him but he blocked all her attempts and at the same time did not want to hurt Stacy. He grabbed her arms and pulled them down to the sides of her body and wrapped his arms around her. Talk about bad timing, for some reason he became sexually aroused but when Stacy felt his erection, she snapped again.

"Keith get off me. You are sick and perverted, I can feel your nasty hard on against my body, let me go Keith." She yelled.

Stacy continued yelling for him to get off her and tried to get loose but the more she struggled the more aroused he became, and she found this disgusting. She managed to get her arms loose and smacked him hard. Keith would never hit Stacy because he loved her. His sexual desire for Stacy now was incredible, so he pulled her skirt up and grabbed her butt.

"Are you crazy? Get your damn hands off me Keith and I mean it. Stop it. You betrayed me and now you want to have sex, how perverted is that. You crossed the line with me." She swung hard at him but missed again because he leaned back.

Keith got her skirt off and pulled Stacy's panties down then pushed her against the wall kissing and sucking her neck. This was the last thing she wanted but her deep sexual passions caused the erotic part of her personality to manifest. She kissed Keith hard on the lips while massaging his erection and unbuttoned his pants, pulled it and his underwear down quickly. Keith kicked his shoes, pants, and underwear away. They stared at each other and Stacy got on her knees and started sucking his dick like it was her air to breathe. She licked and sucked his balls and slid her tongue on the sides of his dick and sucked on just the head and looked up at him with anger.

"If you cum right now I am biting your dick, believe that."

Keith looked at this woman like she was crazy and used all the discipline he had not cum but it felt fantastic.

Stacy grabbed his dick and squeezed it to help him not cum because she had plans for him. She stopped and hopped up on him and put one hand around his neck while using the other to slide his dick inside her then put her hand on his neck and started riding his dick. She rode him so hard he leaned back against the wall to keep from falling. You heard Stacy's moaning and the slapping sounds of their bodies until she screamed.

"Ahhhhhh Keith, I am cummming. I hate you. I hate you, ahhhhhh." She continued riding him until she felt him getting ready to cum, so she hopped down.

"You know what I want, stop looking at me like that."

Keith thought, *Okay it's like that, no problem.* He saw some big towels in the corner of the room and spread them out on the floor and pulled Stacy down with her back on the floor. He pushed her legs back and licked her pussy up and down slowly and pushed his tongue inside. His oral skills were great, and he knew this, and he knew his wife loved his face all over her wetness licking and sucking at the same time until she climaxed hard on his tongue as it pushed inside her back and forth. While Stacy's body was on fire, he grabbed her ankles and pushed his dick inside her while she climaxed, and fucked her the way she wanted him to.

Stacy enjoyed every second of his loving because it made her feel so good despite what happened, but she wanted more and pushed her body into him moving and sliding on his dick. She felt another orgasm building so she pushed him off and grabbed his dick, and her mouth engulfed it. When she tasted her juices on his dick it turned her on even more as she sucked and slobbered all over it. They changed positions to a sixty-nine with Keith on his back and they sucked and licked each other with great passion, trying to see who could make the other cum first. Keith felt himself on the edge, so his lips sucked Stacy's clit and he slid a finger in her ass. That was it for her, she stopped sucking his dick and screamed from such great pleasure.

"Ohhhh it feels so good, ahhhhhh." She hit the floor repeatedly with the palms of her hands because she climaxed so hard.

Keith moved her body and got on top and slid his hard dick inside and looked at her eyes while thrusting back and forth. He saw her pain and love at the same time which caused him to slow his pace because he wanted to make love.

Stacy did not want him to slow down, and she did not want him looking at her the way he was right now because she saw so much love in his eyes for her. So, how could he do what he did?

"No Keith, don't slow down, fuck me."

This was not what he wanted and ignored her words and continued moving slow and deeply inside her until he felt her body trembling underneath him.

Stacy's emotions and love for Keith betrayed her and she had a deep explosive orgasm while looking into his eyes.

He could not hold out any longer and came inside Stacy while kissing her lips which made her finally break down and cry hard.

"Why Keith? Why did you do this?" She continued crying while he kissed her lips very softly and held her tightly knowing she cried hard because of him. It broke his heart knowing he hurt his only true love.

They laid there for a while and then cleaned themselves and got dressed. Keith tried to hug Stacy, but she gave him a look that let him know she did not want to be touched. They walked out of the room toward the VIP section and Stacy saw Shantai standing at the bar. Their eyes locked and all Shantai saw was a rage in Stacy's eyes so she ran out of the club. Stacy ran after her and Keith ran after them. Ron and the others saw this and Ron ran after them. As Shantai ran out of the club and was crossing the street, a car was coming and she jumped up to avoid being run over but the car hit her.

Stacy, Keith, and Ron ran outside in time to see Shantai get hit by the car and her body fell to the ground.

"Noooo!" Stacy screamed and her rage for Shantai instantly left and felt heartbroken seeing her body lying on the ground, possibly dead. She turned to Keith and buried her face in his chest crying and held him tightly.

# CHAPTER THIRTY SEVEN

*The Hospital*

Shantai laid unconscious in bed in a large private room at the hospital. Pastor Williams, Sheila, Zechariah, Ron, Diana, Cynthia, Rick, Tonya, Keith, and Stacy were in her room. Doctor Clifford walked in and waved at everyone. He checked the tubes connected to her body and made notes on his tablet.

"Doctor Clifford please tell us what is wrong with her and why is she still unconscious?" Stacy said.

"Well, the good news is she has no broken or cracked bones, which is amazing considering she was hit by a car and the fall she took. But I was concerned about the bad bruise on the side of her head, so I ordered a CT scan. The bad news is she has a bad concussion and a small blood clot pressing on the brain. She is receiving warfarin medication which is a blood thinner, and this should take care of the clot. But we will not know the extent of her injuries until she wakes up."

"Doctor, when she wakes up what are some of the things she may deal with?" Pastor Williams said.

"Well, it varies but one of the most common symptoms is amnesia, memory loss before the injury. The fact she was knocked unconscious and has not wakened yet is a major concern. But she will wake up and it could be at any time, we just do not know."

Stacy started crying.

"This is all my fault. I feel so bad but at the time all I felt was anger and rage. Lord forgive me."

Keith kissed her on the cheek and put his arm around her waist. Stacy gave him a mean look because she was very angry with him and she knew Shantai would not be lying in this hospital bed if it was not for him. She blamed him for all this, but her heart was hurt seeing Shantai in this condition. Suddenly, Shantai's body moved, and she began coughing and Stacy leaned closer and her eyes opened. The first person she saw was Stacy.

"Hi Stacy," She looked around at everyone. "Wow, hello everyone but what happened to me, and how did I get here?"

Doctor Clifford stepped closer to her bed.

"Shantai, I am doctor Clifford, the chief neurologist at this hospital. You were in an accident, and I need to ask you some questions to help us find out your medical condition."

"Sure doctor Clifford but I don't understand any of this and definitely don't remember getting in an accident, but ask away," She waved at everyone. "Hello everybody and Pastor Williams."

Everyone waved and spoke to her.

"Well, you answered one of my questions. Tell me what you do remember?"

"The last thing I remember was sitting in the VIP section of the club laughing and having fun. Now I am in this place, I have a serious headache, and my vision is a little blurry. I am also very thirsty. Other than that, I am fine. How was that? Now you tell me what happened and my medical condition."

"Not a problem. After walking out of the club, you were hit by a car and have been here for three days unconscious until now. You suffered a serious concussion, and you have a small blood clot pressing on your brain. The blood thinner you are receiving is taking care of the blood clot, so we don't feel this will be much of a problem for too long. Your concussion is our main concern. So, you have no memory before the accident?"

"Not at all. Why, did I do something crazy," she laughed but noticed the way Stacy looked at her and the mean look she gave Keith. "Something must have happened at the club, so is anyone going to tell me the truth," she stared at Stacy. "Stacy, I know you know something so tell me the truth. What happened at the club?"

"Shantai, the most important thing right now is for you to get your rest and heal. Nothing is more important than that." Stacy gave her a fake smile.

Shantai knew Stacy was hiding something from her but now was not the time. Sheila caressed the side of her face.

"Shantai please focus on getting better. All our prayers are focused on you."

"Thank you very much and I appreciate everything everyone is doing," she looked around the room. "This room is big and very nice, but I cannot afford all this."

"Shantai, please don't think about any of that, you are totally covered."

Stacy gave Keith a look that said, *this is all your fault.*

"Well, she needs her rest now, so you all have to leave. Shantai, I will be back first thing in the morning and if you have any problems, please just push the button by your bedside." Doctor Clifford said and walked out.

Everyone hugged her and walked out. The pastor was the last one in the room and he prayed for her and then walked out. Doctor Clifford disliked this part of his job, but it had to be done. He did not know who to approach so he chose Sheila.

"May I talk with you for a minute please?"

Zechariah moved closer to Sheila.

"What's up doctor? Is there more bad news you did not want to mention to Shantai?" Zechariah said, and he was very protective of Sheila.

The others noticed them talking and wanted to know what was going on, so they walked closer to them.

"What's going on Mom?" Ron said.

"I was about to inform Sheila because Shantai was brought in unconscious we have no record of any medical insurance on her and her medical treatment is very expensive and will increase. Without insurance, we will be forced to release her once she is stable. I wish things could be different but unfortunately, they are not."

Ron got angry at the very thought of Shantai being kicked out before she had time to fully heal. Keith saw the look in his eyes and knew his friend well because he felt the same way.

"Doctor Clifford, I know you are only doing your job but if you release her from this hospital before she is fully healed, it's going to be some problems. She has a full-time job, and she does have insurance, the best. I will take care of all her medical bills that have accumulated so far," he and Keith pulled out American Express Black cards. "Where do we go to take care of this?"

"Okay, I thank you sir for such a kind jester. If you walk over to the desk they will be glad to assist you."

They handed the cards to Cynthia because she was the club manager and she and Rick walked over to the desk. Keith knew this was not the place, but he wanted to talk with Stacy. He whispered in her ear.

"Baby, we need to talk."

"Not now Keith, this is not the place or the time to talk." She whispered back to him.

"Yeah okay. So, let's leave now so we can talk."

She gave him a look of defiance because the last thing she felt like doing was talking to him but since he was being so persistent, so be it.

"Fine Keith, since you want to talk so badly, we can leave and talk."

Keith and Ron talked for a while and Cynthia walked over and handed them their cards back. They mentioned to everyone they were leaving, and he and Stacy walked out of the hospital holding hands.

# CHAPTER THIRTY EIGHT

*Stand your Ground*

They all remained at the hospital for a while talking and then left. Keith and Stacy were quiet the entire ride home until they walked in the door and Stacy turned around and pointed her finger at Keith.

"I don't care what you say, this is all your fault, and you know it. I cannot believe you had your tongue in her mouth and hand all over her ass, the same time you were out with me. What's wrong Keith, are you getting bored with me and had to venture out and try you some new booty?" She stepped closer to him. "You know what Keith, the only reason you are still breathing is because I gave my life to Jesus, other than that, I would have fucked you and slit your throat that same night."

"I am going to overlook your threat to cut my throat because you need prayer and you are right, I messed up. But before you get ahead of yourself do not forget what you did and how I handled it. Betrayal is betrayal Stacy and when you had your tongue in Diana's mouth and grinding all over her body, you were betraying me. That was an incident of Shantai having too much to drink and me not pushing her away as I should. No matter what you saw, that was as far as it was going to go."

"So you tell it Keith. Fact is, we will never know. I wonder if I walked in ten minutes later would I have seen your dick inside her." She looked at him with disgust and anger.

"You are being very dramatic, and you know it but since you went there, I wonder what I would have seen if I walked in on you and Diana ten minutes later, your face buried between her legs?"

Stacy staring at him realizing she was being such a hypocrite. How could she possibly be angry at Keith when she did so much to betray him, many times over. If he only knew the truth and she wanted to tell him everything. This was too much weight for her to carry and it affected her mind and spirit greatly. So, before she realized it, she blurted it out.

"Keith, I am attracted to women and have been for years even before we met. I know you will leave me after this, but I can't take the pressure anymore. Yes, I have been with other women and the details do not matter because it was all wrong. Yes, Diana and I have been together sexually. No, Ron does not know it and no I have not been with any other man. I will never do anything like this again, please forgive me."

Words could not express how she felt now after confessing all that to Keith. She felt free but realized her marriage was over. Keith stood there looking at her in astonishment and not sure what to say. So, he walked away.

"Keith, where are you going? I poured my heart and soul out to you and you walk away from me. You have nothing to say to me? Yell, scream, say something."

He stopped walking and turned around.

"I am going for a walk Stacy. Anything I say to you now would be very destructive." He walked out in the backyard and sat down and was unable to control his hurt or pain. Tears came to his eyes and down his cheeks. He was heartbroken and did not know what to do, so he sat in the chair while the tears continued to flow.

Stacy kept her distance but she saw Keith crying. He was crying and for him to cry or show this degree of emotion, she knew he was hurting beyond measure and this made her cry. If there was any hope of them remaining together, she knew now it was over for them, so she went to her room and laid face down on the bed and cried uncontrollably until she fell asleep.

An hour later, Keith walked into the house and to his bedroom and saw Stacy asleep on the bed. He took a shower and got out with a towel wrapped around him and saw Stacy sitting on the bed looking at him with swollen eyes from crying so much. Yes, he deeply cared but right now he needed to get away from her. He started getting dressed when Stacy touched his arm.

"Keith, where are you going?"

He turned around and looked at her with great pain in his eyes.

"Away from you before I do something I will regret."

"Keith, I know I did some horrible things but only God knows how much I love you and want us to be together, please don't leave me, please."

He ignored her words and continued to get dressed. He walked towards his bedroom door when Stacy ran and closed it and stood in front of it.

"No Keith, don't do this to us. If you walk out the door now in the mental state you are in, something bad is going to happen."

"Stacy something bad has already happened. Now, I am asking you to please get out of the way before this scene gets ugly fast."

"No, I am not moving so you will have to physically move me, and I am not going to let you walk out on us. Keith, I know you are hurting tremendously right now but what about, for

better or worse? What about all the things we have been through together to get us here. Ride-or-die to the end remember?"

As badly as he was hurting now and wanted to get far away from Stacy, he knew if he tried to move her away from the door, this situation would get much worse. He saw that determined look in her eyes he has seen many times and knew she would fight him to the end. He was getting sick of this.

"Stacy, get out of the damn way, now!" He yelled.

"No," she yelled back. "I am not moving, and you are not going anywhere either, so do what you got to do Keith. But if you touch me, we are going to fight, and I mean it." She took her shoes off and put her hands up and got in a boxer's stance ready to fight. "You may as well go ahead and dial 911 because we are going to be two bloody people by the time they get here."

Keith looked at her like she was crazy but knew she was serious as she stood there in this boxer's stance ready to fight him and that told him a lot. He tried hard not to, but he could no longer hold it in. He burst out laughing.

"You are something else you know that. Standing there ready to fight me because I want to leave."

Still in her boxer's stance rocking slowly from side to side.

"Don't laugh at me Keith. I mean it if you try to walk out that door it is going to be bloody. Your mind is not stable, and you might do something stupid like be with another woman to get back at me. The very thought of you having sex with someone else is heartbreaking and I would do something to you Keith and you know it. So, no you are not leaving." Tears flowed from her eyes as she held her arms up ready to fight him if she had to.

With all the pain he felt, he loved his wife. Keith stepped closer and kissed her on the lips. Stacy wrapped her arms around his neck, and he carried her to the shower. The water soaked their clothes, so they removed them. This was the longest shower they ever took together. The entire time was spent washing each other over and over. They got out and dried one another off then put lotion on each other. Getting in bed together was so natural for them but not this time, it was emotionally difficult. They needed a much stronger connection than what making love would do, so they prayed, holding on to each other physically and emotionally very tightly. An hour later they were still praying.

"I love you Keith Washington and you know this."

"Yeah, I love you to Stacy but..."

She put her fingers over his mouth.

"Please Keith, say no more. We still love each other, and God will do the rest. I realize it is going to take some time, but we cannot fix this situation or get healed on our own. Only God can make us whole again in friendship and husband and wife." They began kissing slowly until they fell asleep.

# CHAPTER THIRTY NINE

*The Power of Prayer*

Two weeks later Shantai was out of the hospital and fully healed, not even a scar on her head. The Pastor and many others prayed for her complete recovery. The Doctors could not believe her recovery and healing with no scar at all. This was impossible but prayer removes the impossible for those who believe. Before she was released from the hospital, Stacy came by, and they talked for hours. Seeing her fully healed was amazing. It was difficult for Stacy to get answers from Shantai because she had no memory of the incident between her and Keith. So how can you fuss at someone about something they have no knowledge of? Shantai told Stacy it was like a bad dream. One minute she was in the club drinking wine laughing and having fun and the next thing she wakes up in the hospital. So, they talked about other things, like how she was attracted to one of the *Young Wolves*. Stacy laughed.

"Not you as well. What is it about these guys that attract women so hard? First, it was Tonya and Derrick, and now you. Okay, so which one is it, no do not tell me, I think I already know because I have seen the way he looks at you. It is Shawn, the brother with those white teeth, a pretty smile, and muscles for days. And he has a wide thick back."

"Yes, to all you just said and the brother is fine, but he is more than looks. He has a degree in business, he speaks three different languages, and he likes fixing up houses and selling them. He designed and built his five-bedroom, three-car garage house in Bowie, MD. Girl, that house is nice, big basement and a large master bedroom."

"Wow, I'm impressed. So, if he has all that going for him why are you two not closer? Did you give him some booty? Did he take his time and put that thang on you? Don't tell me, baby momma drama it never fails."

She looked at Stacy and laughed.

"You are something else. No, I did not give up the booty and no baby mamma drama, not this time, not with him. He was involved with this young lady for a while and then it ended but he must have put it down because she will not leave him alone. She keeps coming around after he told her many times it was over between them."

"Okay, sounds like a typical story but that is his side of the story what about her side. Is he still having sex with her, and have you seen her?"

"Yes, I have seen her and before you ask, yes, she is good looking, but I am definitely a step up. We talked and she was straight up with me. Told me it was over between them, but she throws herself at Shawn every chance she gets. And he never turns her down."

"Girl please, we know how that game goes. What man is going to turn down some ass when it is staring him right in the face?"

They looked at each other and laughed. They continued talking for a while and then Stacy hugged her and left.

Keith did not want to but Stacy was persistent in going to the Pastor for counseling. They discussed everything which Keith did not like because he believed a man handles his problems, but he was married now and realized things were different. He saw the positive difference it made in their relationship. They had not been together sexually but healing was taking place and they became closer mentally and spiritually which was by far more important and lasting. First thing in the morning and each night before they went to sleep, they prayed together asking God for continued healing and forgiveness. They also read the bible to one another instead of having sex and all these things combined with the deep love they had for one another made them closer.

# CHAPTER FORTY

*Prayer is the Answer*

It was Saturday afternoon. The day Rick, Cynthia, Derrick, and Tonya would be joined together in Holy matrimony. They spoke with the Pastor and informed him they were not interested in a lavish wedding. He understood and respected their desires. Sheila, Zechariah, Ron, Diana, Keith, Stacy, Shantai, Christine, Sandra, James, Catarina, the *Young Wolves,* and members of the church were there. Cynthia and Tonya wore white dresses and Rick and Derrick wore black Armani suits. Each spoke their wedding vows to each other and put the rings on one another's fingers. Pastor Williams prayed over them individually and as a group until he finally said the words these four looked forward to.

"Giving God all the praise and glory for his blessings on this day. I now pronounce Rick, Cynthia, Derrick, and Tonya husband and wife. You may now kiss your brides."

They kissed and music began playing and everyone started clapping their hands. The church members were so happy to see such a wonderful sight of God bringing these people together as one. The reception was at the church with plenty of food and more music. Shawn walked over to Shantai and asked to speak with her and they walked away from the others. He told her she looked great in her dress, and he was concerned about the medical condition she was in, but he knew God would heal her.

"Shantai, when can we start spending more time together? You know I am very interested in you."

"No Shawn, I don't know how interested you are in me and besides you already have a woman in your life, and I don't do seconds. It is either all or nothing with me and I don't have time for games, so you can keep it moving."

"Good, we are on the same page, and I feel the same way. You know there is no one in my life but that stalker and that's not my fault."

She wanted to slap Shawn for insulting her intelligence.

"Shawn, you are full of it," she stepped closer and whispered in his ear. "She would not be a stalker if you would keep your thang in your pants." She walked away from him toward the Pastor and started talking with him.

Pastor Williams noticed how hard Shawn looked at Shantai.

"Sister Shantai, I see you have an admirer. Is brother Shawn trying to put the moves on you?"

"Pastor you don't miss much. Yes, he is, and I would talk to him because I like him and he has a lot going for himself, but he has to get his priorities in order."

"Wise women my dear and stay that way." He patted her on the shoulder and walked away talking to the married couples and giving them words of wisdom. Pastor Williams's wife died before he became a Pastor, but this never caused him to walk away from the calling for his life. God gave him a spirit of an abundance of love for all people.

# CHAPTER FORTY ONE

*Catarina's Anger*

Everyday Catarina and James spent together as husband and wife was a blessing in so many ways. She loved this man deeply. However, she was dealing with anger and it was building up inside her. She always appreciated everything her dad did and how hard he worked to accomplish his goals. No, she did not like some of his business ventures, but her dad was all she had and now he was gone. He did not die but was killed by Leticia Wilson and her evil team members. She prayed daily asking God to remove all the anger and hatred she had for Leticia but so far, it was not working. The last thing on her mind was money, but James said they needed to talk so she put her emotions on hold for tonight and walked to the den where James sat wearing sweats and a short-sleeved shirt. She wore tight shorts and a T-shirt tied in a knot at her waist and no bra, to flirt with him. She walked past the sofa where he sat and purposely bumped into him when she sat down in front of him. Relaxing with her husband was always good. When Catarina bumped into James he laughed and watched her walk by in those tight shorts. She has so much going for her, and Catarina was stunning any day of the week.

"So, my darling sweet husband what is it you want to talk with me about?" Giving him her sweet innocent look.

"Well, I wanted to talk with you about your huge financial situation and investing. However, since you walked by wearing those booty shorts and your nipples are hard, my thoughts have been interrupted. We can put that conversation on hold for sure,"

He leaned forward and caressed one of her legs with his hand. "Bring your sexy body over so I can taste you." He laughed and rubbed her leg.

She hit his hand and crossed her legs tightly.

"James, stop being nasty and stay focused please so we can talk."

"You don't want to talk that is why you came over here dressed in your CFM outfit. You are trying to get bent over this sofa and get some of this DD and PT. So, stop faking and come here."

"I know I should not ask this but what does CFM mean?"

"Now you are playing games. CFM means, come fuck me."

"Why did I ask. You have a one-track nasty mind sir. I do love your DD and PT very much. Otherwise known as, diamond dick and pearl tongue."

"I am so glad you said yes to marry me. Change of plans let's not talk business tonight at all" he patted the sofa. "Let's be nasty all over this sofa?" He moved on top of her kissing her lips and pulled her T-shirt up, licking and sucking on her nipples, and working his way down.

Catarina leaned her head back enjoying his touch and wanted him to continue but she knew they needed to talk about business.

"James, you are making me feel so good, but we do need to talk baby." She pulled her T-shirt down and raised his head. "That was not easy for me to do because you know my body so well. Now back to business dear."

James looked at her wondering if he should snatch her shorts and underwear off but business first.

"You are such a tease, but the night is young. Okay, to the business at hand. You are worth fourteen billion dollars and..."

She leaned over and kissed him.

"No James, we, are worth fourteen billion dollars. I grew up around money, lots of money all my life, and saw how it brought out the worst in so many people. I have no idea what to do with that much money."

"I agree with you, money does expose the true spirit of a person. I have thought about investing a small portion of the money in feeding people in this country and providing real affordable housing. We could establish a chain of non-profit restaurants. The facility would provide three free meals a day, seven days a week for anyone. I am talking about good food, not just some frozen patties thawed out and cooked. There would be a seating capacity of two hundred. The goal would be to have one in every major city in the country and several in the larger cities and we would provide bus transportation to and from each facility. I would like to build three-bedroom homes and sell them for a hundred thousand dollars. No, this will not happen overnight, but it can be done. So, what do you think?"

Catarina looked at James and held back her tears because of everything he had said and how beautiful his heart was. She knew she married the right man.

"James, I think it is a wonderful idea and would like to get started on these projects right away. You do not have to go to other countries to find hungry people. Right here in the United States people go hungry every day and it is a shame because it can all be prevented. So, do you have a financial goal for this project?"

"Yes, I do. If you agree, it's your money."

"Please, stop saying that, I don't like it at all. You are my husband, and we are one in everything so stop saying, my money. So many married couples fight over money and what belongs to whom. That is the wrong spirit to have in a marriage. If that is how a person feels they should not get married. Now, back to the financial goal for this project."

"Thanks, and I won't say it again. The total financial goal I had in mind was two billion dollars. A billion for each project. We would establish one major business entity that would oversee all of them across the country. There would be a team to ask for donations year-round and something like this would give us state and federal tax incentives and tax breaks."

"Again, a wonderful plan and I am all for it because the cause is so important. James, thank you for talking to me about all this and I know it is just the beginning of many things we will do together. My heart is still very heavy concerning the loss of my dad. He was murdered James by that evil greedy woman, Leticia Wilson. I have prayed so hard asking God to take this bitterness out of my heart. James, please listen to me, she must go. I want her gone for good, forever. Do you understand where I am coming from?"

"Yes, I do, and my thoughts are the same but there is a right and wrong way to go about this..."

Her emotions were getting the best of her.

"No James, I don't want to hear any legal terms or long battles in court. I want her gone!" She yelled.

"So, you want revenge."

She stared at him with the spirit of anger in her eyes.

"Yes James, yes I want revenge."

"I do understand your anger but how do we get blessed by the hand of God by taking revenge?"

"I knew this was coming. Well, where was God when my dad was being murdered James, tell me that."

"You have every right to feel as you do but deep down inside you know this is not the path for us to take."

"Fine, so we sit back and do nothing and allow this evil woman to keep killing people with impunity. A license to kill and destroy is that it James? She is the devil incarnate and you know it. I know a lot about Mr. Bones and the many evil things he did to so many people. So, do not expect me to sit back and act like everything is going to be alright when we both know it is not James."

What words could James possibly say to his wife to comfort her when he knew everything, she said was the truth. He also knew you cannot fight a spiritual battle with earthly means. He moved closer to his wife and caressed the side of her face and kissed her.

"For me to say I know what you are going through would be a lie and I know especially at times like these it is important to remain close to God so we can hear his instructions for our life. So please allow me to do all I can to protect and love you."

"You always know what to say to me James because I was about to go off."

"You have a right to be angry but for tonight, allow your husband to spoil you." He kissed her and walked away.

"James where are you going in such a hurry?"

He came back with several large towels, pillows, and lotion in his hands.

"I will be your masseur for tonight. All you have to do is relax and put yourself in my loving hands." He spread some towels on the floor, two pillows, and put the lotion by the pillows. He laid the rest on the sofa. Then stood Catarina up from the sofa and started undressing her until she was naked. He stared at her gorgeous body and instantly became aroused.

She looked down and saw his erection and wanted to have some fun with him.

"Sir, I noticed you have an erection. I think it is company policy for you not to become aroused and tempt the patrons." She smiled and rubbed his leg.

"Please, no talking," he whispered in her ear. "You will get the DD and PT later." He bit her ear and laid her down on the towels and pillows and began massaging her body.

It was difficult for James to remain focus while massaging his wife because she is so attractive, and her body is flawless. His dick was so hard it could break through a slab of concrete, but he wanted to help his wife relax. As she laid on her stomach, he massaged her neck down to her feet paying extra attention to her lower back. Thirty minutes later, he turned her over and began massaging her shoulder area, breasts, stomach, arms, and legs.

Catarina fell asleep twice during her massage because James was good and she knew it was hard for him to stay professional, but he has, and she loved every second of it. Having his strong warm hands slide all over her body was incredible and she wanted more, so she turned back over on her stomach.

He knew she loved the massage, and this was his desire from the beginning. He massaged her lower back, butt, then moved her legs apart gently to massage her inner thighs. After all his massaging, caressing, and warm touch, when James massaged her butt and inner thighs it almost gave her an orgasm. James pulled off his sweatpants and underwear and laid over his wife and slid inside her.

That was it for Catarina, she moaned and had her first orgasm.

"Oh James." She raised her butt back and forth to meet his thrusts and continued to do so.

James' made love to his wife slow and delicate. Hours into their lovemaking they expressed how much they loved one another with words and actions of the body. After James made her climax twice, she stood up and pulled him closer, and looked into his eyes.

"You started this tonight, but I am going to finish it. Your wife is going to make love to you and look in your eyes every second until I drain you. I will be right back and don't you move." She walked into the kitchen quickly and came back with a small plastic bowl of ice. "Lay down James."

He laid down and she lowered herself on his full erection very slowly and put the bowl of ice close to them. Catarina rode James slowly and when his dick was completely inside her, she would grind on him hard. Gyrating her body on his dick. She lifted herself almost off him then back down slowly. She did this repeatedly, never taking her eyes off his and when she knew he was going to cum she stopped. Catarina gripped his dick hard and grabbed an ice cube and rubbed it across the tip of his dick. She licked and sucked the tip and rubbed the tip with the ice again. James' legs shook, and he was ready to bust at one moment and felt his dick was going to freeze the next. Feeling Catarina's warm tongue and mouth on the tip of his dick and the ice was driving him crazy. She lowered herself on him and stared into his eyes but never increased her pace. Up and down slowly grinding on his dick. She felt his dick pulsating inside her and got harder and felt it throbbing. So, Catarina began winding her hips, back, and butt hard on his dick but slower until he erupted inside her and their eyes never left each other. She smiled at him.

"You are the King of this house, but I am the queen, and don't you ever forget this. I love you James."

# CHAPTER FORTY TWO

*Attack*

Diana was home and enjoyed being pampered and catered to by Ron this Wednesday morning. They walked around in sweats. Being pregnant has its perks, although he spoils her anyway but like most pregnant women, she was not feeling sexy. Her hips and butt were bigger, and she did not like it, but Ron thought it was great and it turned him on even more. He constantly rubbed her hips and butt and said sexy remarks to her. She looked at him and shook her head.

"Ron, I am glad you still find me attractive although I feel fat and unattractive. My clothes do not fit so can we spend the day together and go shopping. Tomorrow is Thursday, so I know we will not spend much time together because you will be working in the club. I dislike you working in a club, and it is not a good place for you or Keith. The environment is all bad Ron, half-dressed women, alcohol, and wild nasty music. It's like Sodom and Gomorrah every day."

Ron laughed and walked up behind her and put his arms around her waist and pressed his body against her butt.

"Relax Diana, I am not corrupted, and I gladly come home to you every night. It does not matter what I see. My heart is with you so relax. Besides, you are looking so sexy to me with all this body you got." He kissed her and rubbed her hips while pressing his erection into her.

Diana became angry and pushed his hands down and backed away and turned around to face him.

"Stop it Ron! This brings back bad memories for me. It reminds me of when you got out of prison, and rebelled against God while working with Keith. Your mouth was so foul, every time you saw me you made nasty comments about my body and what you wanted to do to me and always kept trying to put your hands on my hips and butt. I am more than that Ron. That is all you men talk about is a woman's hips and the size of her butt. It can be degrading at times. Women are not walking pieces of meat for men. We have brains, feelings, and emotions."

"Well, tell me this Diana. Why do so many women dress to show off their hips and butt? Because you want men to see the contours of your hips and booty." He laughed and caressed her butt.

Diana looked at him and began crying. He hugged and kissed her.

"Don't cry Diana, you know how much I love you and it is not my fault."

"What are you talking about Ron?" she wiped the tears from her eyes. "What is not your fault?"

"It is not my fault you have all that power, hips and butt for days. So, do not get upset with me Sister. Blame your mom and dad and God, not me. I am your wonderful sweet loving husband who right about now desires very much to wax that ass, wax that ass and wax that ass." He said that knowing it was silly and immature but hopefully it would make her laugh.

Diana looked at him trying not to laugh but burst out laughing anyway.

"Okay, you made me laugh and you are right, just this once. Anyway, let's get dressed and go shopping so I can find some jeans to fit all this power into, so you tell it."

He caressed her face with the back of his hand and kissed her.

"That is what I am talking about. Before we go can I have some of your power, it has been two weeks and I am feigning for your body baby. I am a junky for your love and in need of a fix."

"Lord Jesus, help me. Come on Ron." She grabbed his hand and they walked to the bedroom.

"Oh, don't act like it's just me and you don't like all this good loving. I know you like it because when you have an intense orgasm from me putting all this work in, you make those sexy ugly faces," he made a face at her. "Oh, and then you talk to me, and every man knows when a woman talks to you and threatens you during sex, you got her. You do threaten me. You scream at me while I am putting all kinds of dick in you."

She waved her hand at Ron while laughing so hard at him.

"Ron stop, you are making my stomach hurt from laughing so much and I don't make ugly faces or threaten you. And you do not put, all kinds of dick in me as you say, so stop exaggerating."

"Oh, I am not exaggerating. You scream, yes Ron, that's it baby, give me all that good dick, don't make me kill you Ron." He fell on the bed laughing at her.

Diana shook her head and looked at him with hands on her hips and a condescending look.

"Whatever Ron, I am going to take a shower and get dressed." She removed her clothes, threw them on Ron, and walked into the shower.

He sat up and looked at her hips as she walked away like he was hypnotized. He could not undress fast enough and followed her into the shower. Their lovemaking was passionate and intense.

An hour and a half later they were riding in his Bentley. Ron wore dress shoes, dress pants, and a long-sleeved dress shirt. Diana wore a dress and jazz music played in the car.

"You look good in your dress Diana. I did not say anything about your hips and butt." Smiling at her.

"Thank you for your compliment Ron and for not mentioning my butt or hips."

"No problem. Besides, I do not have to mention anything about your hips or butt because you were throwing all that back on me while we were in the shower. And yes, you did threaten me repeatedly. Oh Ron, don't make me do it, don't make me do it, ahhhhh." He hit the steering wheel because he was laughing so hard.

"I am not going to comment on anything you just said and stop laughing at me and pay attention to your driving." She hit him in his side. "I am calling Stacy and Keith so they can join us." She called Stacy on her cell phone.

Ron and Diana met Keith and Stacy at a restaurant in DC. Diana was glad to see Stacy and have another woman to talk with. As usual, Stacy looked great, and she noticed Keith and every other man walking by could not keep their eyes off her. She did look great in her jeans as always. Ron tried to play it off, but she caught him looking at her as well, she shook her head. They sat down to eat. Ron and Keith were discussing business as usual. Stacy shared with Diana how she and Keith became closer by talking more and praying together. They ate and talked for two hours then went shopping. Nine thousand dollars and four hours later, Keith and Ron carried all the bags but had nothing in the bags for them. After putting the bags in the cars, they decided to go to the park in Haines Point and go for a walk.

It was evening time, and the park did not have many people walking around. Keith held Stacy's hand and Ron held Diana's. It was a romantic moment with each couple teasing the other. A hundred yards away behind them stood Leticia Wilson and a black wolf. This was no ordinary wolf. It stared at them and dropped its head as its eyes turned red. She leaned down and whispered in the wolf's ear.

"Attack!"

The wolf took off running covering a distance faster than a Cheetah and headed straight for Ron. Two and half seconds later it was within inches of Ron with his mouth open wide to bite. Keith saw it and pushed Ron out of the way knocking him and Diana on the ground hard. The wolf kept running but it had blood in its mouth. Keith was on the ground bleeding badly from the wolf's bite on his left thigh. Diana was on the ground crying and holding her stomach in pain because she was hemorrhaging. A few people ran over to help and called 911. Emergency vehicles arrived and took Diana and Keith to the hospital. Ron and Stacy rode along.

While en route to the hospital Stacy felt compelled to call Pastor Williams explaining to him what happened. At the hospital, doctor Clifford and others worked on Keith trying to stop the bleeding on his leg. He had a serious infection that was spreading from his leg to the rest of his body and the doctors could not stop it or figure out what it was. Diana was in the emergency room while the doctors tried to stop her hemorrhaging and she passed out from the pain. Pastor Williams, Sheila, Zechariah, Christine, and Sandra waited with Ron and Stacy. Doctor Clifford checked on Diana and then walked out to the family.

Ron walked up to doctor Clifford with the others walking behind him.

"Doctor Clifford, how is my wife and Keith doing?"

"Diana is heavily sedated, but she will be fine with rest," he looked down and then looked at Ron. "We tried everything we could, but her blood loss was too great. I am sorry but she lost the baby, and may never be able to have children. I am so sorry."

It was as if Ron were in a trance and seconds later the doctor's words hit him, and he screamed so loudly his screams could be heard outside the hospital. He fell to his knees with his face down and his hands bawled up tightly in a fist screaming and crying.

"Nooooo!" He yelled and was crying so hard his entire body was shaking and he began to sweat.

No mother ever wanted to see her child in so much pain and it made Shelia's knees buckle. Thankfully, Zechariah was there to hold her. Sandra and Christine were crying. Pastor Williams felt nothing but evil forces at work in this situation. He laid his hand on Ron's head and prayed for his strength.

"Doctor Clifford, how is Keith doing?" Stacy said.

"He is being worked on and I was told he was bitten by a wolf," he shook his head. "In the city, unbelievable, but anyway his bite is bad but it's the infection from the bite that is causing the most damage to his body. It is spreading and all our efforts to stop it so far have failed. Truth is, he is dying and there is nothing we can do if we can't stop the infection."

Hearing Keith is dying hit Stacy so hard she shook from the inside out until her body could no longer contain it and she passed out, but Christine and Sandra caught her before she hit the floor.

When Ron heard Keith was dying it sent a shock to his very soul and he stood up with tears still coming from his eyes. He looked at Dr. Clifford.

"Keith saved my life and I know it. No more deaths today doctor, take me to him."

"Sir, I understand the care you have for your friend, but the doctors are still trying to save him and..."

Ron stepped closer to Dr. Clifford.

"I said take me to him."

What doctor Clifford saw in Ron's eyes was unlike anything he had ever seen, and felt compelled to let him go. They walked to Keith's room and what Ron saw made his knees weak but not his spirit. Keith laid there with a gash in his leg, but his skin tone was almost grey, he looked dead. Ron waved his hand for the others to move away, and they did as he approached Keith.

Keith turned his head slowly in Ron's direction and spoke almost in a whisper.

"Ron, it is good to see you my brother. You do not have to tell me; I know I am dying. You saved me from a life in prison, saving your life was no problem. Tell Stacy I love her." He started shaking, coughing up blood, and his heart rate instantly dropped. Ron knew he was dying. The doctors moved forward to do what they could but again Ron waved them away. This time they felt the wave from his hand.

Ron placed one hand on Keith's chest and the other on the wound on his leg and spoke with authority.

"In the name of King Jesus, I command the forces of darkness to leave his body and I speak healing from the inside out and the outside in. For with God nothing shall be impossible."

RONALD GRAY                                                       219

Keith stopped shaking, his blood pressure and skin tone went back to normal, and the wound on his leg instantly closed. His eyes opened and were clear and full of life. The doctors and everyone else in the room could not believe what their eyes just saw. Keith stood up and hugged Ron then dropped to his knees thanking God for once again saving his life. He and Ron walked out and joined the others.

Stacy sat in the chair with the others with a blank look on her face and she looked up and saw Keith and Ron walking towards her. She jumped up and ran towards Keith and wrapped her arms around his neck and kissed him hard on the lips. The others joined them and hugged Keith. Pastor Williams looked at Ron because he knew what took place and so did Zechariah and Sheila. Ron hugged them all and then walked away to see Diana.

Diana was in the recovery room when Ron walked in wearing a hospital gown and top. She looked over at him and immediately started crying because she was still in shock and her heart and spirit were deeply hurt.

"The baby Ron, it's gone. The baby is gone."

He leaned forward and kissed her and held her hand.

"I know Diana, doctor Clifford told us, and I am so sorry this happened. If there was anything I could do to change this situation, I would. We still have each other and we are young."

"Yes, we are young. What is that supposed to mean and what took you so long to come see me, Ron? I thought you would have been here a lot sooner to see your wife."

"Yes, I would have come sooner but Keith was dying and once again God used me to save his life."

Hearing these words in her current mental state did not register with Diana well. Her face became so full of anger and resentment, she snapped.

"What!" She yelled. "Your wife was in here fighting for her life and our baby's life and you did not come to see us, but you go save Keith's life. You make me sick," her words came out so full of venom and hatred. "Don't look at me like that. You think I am crazy don't you? Well, I am not crazy Ron, and I see the picture very clearly now. It has always been you, Keith, and Stacy. Yes, you married me, but I know secretly you always wanted Stacy. How could you Ron, how could you not put me first, for once put me first. Your wife!" She was crying and stared at Ron.

"No Diana, you are wrong about everything. doctor Clifford came out and told us you were heavily sedated and would be okay, but you lost the baby. You will never know how hard that hit me or the effect it had on my heart. Then, he told us about Keith."

"So you tell it Ron. You think I am stupid. I know you and Keith have your dirty little secrets. All that money you two were making, spending time in the club with all those nasty women. I can't stand that place," she pointed her finger at him. "I see the lust in your eyes when you look at Stacy, watching her shake her ass when she walks. I see you Ron, Christian husband. You are like every other man on this planet, with wondering eyes and thoughts. For all I know you probably already had sex with her. What, I was not good enough for you dear husband. Didn't suck your dick good enough, was not freaky enough for you in bed?"

"Diana that is enough and you are being totally ridiculous. You are dealing with a great deal right now and your emotions are all over the place. You are the only woman I have ever wanted for my life, and you are the only woman I love and am in love with, there are no others. Never have been."

She stared at him and cried while gripping the sheets.

"Oh Ron, our baby is gone. Why Lord, why did this happen to my baby."

He sat next to her and held her hand and prayed.

# CHAPTER FORTY THREE
*Target from the Past*

The guy who bumped into Diana at the club and was slammed to the floor by Zechariah was Karl who was the cousin of Dwight and Chuck. These were the two men who harassed Diana and Stacy at the jewelry store and later were destroyed by Mr. Bones and Mr. Case at their house. They were burned and eaten alive, and he was supposed to be there that night. Karl was humiliated and thrown out of the club by the *Young Wolves*. During the entire ride home, he was plotting how to get revenge on Zechariah.

Karl lived a double life. As a profession, he is an experienced computer programmer in Washington, DC, making a hundred-twenty-five-thousand dollar a year living in a nice condo that his computer programmer job affords him, driving a Tahoe SUV. He is also a hacker and an exceptionally good one. He owns a four-million-dollar house in Miami, Florida with two Bentleys and a Lamborghini in the garage. Karl receives requests to hack into certain places, retrieve information, and pass it on to his client. His clients have never seen him or know where he lives. Years ago, he started out changing college student's grades and DMV records for two hundred dollars per transaction. Now he does not take a job under twenty-five thousand. So far, he has not come across anything he could not hack into, and he has over a million dollars in various computer equipment he kept in an old house in the country. This is an ugly house that would not attract anyone's attention but the house was upgraded with special doors, windows, power generators, and an escape hatch in the floor which leads to a tunnel across the street to another house he owned that was not in his name.

On the night he was thrown out of the club he went directly to the computer house, as he likes to call it, and did research on Zechariah, Keith, Ron, and everything about them. He found a lot of information, but the best information was finding out they were responsible for his cousins' death, at least that is the way he saw it. He decided to destroy Keith, Ron, Zechariah, and anyone associated with them. He planned to get next to Ron's sister Christine, which for some reason she stood out to him more than Sandra. He knew about their walk with God, but he was going after her anyway. If all else fails, he would have kidnapped her. He tapped into Christine's cell phone, email address, and the GPS in her car. He knew of her past problems with porn from her many website visits and this was another doorway into her life. He knew of Catarina's worth and Leticia Wilson and her evil ways and wanted to meet her. He contacted her hotel and made an appointment to meet her offering his computer programming service but wanted to show off his hacking skills. Leticia was impressed with what he could do and hired him on the spot. He mentioned his run in with Ron and his crew and how much he hated him and had plans to get to him through his sister Christine. Leticia gave him a small bottle of liquid and told him to put a few drops into her food or any liquid drink and he could do whatever he wanted to her after that. Just speak his desires to her.

Christine was in a grocery store and Karl was there watching her. She was a very attractive lady but was conservatively dressed in a skirt and a blouse. Although she was dressed conservatively, anyone could see she has a great figure and Karl was having various perverted sexual thoughts about what he wanted to do with her. He purposely bumped his shopping cart into hers.

"Excuse you but you need to watch where you are going." She looked at him frowning.

"I apologize it will not happen again," he backed up with his cart and walked away. "Bad attitude and a nasty spirit."

Christine heard him and felt bad because she does not have a bad attitude, she was just cautious. He was nice looking. She pushed her cart quickly to catch up to him.

"I heard what you said about me and for the record, I do not have a bad attitude or a nasty spirit."

Karl looked at her and smiled and extended his hand out to her.

"Hi, my name is Karl."

She shook his hand.

"Hi Karl, I am Christine. So, what do you do when you are not bumping into women in grocery stores?"

"I am a computer programmer in DC. I am looking for a nice church to attend but tonight I want to go to the movies."

"Well, I am a member of a great church you should visit."

"Sounds good. I have an idea; I will visit your church this Sunday if you come with me to the movies tonight. You drive your car and I drive mine, we watch the movie, afterward, you go to your home, and I go to mine. No pressure or stress. What do you think?"

She stared at him trying to read his spirit and size him up.

"Normally I would say no but I like movies and I am in the mood to go. So yes, we could do this. Oh, just for the record, you are not getting any booty when the movie is over." She looked at him and smiled.

"You are something else. Not a problem. I'll meet you tonight at the mall in Columbia at seven thirty."

"See you tonight Karl." She walked away pushing her cart and tried not to wiggle too much because she knew he watched her.

They met at the mall and went to the movies. She wore jeans and a long-sleeved thin shirt. Karl had on jeans and a short-sleeved shirt. He ordered food and drinks from the concession stand while Christine went to the bathroom. This was a big mistake on her part because Karl put drops of the liquid Leticia gave him in her food and drink. He was curious to see what was going to happen. This liquid was a mix of demonic sexually perverted curses and mind and body altering chemicals. The chemicals numb the body of its senses causing it to desire whatever words are spoken in the ear. Christine enjoyed the movie and Karl's company. He was a perfect gentleman but for some reason, she was extremely horny. They just met and she wanted him so bad she kept her legs crossed at the ankles and was very sleepy. She leaned her head on his shoulder.

"Are you okay?" He kissed Christine gently on the lips to see how she would react.

Something as simple as a kiss instantly affected her so she kissed him back and slid her tongue across his lips and moved her hand to his crotch caressing it.

"I want to taste your body and fuck you so bad." He whispered in her ear as he caressed her thighs.

"Yes Karl, I want you too, let's go." She could not believe her words or actions, but everything was incredibly compelling.

The movie was going off anyway and they walked out holding hands. She agreed to ride in his car and he would bring her back later, but Karl said he had a surprise for her. He drove to BWI airport, and they caught a private flight to Miami. A limo was waiting, and it took them to his house.

Christine never had any man treat her this good, the limo was very nice but the private plane was great. She thought, *I feel like a serious VIP and if he only knew how badly I want him and would have given in if he made moves on the plane, but he did not.*

Karl put more drops of the liquid in her wine while on the plane. Christine felt like she was having an out-of-body experience, seeing and hearing but not believing any of her actions tonight for someone she just met. The only thing on her mind was sex. When the gate opened to his house, she was impressed but more so when they walked in. His home was immaculate. They sat down on the sofa to talk, and he pushed a button on a remote, and music started playing. He asked her to dance and of course, she said yes. The music was slow, and Christine enjoyed slow dancing feeling his body pressed against hers and felt his erection, and feeling his hands caressing her butt felt good to her. Karl was kissing her neck while taking her top and bra off and then her jeans until Christine stood in front of him naked. Damn, her clothes hid her body well, she was very sexy. In seconds, he was naked. His body looked great to her, tight and muscular.

Every image Christine saw in porn movies she watched, came to her mind instantly over and over. Her thoughts, desires, and focus now were sexual satisfaction and that is exactly what she was going to do. Karl walked her to his large master bedroom and they showered together washing each other. He washed her with such tender care. All this was a set-up for what was to come. After getting out of the shower, Christine wasted no time on what she wanted. She pushed Karl on the bed and started sucking his dick like a pro until he was rock hard and then rode him until she climaxed. That was the beginning of three days of food and sex. Christine let him do to her whatever he wanted, repeatedly, like she was possessed with lust. Each sexual position was more of a turn-on than the next. The more intense, nastier, and more erotic, the more she liked it and could not get enough. Vaginal penetration and anal penetration, whatever, they did it. First thing in the morning she sucked him and several times during the day. He licked and sucked her pussy, ass, and entire body twice a day and he brought home another woman so they could have a threesome. Christine loved it, having hands caressing all over her body and being kissed, licked, and sucked all over was incredible. But later she wanted the girl gone so she could have Karl to herself, so she asked him to get rid of her and he did. She thanked him by sucking his dick and laying on her stomach on the bed with pillows underneath her waist. Karl knew exactly what she wanted him to do. His hands began rubbing her butt, followed by his lips and tongue. It felt good to Christine having his warm wet tongue slide between her butt cheeks and licking her anal entrance. He spat in and licked her ass and she liked feeling his dick slide slowly in her ass. At this point, she enjoyed the anal penetration a lot it gave her intense orgasms. She wanted this man in her life permanently.

Christine woke up early after one of their long sex sessions and her mind and body felt tired. Karl was sleeping hard. Reality hit her spirit and everything she did with this guy was shocking and so disgusting. She walked quickly to the bathroom naked, closed the door, and vomited repeatedly until she felt dizzy and laid down on the bathroom floor crying out to God to save her. She repented repeatedly and got up and looked at herself in the mirror. What she saw was another person. How could she do those sexual things to a stranger? Having him inside her precious body, sucking his penis, having it in her butt, and enjoying it. All of this was so perverted and sick! It made her vomit again until it hurt to breathe. He must have drugged me somehow, she thought. While brushing her teeth, rage set in, and she wanted Karl dead. Since God would not save her, she decided to save herself, at that moment Christine's heart became cold towards God.

She walked to the kitchen and got a knife and walked very softly back into the bedroom. Karl laid on his back and was snoring. She lifted her arms with the knife clutched tightly in both hands, trembling from fear but determined to make herself stab him in and run. She could not do it, despite all the evil he did. She does not know how she allowed him to violate her body so quickly. Tears flowed from her eyes as she walked away and put the knife back in the kitchen and began looking around his office still naked. She opened a drawer and found American Express Black cards which she took and in one of the closets, she found a safe. She knew it was locked but pulled the handle anyway and to her surprise, it opened and what she saw made her mouth drop open.

Christine never saw so much cash in her life. She grabbed some of the stacks, it was hundred-dollar bills in ten-thousand-dollar stacks. She looked around and saw an empty gym bag in the corner of the closet and filled it quickly with money, along with the credit cards and a set of house keys. She walked quietly back to the bedroom and slid the gym bag under the bed just in time because Karl woke up with an erection. She assumed he was taking something because his dick stayed hard.

"You are a very beautiful woman that I can't seem to get enough of, now come here." He reached over to grab her arm, but she moved out of the way.

She gave him a fake smile thinking, *what should I do now? If I suddenly stop having sex with him, he is going to become suspicious and hurt or maybe kill me. The very thought of him touching me again is repulsive but I must pretend and deal with it, no matter what.*

"No, you come to me." She laid down and spread her legs and pointed her finger at Karl then between her legs.

He got the message and began licking her inner thighs, and moved his way up, tasting Christine's wetness.

"Ahhhh, that feels good baby." She hated him but he made her body feel incredibly good. She was moaning and gripped his head and pressed it between her legs, moving it from side to side, up and down slowly until she climaxed all over his face. "Ohhhhh my goodness, baby don't stop." After calming down, she felt sick and wanted to throw up again.

The forces of darkness were working hard to destroy Christine, but unknown to her, the spirit of God was moving to protect her. Sandra called her mom and said she had not seen or heard from Christine in over three days. Sheila and Zechariah prayed hard and God revealed she was in great spiritual trouble. Zechariah called Ron and he snapped then called Keith and everything after that was more phone calls. Sheila called Pastor Williams and he had the entire church praying for Christine.

The next day Christine woke up feeling sick and repulsed after having more sex with him but enjoyed it at the same time. Karl was in the backyard having a heated conversation with someone on his cell phone. Christine watched him as she called Ron.

"Christine, tell me where you are."

"Ron, please come and get me, I have been drugged, please help me. I will text you the address and…oh God he is coming back in the house." She hung up the phone and text Ron the address. Her fingers never moved so fast.

Ron was beyond angry and asked God to forgive him for what he was about to do. Zechariah wanted to come with them very badly, but Ron needed him with his mom in case everything went bad. That evening, Ron, Keith, and twenty *Young Wolves* were on a private plane to Miami and there was enough firepower on the plane to start a small war. Keith had friends in Miami and arranged transportation for them at the airport.

To avoid Karl from becoming suspicious she had to continue acting the same and it made her sick. She laid face down on the bed naked, with tears coming from her eyes while he laid on top penetrating her. She told him she felt sick and for him to get up. Christine ran to the bathroom and vomited then rinsed her mouth, brushed her teeth, gargled, and came out to the dining room. Karl sat at the table with a cup of warm tea and a smile on his face. Before Christine came out, he put more drops of the liquid in her tea. She sat down and gave him a fake smile, wondering should she drink the tea. She did because she could not deviate from her past actions. An hour later, Christine was on her knees sucking his dick. Karl did not want to cum yet, so he told her to stop and assume the position. She leaned across the sofa and he slid inside her and began fucking her slow. This felt so good to Christine, but she wanted more. She looked back at him.

"Stop moving so damn slow all the time," she yelled. "You wanted me, now you got me, so fuck me like a man and not a little boy. What's the matter, you cannot handle this young hot pussy. Fuck me!" She yelled and stared at him hoping her words would irritate him and he would take it out on her body.

Karl knew what she was trying to do but he did not like to be provoked, especially by Christine. He gripped her hips firmly and began thrusting inside her.

Christine was cursing and screaming while having multiple orgasms, hating and loving the moment at the same time.

"Yes, that's it, ahhh. Make this pussy grip your dick. Ahhhhh baby my pussy is on fire. " She exploded with an orgasm.

He pulled out but Christine wanted more so she turned around and started sucking her juices off his dick. It was so hard, so she bent over, gripped his dick, and guided it inside her. Fucking him hard until she climaxed again. The sex lasted for two hours until they were exhausted. They showered and went to sleep.

Three o'clock in the morning, several black SUVs pulled up close to Karl's house and everyone got out dressed in black and carrying automatic weapons and wearing night goggles. Their faces were covered with masks. When they climbed over his fence an alarm went off inside the house which woke up Karl and Christine. He grabbed his gun from his nightstand, but it was too late. His front, side, and the back door exploded, and they came in through the doors and windows in his bedroom. He got off five shots, but everyone wore body armor and Karl was shot thirty times with automatic gunfire. Christine was balled up on the bed crying, screaming, and shaking under the sheets because she was terrified, not knowing what was going on.

Ron pulled his mask off and tapped Christine on the leg.

"Christine it's me, hurry up and get dressed."

She uncovered her head.

"Ron." She hugged him then covered her body with the sheet and got off the bed and grabbed the gym bag underneath and rushed toward the bathroom.

Christine walked so quickly she stepped on the sheet and her naked body was exposed from the back. Ron closed his eyes and looked down quickly, but Keith stared because he did not know Christine's body looked so good. He thought, *damn, she is sexy, I could fuck her for days. Forgive me Lord.*

Christine grabbed the sheet quickly and covered herself and kept walking making sure not to drop the gym bag.

Ron assumed the gym bag was her personal belongings. If he only knew! Keith and Ron escorted Christine from the house to one of the SUV's. The *Young Wolves* wrapped Karl's body in plastic, taped it up, and took it with them. On the way to the airport, Karl's body was tied to chains and bricks and dumped in the ocean. They were back on the private plane in one hour and in the air back to Maryland. Keith made a call to some people he knew in the Miami area to come and fix the house as if it was never touched. The entire ride home Christine cried and held on to Ron.

# CHAPTER FORTY FOUR
*Free Will*

Sheila was so glad to see Christine and have her home with her and Zechariah. Sandra and Ron being there made it better. Pastor Williams was over earlier talking one on one with Christine and praying with her. He prayed with many people but it seemed as if Christine's inner will was fighting not to be delivered and this made no sense to him. While Christine rested he talked with Sheila and Zechariah explaining things to them and then left. Zechariah, Sandra, Ron, and Sheila sat downstairs in the basement talking.

"Mom, why do so many bad things keep happening to this family? It is as if we are cursed or something. Time goes by when things are great and then more bad events. I still cannot believe Christine would go off with a stranger to Miami and do God knows what. Okay, she mentioned being drugged but we still have free will and I know she had sex with him."

Christine heard the conversation as she walked down the stairs and for the first time she had resentment toward her sister.

"What if I did Sandra? What would you rather I do, let him beat me, rape me, and kill me? I did whatever I had to do to survive and would do it all over again if I had to. I dealt with a living hell. What about you Miss Perfect, what would you do? Keep praying until he slit your throat? I did pray, repeatedly and nothing happened." She looked at Sandra with contempt and she knew from this moment on they would never be as close as they once were for so many years.

Ron stood and walked over to her.

"Christine, you don't have to explain. It would be easy for me to say what I would do in a situation, but the fact is, you never know exactly what you would do, until that time. Self-preservation is motivation to do whatever to survive."

"Christine come over and sit down." Sheila said.

She hugged Ron and had to hold back the tears because she loved him so much and not just for saving her life but for never giving up. She walked past Sandra, rolled her eyes, and bumped into her leg on purpose. Zechariah and Sheila hugged her.

"It's truly a blessing to be here but enough talk about me. Mom how are you and Zechariah doing in this big house."

She and Zechariah looked at each other smiling.

"We are doing great and enjoying our house fine thank you very much. Plenty of space to pray." Sheila looked at everyone and could not help but laugh.

Zechariah leaned toward Sheila and kissed her on the cheek.

"Tell them again baby, we have plenty of room to pray."

"That's not all you two are doing in this big house." Christine said smiling.

"Hold it. I am not old enough to hear conversations like this and besides, I am hungry." Ron said.

"Son, you are always hungry. Come on girls let's go cook."

Sheila, Sandra, and Christine went into the kitchen to cook while Ron and Zechariah talked. Thirty minutes later, Diana, Stacy, and Keith came by, and the circle was complete. Diana and Stacy joined the others in the kitchen and Keith sat down with Ron and Zechariah.

"Alright you three, dinner is ready, so come to the kitchen and wash your dirty hands so we can eat." Sheila yelled.

All three washed their hands and sat down at the dining room table to eat fried catfish, greens, baked macaroni and cheese, candied yams, cornbread, and iced tea. There was homemade coconut-sweet potato pie with spiced crust and ice cream ala mode. Ron clapped his hands.

"Wow, now this is what I am talking about. Some serious home cooking, very nice."

"Say it again my brother. This is the way to a man's heart." Keith and Ron dapped up.

Stacy and Diana gave Ron and Keith mean looks.

"Ron, you and Keith need to stop acting like Stacy and I do not feed you two very well at home. Neither one of you look like you are suffering from malnutrition so you can stop all the drama and trying to make us look bad in front of your mother." Diana said and looked at Ron.

"My brothers, my advice for you two is when you get home, pray and pray some more." Zechariah started laughing.

"Alright, enough of all that. We all are blessed, now let's eat. Zechariah will you bless the table please." Sheila said.

"Lord, we thank you for blessing us for gathering in your name and as a family. We ask you to bless this food and purify it, in Jesus' name, Amen. Let's eat."

For the next hour, there was eating, smacking lips, and plenty of talking. It was a while since they were all together like this. You felt the love in the room. Christine excused herself, got up from the table and walked to the bathroom, and sat down. She lowered her head, wrapped her arms around herself, and cried like a baby. She was having flashbacks of what took place in Miami and all the sick and perverted sex. Reasons beyond her thinking, she missed the excitement, the rush, and the incredibly satisfying sex. She hated herself for admitting it, but she wanted more and soon. Christine smiled as she thought about all the cash in the gym bag at home and looked forward to counting it.

Sandra drove and she and Christine rode home together but there was tension between them. Christine was still upset about the comments Sandra made but tried to get past all that. She was thinking how wonderful it was spending quality time with her family and how much she wanted more of this family time. First, she wanted to find out how much money was in the gym bag. Sandra looked at her, but Christine rolled her eyes at her.

"Christine, I know you are still upset with me for what I said about you. Please forgive me but you will never know how worried I was about you. The thought of you having to do sick perverted things with some guy to stay alive angers me beyond words. I am sorry very Sis."

"I thought you of all people would understand because of all the things you have been through. Don't worry about it, I will get over it like I have everything else in my life. By the way, how come you do not have a man? You can't tell me you don't want a man in your life to love you."

"No, I don't have a man in my life, but God will bless me and yes, I want a man to love me but not love on me. That is not love, that is lust and of the devil."

"Yeah okay. You are a very good-looking woman Sandra, we both are, and life is passing us by. If we are not careful, we are going to wake up one day and be old single ladies living with cats. But not me Sandra, I am going to start living."

"What in the world is that supposed to mean? You are going to start hanging out with low-life thugs and having sex and you call that living. That is not living Christine, that is dying."

Christine smiled and then laughed.

"Wow, you need a man to put it on you. I am talking DD and PT to the fullest."

"What! So, having sex is going to make my life better. What are DD and PT?"

"DD and PT stand for Diamond Dick and Pearl Tongue. This is what you need on a regular." She started laughing

"Oh God Christine. What happened to you, your mind and spirit are so disgusting. You need to be delivered and quick."

They arrived home and went to their rooms. Christine pulled the gym bag from underneath her bed and dumped all the money out. Ten-thousand-dollar stacks were tied together, and she stared at so many. She counted two hundred stacks, that's two million dollars in cash. So many thoughts went through her head as she sat on the bed staring at all this money along with the many conversations Karl shared with her. No one knew about the house in Miami. The cash she left was possibly still in the safe. She could take a trip back there to at least check things out but who could she trust? One of the *Young Wolves?* Which one, she wondered because they were all loyal to Keith and Ron but just how loyal? Maybe she would meet someone. Christine began smiling and talking to herself.

"I am a good-looking woman, a freak in bed, and now I have plenty of money. I can seduce any man. Men can talk all that noise, but it would be very difficult for a man to turn down a fine woman giving up throat, pussy, and ass. No man is going to be talking about God if you have his dick in your mouth, deep throating it. Yes, it is my time. Free will baby," She continued to smile. "Free will."

# CHAPTER FORTY FIVE

*Seduction or Trap*

Christine started going to the same gym where the *Young Wolves* worked out. They always came as a group. People knew who they were and always gave them space. She was on a mission and came to the gym dressed very conservatively in dresses but when she came out of the dressing room it was a different look. She wore tight spandex shorts with a matching top showing her tight abs. Christine had a very attractive body and she knew how to work it without appearing too obvious. Guys tried talking to her, but the *Young Wolves* always intervened, until word got out she was not to be talked to. This was not part of Christine's plan, how was she supposed to attract a man if no one would approach her anymore? This was not good, so her only option was to select one of the *Young Wolves,* and there was one she noticed would watch her more than the others. She did not know if he watched her for business or pleasure. Well, it was time to find out, so she walked up to him one day and asked for his help with doing squats. She noticed he did a lot of squats and his legs looked good and he was strong. On this day, she wore pink and black tennis shoes, pink tight shorts, and a pink and black top to match that came just below her breasts. His name was Sonny, he was dark skinned complexion, thirty-two years old, six feet two, and two-hundred-thirty-eight pounds. With his looks and build, he could be a model he was so fine. She watched him do his set and now it was her turn.

"Thanks for helping me Sonny I appreciate it a lot. Yes, I know how to do squats, but I am trying to get stronger and tighten my butt," she turned to the side. "So, what do you think, how much work do you think I need?" Smiling at him.

"You look great Miss O'Neil." He was careful of what he said. Not knowing if this was a setup, either way, he was not falling for it. He loved his job and he liked breathing.

Christine put her hands on her hips and looked at him.

"Please do not call me that, my name is Christine, and don't call me Miss Christine either." She walked up to the squat rack and Sonny helped her put the bar across her shoulders with twenty-five-pound plates on each end. She did ten reps of deep squats with Sonny directly behind her, squatting as she squatted as it should be for a real spotter. With each rep, Christine made sure her butt lightly brushed up against his crotch. She turned around and looked at him.

"So, what do you think, how was I?"

"Good reps and good form. All you have to do is stay focused and consistent and you will be fine."

"Thanks again Sonny for your help. Can I talk to you for a minute please, I need someone to talk to?"

"Sure, no problem but let's finish this work out first, and then we can talk.

This was not what she wanted but okay. Besides, she was able to rub her butt against him some more. They did four more sets of squats, leg curls, calf raises, and some shoulder work. After all this, Christine was tired and did not feel like talking, all she wanted was a hot shower and some rest, but business was business. They sat down in the lounge area.

"Great workout. So, what is on your mind Christine? Are you okay from the Miami incident? I know it was horrible for you." He tried to stay focused, but she was incredibly attractive.

"Thanks for asking and I will be alright in time, but I will be direct with you. I want to change some things in my life and not walk around in fear. I would like to go out more but as soon as the person finds out whose sister I am, then that is it, he is gone. No one will take me out, everyone fears my brother or Keith." She said this on purpose knowing it would get to him, a man thing.

"I can only speak for me, but I fear no man. It is respect and honor I have for you and your family. You stay in church and all will be well."

"Yeah, okay. Sonny, I have some serious plans for my life, and I need the right man to be by my side," she leaned closer to him. "Will you take me out, please? Just one time and if we don't connect then I will not bother you anymore."

He was still cautious of what to say but was willing to take a chance and see what happens.

"No problem we can go out. When and where?"

"Tonight, but let's do something a little different. I would like to go out to eat, go swimming, and then see a movie. So, what do you think?"

"Well, it all works for me. But do you have the energy for all that after our workout?" He was being smart to see her reaction.

"All I need is a hot shower and I will be good as new. This is my thought and please do not give me that look or get the wrong impression. We can get rooms at the Hyatt Regency Hotel on Capitol Hill because they have nice restaurants and a pool and then go see a movie in China Town. Please do not judge me and say yes, so we can have some fun and still be respectful. Say yes and I will make the reservations now."

Sonny stared at her and various thoughts came to mind but why not. To him, it will be a clean date with the Christian girl who was bored.

"Make the reservation."

Christine was happy and hugged him but did not realize other *Young Wolves* were watching them since she was in the gym. She made the reservation and they had rooms G405 and G406 and agreed to meet in the hotel lobby in three hours. Sonny walked Christine to her car, and she hugged him tightly and kissed him on the lips and got in her car and drove away. He walked off and was thinking, *okay she wants to play games pressing her body on mine and kissing me. No problem, we both can play that game.* He drove away.

Leticia Wilson was aware of all this and transformed into a mist. She went to the rooms at the hotel and changed back into human form once she was inside each room.

"Every lustful desire and imagination will transpire in these rooms on this night, I speak demonic curses and manifestations of lust in this place." She continued to speak demonic curses in each room and spat all over the beds and furniture and then walked out of the rooms.

The entire ride home Christine hoped Sandra was not home to avoid the questions. She walked in calling Sandra but there was no answer. Great, she thought and moved fast to get out. She showered quickly and put on lotion then sprayed one of her favorite perfumes lightly between her legs, on her neck, her lower back, and the back of her knees. She put on pink thong panties, a matching bra, dark blue tight jeans that hugged her body well, heels, and a light blue mid-riff top. She looked in her full-length mirror and liked what she saw. She prepared her overnight bag and was out the door with five grand cash in her bag.

When she walked into the hotel lobby an older couple was coming out and the man turned his head to see Christine's butt as she walked by and shook his head. His wife slapped him in the back of the head.

"Stop looking at that young girl's butt because she does not want your ten-bottle, medication taking ass. She will give you a heart attack old man."

Christine laughed and kept walking to the front desk.

Sonny saw her when she first came in and was impressed and watched the man getting slapped made him laugh. He walked up behind Christine and put one hand on her shoulder while holding his weekender bag in the other. Christine turned around and liked what she saw standing before her. He wore brown suede Penny Loafers, black Ralph Lauren *Moto Jeans,* and a tan and black dress vest with no shirt on underneath. He looked like a bodyguard and model all in one. The man was ripped, and he smelled so good. Christine hugged him.

"You do know how to get a women's attention. You look good Sonny."

"Your entrance was much better than mine. I saw that old man get slapped while looking at your butt. You do look good and your jeans fit you very well."

"I do squats baby, lots of squats."

They laughed and hugged each other again. Sonny paid for the rooms, and they dropped their bags off and came back out. They sat down and ate in one of the restaurants in the hotel. You would have thought they knew each other for years with the way they talked and laughed because the connection between them

was instant. After eating, they drove to China Town in DC to see the movie, *Miles Away* starring Sid Burston. Christine held his hand at times in the movie because she was so drawn to him and was very horny. It was eleven thirty when they got back to the hotel holding hands and laughing as they walked in.

"Christine, tonight has been great, and you know I have enjoyed your company, but if you are tired, we can go swimming another time."

Christine looked at him and thought, *he is mistaken if he thinks I am not getting him in that pool.* She smiled at him.

"Thank you for your consideration but I am not tired so let's go up to the rooms, change and get in the pool."

"Works for me, let's walk."

Sonny walked Christine to her room and was about to walk away when she grabbed his arm and pulled him back.

"Can I at least get a kiss before you change clothes?"

He kissed her but Christine only wanted to kiss him to get his mind and body going for what she had in mind. She licked his lips slowly and slid her tongue in his mouth enjoying the warmth of it. She smiled and walked into her room, and he walked to his.

Sonny walked out of his room carrying towels and wearing sandals, swim shorts, and a T-shirt. He knocked on Christine's door and she opened it wearing sandals, black sweatpants, and a T-shirt. Sonny laughed.

"Is that what you are wearing to swim in?"

"Oh, you got jokes. No, I am not going swimming in this, but I am not walking down any hotel hallway wearing a swimsuit."

They reached the pool room and were the only ones there. Christine took off her sweatpants and T-shirt making sure she stood in front of Sonny with her back to him so he could see her bending over. She wore a pink two-piece bathing suit that did little to hide her curvaceous body. Sonny stared and got hard quickly looking at her, he got in the pool to hide his erection. Christine saw it and wanted him. They laughed and played in the pool for hours until it was three o'clock in the morning and they decided it was time to leave. Sonny dried himself off and then Christine and they got dressed and left. He stood by her room door.

"Christine this was the best time I had with a woman in a long while and I would..."

Christine hugged and kissed him while rubbing his penis through his shorts. He enjoyed all of this but once again caution came to him and he stepped back.

"I don't know what kind of game you are playing but I don't play games so this seduction thing you are doing is for children if you are not for real."

She wanted to slap him for talking to her like she was a hot ass little teenager. But she was too close to allow her emotions to get in the way.

"Sonny, I know what you might be thinking. I am not trying to set you up, get you in any trouble, or play any games. I am a grown woman like you are a grown man. You know I am very interested in you or we would not be here. Will you give me enough time to shower and come back to my room please?"

"Yes, I can do that." He kissed her and walked away.

Thirty minutes later, Sonny walked to Christine's room wearing sandals, sweatpants, and a T-shirt. He knocked on her door and she answered it with a big towel wrapped around her body. She grabbed him by his sweats and pulled him in. For the next four hours, Christine and Sonny did everything she did with

Karl while in Miami, but it was better. She had real feelings for Sonny and wanted to be completely open to him in the bedroom and out but right now, it was all about sex. Everything they did was more intense than what she experienced in Miami but could not figure out why. They fell asleep but woke up having sex like it was the beginning. Sonny made her climax five times and three were from oral. His dick was so hard and the right size for her, not too small but not huge either to make her sore. She gave him her entire body and loved it. Christine knew he was the one for her. She rode him while sitting in a chair.

"Ahhhhh Sonny." She leaned forward grinding on his dick and passionately kissed him while climaxing hard. His touch was so warm to her mind and body.

About nine in the morning, they were still in Christine's room taking showers together but as great as all this was, Sonny was no fool by any means. He knew no woman would do all this without some angle. Christine stood in front of a long mirror close to a chair, getting dressed putting on a mini skirt and a top when Sonny walked up behind her. He put his hands on her hips and pressed his body into hers. He kissed both sides of her neck while caressing her hips under her skirt.

"So, do you want to tell me what all this is really about? Be straight up with me." He was sucking her neck and his hands moved underneath her panties.

It was either now or never and this was the best chance Christine was going to get to lay everything out. It was hard to focus on business with his warm mouth and tongue on her neck, his hands between her legs, and feeling his growing erection against her butt.

"Okay, but you need to stop. How am I supposed to focus on talking about business when you are making me horny all over again? So, let's sit down and talk." She tried to walk away but he wrapped his arms around her.

"Anyone can focus in ideal circumstances. I am going to show you how to get it all done no matter what. So, you talk, and I will listen and please you at the same time." He pulled her panties down, her miniskirt up, got on his knees, put his hands on her hips and began licking her butt. "Start talking."

Christine looked back at him and gripped the chair.

"Okay, fine I will talk and ignore you," Easier said than done. "Sonny I went through so much in Miami and owe all of you for coming to get me and possibly saving my life. But while I was there, I came across an interesting situation. I found a lot of money and took some with me, but a lot was left, and it could still be there. I learned some valuable information. Yes, I have been sheltered in life because of how I was raised but I am far from stupid and..."

Sonny spread her legs as she talked and licked between Christine's legs and the moment she felt his warm tongue it made her stop talking.

"That feels so good."

"Keep talking." He smacked her butt and continued licking.

"Yes, oh, okay whatever you say." This was not easy, but she was determined not to allow him to get the best of her. "I think we could make a good team. You be my man and watch my back as I watch yours and we do this together. Trust is everything."

He pushed Christine over the chair and slid his tongue inside her moving it back and forth.

"Oh, Damn Sonny, baby..."

RONALD GRAY

247

He smacked her on the butt twice but not hard.

"I said, keep talking." He buried his face between her legs.

Christine knew she was close to orgasm but thought he would consider her weak if she climaxed and laid down on the bed like some weak little girl. So, she pushed back her emotions and feelings. She wondered how he could have his face pressed so tightly between her legs and still breathe. She shook her head and tried not to climax so quickly but damn; this man could eat some pussy.

"I need you to come with me back to Miami and keep this to ourselves. Sonny, I will be a good woman to you, don't ever lie or try to deceive me, like I said, I am far from stupid."

He stood up and took his clothes off. Sonny stood behind Christine and looked directly at Christine in the mirror. His dick was fully erect as he slid inside her.

"Keep talking." He smiled as he moved his dick around, in and out, and rubbed the head of it against her butt and slid back inside. He increased his pace while holding onto her hips. He continued doing all this while she talked, knowing it was making the emotional and physical side of her go crazy.

Christine was fighting so hard to resist but it was all too much knowing any second now she would explode. So, she started talking quicker but as she did this his pace increased more and all you heard were the slapping sounds of their bodies.

"We could accomplish so much together and have so much fun at the same time."

He gripped her hips harder and pulled her back into him fast. Watching all this happening in the mirror was more of a turn on.

"Baby I am trying; I am trying to..." It was too late because her orgasm came upon her like an erupting volcano.

"Ahhhhh Sonny you are making me cum." Christine pushed back into him fast and hard with each wave of her orgasm hitting her body repeatedly. She wanted to drop to the floor but seeing that look on his face like he got the best of her, gave her energy she never thought she had. Christine pushed him back with her body and got on her knees and grabbed his dick with one hand and started sucking it with vigor. Never taking it out of her mouth although he tried to get away, but she squeezed it harder and sucked harder.

Sonny did not expect her to do this, and it was fantastic.

"Stop Christine and come up here."

She ignored him knowing he was close, so she kept sucking until his body jumped and cum shot into her mouth, but she kept sucking. She sucked every drop and seeing his knees about to buckle under gave her satisfaction regardless of what he might say after this. She licked and sucked his balls and licked along the sides of his dick and sucked the tip. This was the icing on the cake for her because she made him jump and he tried to pull away from her, but she had a tight grip on his dick. Christine knew he was drained, so she stood up and faced him, not saying a word but looked at him with no expression on her face. She felt cocky.

"Wow! You are incredible." He stared at her and liked everything about her so far and felt she was being straight up with him. He kissed her and held her hand as they walked to the bed and sat down.

"I got you. When do you want to go to Miami? More importantly, is how do we accomplish all this together without your brother or Keith finding out. We both know everyone is on edge right now and seeing me with you will cause your brother and Keith to snap. As I said, I fear no man but I ain't no fool either."

"Well, I have thought about that, and you made some good points. But I am a grown woman and should not have to go through all this, however, sneaking around will get you killed. The truth is the answer. Let me talk to Ron and tell him I am very interested in you and would like for us to get to know each other better."

"Smart move and I like it. Now let's get out of here so we can start this off right."

"We already started it off right." She smiled and kissed him. "But I need you to answer my question before we leave, and you need to think hard before you answer. Will you be my man?"

"My heart is in the right place. Yes, I will be your man." He hugged and kissed her while his hands moved down her back and gripped her butt.

"Thank you Sonny, you made a good choice."

They showered and Sonny went back to his room to change clothes and then back to Christine's room. She had on a different top and a different pair of jeans but just as tight. They kissed and hugged and went downstairs to check out, leaning on the counter laughing and playing. Sonny had his hand on her lower back and let it slide down to her butt, caressing it. They turned around holding hands and laughing and got the shock of their life. Ron, Keith, and seven *Young Wolves* stood there dressed in Armani suits, and the look on Ron and Keith's face was of anger and betrayal.

"Let my sister's hand go and pray real fast homie." Ron unbuttoned his jacket revealing a gun in his holster.

Keith and the *Young Wolves* did the same. Christine walked up to Ron.

"Ron, this is not what it looks like, please listen to me."

He looked at her with disgust.

"Be quiet Christine," He pointed to one of the *Young Wolves*. "Take her to the limo outside."

"Ron wait, you don't understand I..."

The look he gave Christine stopped her from talking. She looked at Ron and then at Sonny knowing she may never see him again and walked away. But she turned back around and walked back to Sonny and stood by his side.

"No Ron, I am not going to let you do this when you don't have all the facts. You and Keith trust these guys with your life so why can't you trust Sonny with me. Derrick is with Tonya, and they are married." She turned to Keith. "Keith talk to Ron please before he makes a big mistake."

Keith was busy mean mugging Sonny because he felt he should have come and talked to him first instead of sneaking around. He looked at Christine.

"Talk to your brother."

Christine looked at Keith and rolled her eyes at him then walked closer to Ron.

"Ron, I love you but please, please don't do what I know you are going to do if I walk out that door and Sonny is not with me," She became angry instead of fearful and got in Ron's face. "Ron, if you do this evil thing, I am telling mom and Pastor Williams you and Keith are out here hurting people again and I mean it." She stared at him with a look of total defiance and bravery, but her heart was afraid.

Ron tried not to show it, but her words hit his spirit hard, and he began to feel bad. He grabbed Christine's hand and walked over to Sonny and placed her hand in his.

"Take care of my sister Sonny and if anything happens to her, I will hold you personally responsible." He hugged Christine and he, Keith, and the *Young Wolves* walked away. He felt like he just lost his sister and held back his tears.

# CHAPTER FORTY SIX
*Family*

Christine and Sonny went to Miami and sure enough, the rest of the money was still in the safe. Three million dollars and she found a small bag of diamonds in one of the shoe boxes in the closet. They took all this and left the house promising to never return. Christine was truly into Sonny, but she was no fool and she knew she could trust Ron and Keith one hundred percent, so she sat down with them and shared everything. When Christine confided in Ron it made his heart feel good and Keith felt this, it made him change his mind about possibly getting rid of Sonny. A friend of Keith and Ron who was very knowledgeable about diamonds, came by their office at the club one night. They showed him the diamonds. The man was impressed and said the diamonds were worth thirty million, but he could get them twenty-two million cash for a quick sale. One week later, Keith and Ron came by Christine and Sandra's house and gave Christine two suitcases with twenty-two million dollars in cash. Christine almost fainted. They told her to be cool and they could work the money through the club over some time. She hugged them and cried. Christine tried to give Sandra some of the money, but she refused and said it was devil's money and she did not want it in the house. So, Christine put the money in safe deposit boxes in different banks in DC, VA, and MD.

Sandra dedicated herself to the Lord and walked in the spirit of great peace. She was talking to a guy at church, but it did not work out. She was approached by another young man who was a member of her church and they spent time together. What she likes most about him was his walk with Christ. Yes, he was nice looking but that meant nothing to her because anyone could look nice on the outside and be ugly on the inside. They enjoyed each other's company a lot and Pastor Williams prayed and kept a close eye on them and so did Ron. His name was Luke.

A month went by and everything was going well for everyone. The club was doing well, and money was flowing in each week. Keith and Ron were in the office at the club talking.

"Keith, I was thinking of how blessed we have been in many ways, but business diversification is important."

"Okay, so you used that long word to say you want us to invest in other things."

"Yes, as I was about to say before you rudely interrupted me. I thought about movies. God brings things back to your remembrance for a reason and at the right time, well this is that time. When I did five years in prison, I did a lot of writing and I wrote a movie script, well, not in the best format but the best I knew how at that time. All three-hundred and sixty-eight pages. I found out later it was far too long for a movie script. Anyway, it is a fantastic story involving drama, action, sex, violence, suspense, horror, prayer, comedy, heartbreaking emotional events, die-hard love, supernatural forces at work, and special effects."

"Wow, that is not a movie my brother that has been our life. What is the name of this incredible story?"

"Yeah, I know, real life on the big screen. The name of it is, *MY CALL*. First, I want to release the book which I have already written and market it well so it will become popular and then produce the movie. We can start our own movie production company, and this will be our first project. So, what do you think?"

"My brother you are always thinking of big ideas. Years ago, you wanted us to become the biggest drug lords in the world. It almost got us killed."

"Yeah, that was something alright but that was years ago, and we were living foul but now everything has changed for the better. So, are you interested, and maybe we can get Christine to invest."

"If you want to get into the movie business, so be it, let's do it. Another source of income for us would be great."

"Great, I will start doing research and making phone calls, but a vacation would be nice before we get into another business venture."

"Amen my brother we all need a vacation. So, go home and talk to your wife and I will do the same."

Ron talked to Diana about his book and going into the movie business. She liked the idea but wanted Ron to take some time off first and take a family vacation because she needed to get away for a while. The thought of losing her child still affected her daily but she was doing much better and so was Ron. He made some calls to the rest of the family. During a meeting at work, Ron mentioned he and Keith would be gone for a few days and Shantai felt left out and wanted to go. She saved her money and could go on her own, but it was not the same as being around people you knew cared for and love you. So, Ron and Keith said they all could go together with them to Barbados. Shantai was happy and was about to hug Keith but saw the look Stacy gave her, so she changed her mind and walked away smiling. Keith and Stacy walked to his office, and she walked up to him.

"Keith, I am not a jealous woman and you know that so don't say anything crazy. I would appreciate it if you would decrease in hugging female employees at work. I don't care who they are."

"No problem baby, I will hug you." He grabbed her by the waist and picked her up.

"Keith, don't you drop me. Put me down." She laughed and enjoyed his attention.

He carried Stacy to one of the sofas in the office and laid her down and got on top of her. All these years and Keith still turns her on by doing the simplest things. She wrapped her legs around his waist and started kissing him.

"You know I love being in your arms, but we need to stop before someone comes in and catches us."

"Relax baby. The only one who comes in here is Ron and he will be busy for a while." He started sucking on her neck and that was it for Stacy. She leaned her head back and enjoyed his touch.

Christine came to the club to talk to Ron, and he was glad to see her. She hugged him and pinched him on the arm as she and Sandra did to him when they were much younger. She saw Sonny walking around and walked over and kissed him on the lips and walked back to Ron. He gave her a mean look.

"Christine this is work and not some hotel, you two can kiss and slob on each other later."

She smiled and loved her brother's protection.

"Yes Ron, I love you too."

"Yeah okay. Anyway, let's go to my office so we can talk about some business."

They walked into the office and saw Keith and Stacy on the sofa. He was on top of Stacy with his boxers on and Stacy was in her bra and panties.

"Oh my God" Christine put her hand to her mouth and was surprised at what she saw.

Stacy and Keith tried to cover themselves with pillows from the sofa.

"Get out." Stacy pointed at them.

"Don't you two have a house for all that? We are gone and clean that sofa when you are finished. Don't make any sense. Two sex addicts." Ron shook his head.

Ron grabbed Christine's hand and they walked out but not before she stared at them for a few seconds. She had images of her and Keith having sex and felt bad about this but Stacy made many comments about their sex life and she would not mind finding out.

Stacy saw the look on Christine's face, and she knew that look all too well and did not like it. It was a look of hunger and lust. She hit Keith in the head with one of the pillows.

"Keith, I told you we should not have done this, now get off me so I can get dressed. Ron and his sister caught us, this was so embarrassing."

"I am not getting off you, at least not yet. We got caught, so what. We may as well have some fun now and get butt naked and do the damn thing."

"No Keith get off..."

He kissed her, pulled his boxers off quickly, pulled her panties to one side, and slid his hard dick inside her.

"Damn baby," she leaned her head back and wrapped her legs around his waist and looked at him. "You are so nasty, but I love it. Now fuck me good." She gripped the sofa hard.

# CHAPTER FORTY SEVEN

*Barbados with a Twist*

$R$on called Sheila and mentioned the trip to her. She was reluctant to go at first because she felt a little uncomfortable being around all these young people. Although Zechariah would be by her side, and he wanted to go. Zechariah could be very persuasive when he wanted to be and she always loved her husband's attention. James will always be family to her married or not, so she called him about the trip, and it was perfect timing. He and Catarina talked about taking a relaxing trip somewhere. They agreed to go if they could take care of the transportation and all hotel expenses. Besides, in his and Catarina's mind what good is having money if you cannot enjoy life. Knowing the hotel business well, Catarina called the manager at the hotel in Barbados before they arrived and requested specific instructions regarding their stay. The hotel manager heard, Silva Management Corporation and that was it for him, he knew money and power were coming and he spread the word to other business owners in the area. Eighteen VIPs were coming and whatever they wanted, they would have with no questions asked.

James arranged limos to pick up everyone at their home and take them to BWI airport. Nine o'clock Monday morning the limos drove into the airport. It was a nice sight to see. Everyone was here. James, Catarina, Sheila, Zechariah, Ron, Diana, Keith, Stacy, Tonya, Derrick, Rick, Cynthia, Shantai, Shawn, Christine, Sonny, Sandra, and Luke. All it took was one phone call and James had one of Catarina's company planes waiting at the airport. The plane was very luxurious inside and it could seat forty people with seats that leaned back and plenty of space between and it had international flying capabilities.

Ron walked up to James and Catarina and hugged them.

"What's up married couple and thanks again for taking care of the expenses for all this but I had it covered."

James put his hand on Ron's shoulder and they stepped away.

"My brother, I know you did but I don't mind because you can't take any of this material stuff with you. When you are worth fourteen billion dollars, you can do a few things." He smiled at Ron.

"What! Good Lord! You two are rolling hard like that? My brother, make sure you keep handling your business, if you know what I mean."

"Yes, I do, and I am on the job." They both laughed and walked back to the others.

It was a warm beautiful eighty-five-degree day when they landed in Bridgetown Barbados four hours and forty minutes later. They were staying at the *Hilton Barbados Hotel* and had private couple suites except Sandra, Luke, Christine, and Sonny. Christine did not like being in the same room as Sonny but she was not about to complain so she and Sandra shared a room and Luke, and Sonny shared a room. Shantai had a room to herself, but she did not mind and so did Shawn. She had sexual thoughts about Shawn but was praying and fighting it. They would be in Barbados for five days and leaving first thing Saturday morning, in the meantime, this was an all-expense paid trip for everyone, compliments of James and Catarina.

This was a different trip than being in Rio because everybody was in a different place in their life, and this felt a lot more at peace. Everyone was in their rooms relaxing or getting ready to go to the beach. Sandra and Christine were having their first argument.

"Christine, I am not trying to lecture you but please do not embarrass yourself and everybody else by wearing a slutty revealing bathing suit to the beach. And other slutty clothes like you are trying to get rent money. Remember whose you are and who you are, a child of God and not the devil. Do not walk out of this room with your butt showing and breasts hanging out."

"You are something and I am not going to spend five days in this room with you treating me like I am a little child. I am the older one, not you."

"Then you need to start acting like it. And since we are having this conversation; I do not want Sonny in my room. Do not bring lust spirits in here."

Christine started laughing.

"You need to get a life. If you think your church friend Luke will not be looking at all the sexy fine women in this place you are delusional. Oh, by the way, I saw him looking at your Christian butt when you walk. He may love the Lord, but he definitely wants to put some dick inside your pussy, mouth, and ass, believe that. Bust his nut." She said that to irritate her.

"You are so disgusting! What happened to you?"

Christine looked at her and changed clothes for the beach. She wore something conservative in case she ran into her mother. She walked straight to Sonny's room and knocked on his door. He opened it and pulled her in.

"I have missed you a lot. Are you okay, you seem a little tense?"

"I am good, but my sister is trying to lecture me about how to dress and how to conduct myself. Forget that," She kissed and

hugged him. "No more talking, I have missed you just as much. I need some loving." She undressed and so did he and they began having sex.

Sheila and Zechariah were on the beach having a great time laughing and talking. She enjoyed Zechariah paying so much attention to her knowing there were so many good looking younger women walking around. She felt good within herself because she looked great from the many years of being in the gym. Zechariah held her hand as they walked, and she loved it and noticed many women looking at him as well because he was fine.

Catarina and James sat in the back of a jeep being chauffeured around the island, but James kept looking at her thighs. She wore shorts and had beautiful legs. He put his arm around her shoulder and whispered in her ear.

"You have gorgeous legs, I have an idea. We can find a secluded spot and you can allow me to taste your legs and..."

She smiled and put her finger over his mouth.

"James, you are so nasty and no we will do no such thing. We have a large hotel suite for that, so behave yourself."

"I don't want to behave myself as you call it. I am trying to get you horny and naked so we can do the nasty."

"I am already horny my husband and you do this to me very easily. We will get naked and do the nasty when we get back to the room."

"Promises, promises my dear." They both laughed and sat back enjoying the ride.

Keith, Stacy, Ron, and Diana were walking around doing some shopping when they ran into Shantai and Shawn. Ron and Keith had on sandals, shorts, and T-shirts and Diana and Stacy wore sandals and island dresses they picked out hours ago. Stacy gave Shantai a mean look because of how she was dressed and did not believe she had no memory of kissing and being all over Keith. Shantai wore sandals and very tight shorts that revealed her butt cheeks when she walked and a tank top she cut to show off her flat tight stomach. She was incredibly attractive with a great body. Diana noticed the mean look Stacy gave her, and she noticed the way Ron and Keith tried hard not to stare at her. Shantai waved at everybody.

"Hi everyone, are you having a good time?"

"What's up?" Shawn said.

Diana was not going to allow any of them to ruin her time in such a beautiful place.

"Hi Shantai, Shawn. You two look nice together."

Ron, Keith, and Stacy looked at her with a mean look knowing she was trying to keep the peace. Stacy was not going for it, so she walked over and grabbed Shantai's hand, and pulled her away.

"Shantai, I am glad you and Shawn are having fun but don't forget you represent Christ. Those tight booty shorts you are wearing are sending the wrong message."

She pulled her hand from Stacy's.

"Stacy, I know who I am but thank you for your concern," looking directly into her eyes. "You know how it goes, either you got it, or you don't." She walked toward Shawn shaking her butt.

Stacy felt an anger spirit trying to take over her emotions and she thought, *Lord, keep me at peace so I don't slap the taste out of her mouth.*

Shantai grabbed Shawn's hand, kissed him on the lips, and walked away shaking her butt hard to irritate Stacy and Diana.

She looked back at them smiling and kept walking. Keith and Ron's eyes were glued on Shantai's body with every step she took. Stacy walked directly in front of Keith and hit him in the stomach. Ron was surprised at what Stacy did and he looked at Diana, she had anger in her eyes.

Keith coughed and looked at Stacy like she was crazy.

"Are you crazy? I thought you got delivered from all your evil ways. I am telling the Pastor I am living with black-on-black in-house family crime, from my wife." He laughed.

"Keith, do you see me laughing? If you do not stop staring at her ass it is going to be some trouble today in Barbados, believe that."

"Ron, I can't believe you would blatantly disrespect me by staring at her butt. I am standing right next to you Ron and you have no shame," she pointed in Shantai's direction. "So, I guess you have already decided to trade me in for a younger girl especially since the doctor said I can't have children. She was being nasty Ron, how come you two cannot see that. Oh, I know it does not matter as long as you could see some butt cheeks." She stared at him and walked away crying.

Stacy felt bad for Diana and was so angry. She looked at Keith and Ron with so much anger it gave her an instant headache.

"You two are something else. I can't believe you Ron." She hit him hard in the chest and walked away fast to catch up with Diana.

Ron and Keith looked at each other and shook their heads.

"We are in trouble again partner. Stacy can punch."

"Yeah, I know. I thought she was past the violent stuff."

Stacy caught up with Diana and put her arm around her as they continued to walk.

"Diana don't believe what the Doctors said about you not being able to have children. Ron's mother was told the same thing and he is here."

"Yes, I know, the miracle child. He is probably getting ready to dump me." She wiped tears from her eyes.

Stacy looked at her with love and thought, *Lord you know I love her, but she is still very dramatic.*

"Diana, I know you are upset, and you have a right to be, but you know for a fact regardless of how many women Ron looks at, he is in love with you and is not going anywhere. Girl, you know that man would drop to his knees and lick your butt." She said that to make her laugh.

Diana looked at Stacy and laughed.

"You are still very nasty and I know he loves me but the licking butt thing, no comment. I know regardless of how much you love and give love to any man; they will always look at other women, but Ron did it right in my face."

"Well, so did Keith but you have to get real, all men will look, and you have to admit, Shantai is very nice looking and she has an incredible body, with a fat, round, tight-looking booty."

Diana looked at her with disgust.

"You do need serious prayer."

"Don't we all but if you put some booty shorts on and walk nasty, I will look at your butt too." She looked at Diana and laughed.

"Lord Jesus, help this child, please."

Ron and Keith walked up behind them and kissing them on the cheek at the same time. They turned around and stared at them then grabbed their hands and walked away.

Sandra and Luke were holding their sandals while walking on the beach close to the water's edge. It felt so good to their feet.

"Sandra, thanks for inviting me, I am having a great time and we just got here. By the way, you look good and don't get all Holy on me because I complimented you."

"Thank you for the compliment Luke and you don't look too bad yourself. I see how the ladies here stare at you and all your muscles. You must live in the gym."

"You only have one body, so we have to take care of ourselves to be ready and in shape to do what God asks."

Two women walked by wearing skimpy tops and thong bathing suits giving Sandra a mean look but smiled at Luke and licked their lips. They spoke loudly so Sandra could hear them.

"Girl, he is fine with that tight body, and he's got a nice butt too. I would ride that dick good, and then suck it." They laughed and kept walking.

Luke was not her man but what they said about him was so disrespectful, but she knew these are the times we live in. No wonder so many men do not respect women, they do not respect themselves. She looked at him.

"Don't act like you did not hear those nasty comments coming out of that girl's mouth."

"It does not matter Sandra, that is not what I want for my life, and I am here with you. This matters to me, the rest is ways of the world." He held her hand and they kept walking. Sandra smiled and felt good.

Tonya, Derrick, Rick, and Cynthia were on the beach playing volleyball. Rick was the oldest, but he had no problem keeping up with everyone else. He looked better and was in better shape than many of the younger guys out here playing, especially after hearing them huffing and puffing sounding like they are going to pass out. Cynthia loved it and did not mind so many of the other women staring at him because she loved her husband and the way he treated her. Tonya and Derrick were obvious newlyweds to anyone paying attention. They kissed every five minutes and looked at each other like they were the last pork chop on the plate. They played five games before calling it quits then rinsed the sand from their feet before walking back to the rooms.

Each of them did their thing day after day and had so much fun. They jet skied, parasailed, and took various private boat tours. Concerts and shows were going on somewhere every night on the island. They took advantage of everything. One night, Catarina and James rented a sixty-foot yacht and stayed out all night with security always close by. On the fourth day, they all played volleyball on the beach together, falling and acting silly with a large crowd watching. Suddenly, everything seemed to stop, and the entire crowd looked in one direction. They all looked as well to see what was going on. Leticia Wilson and her five bodyguards walked close by wearing almost nothing. They wore dental floss with patches of cloth to cover their nipples and crotch area with their entire butt showing.

They walked as if the entire beach belonged to them and with Leticia's money, it would not have been a problem. Leticia was stunning, appreciate or hate her, either way, her looks spoke volumes and the women with her were beautiful. They all had knives strapped to both their ankles and not even the local police said a word to them. Everyone felt the intense sexual tension in the air. Various lewd comments were heard repeatedly from the crowd and many guys grabbed their crotches trying to hide their erections. You also heard a lot of slapping, obviously from girlfriends or wives not appreciating what their men were doing and saying. Diana was the first to speak.

"You have got to be kidding me."

Luke has seen a lot of attractive women, but this lady and her friends were extremely attractive.

"Who in the world is that, good Lord she is fine." He did not mean to say that out loud and he had an erection.

Sandra stood close by and heard what he said, and it irritated her but what made her angry was seeing his erection. She walked up to him.

"I can't believe this from you. You are disgusting." She walked away from him.

Stacy walked over to Keith very closely so no one could hear what she was about to say and looked at him with contempt.

"Keith if your dick gets hard looking at that nasty evil slut of a woman, it's going to be some problems today in Barbados, believe that."

"Stop, just stop with the threats Stacy. Is that all you think about is my dick. All that mouth you have, why don't you put it to work on this dick and start slobbering. Get it real wet, put some spit on it and work your lips." He laughed knowing this would make her angry which is what he wanted because he had a plan.

"What!" she yelled and swung hard trying to hit Keith, but he ducked out of the way and grabbed Stacy and kissed her.

He was still laughing.

"I did not say try to hit me, I said put some spit on my dick woman." He smacked her on the butt and ran away laughing. Stacy ran after him but she was not laughing.

Ron knew what Keith was doing and he followed his lead by looking at all the guys and nodded his head at them. They knew he was up to something. He walked up to Diana.

"Diana, let's go back to the room so I can bend you over."

She looked at him like he lost his mind after staring at that nasty woman and now he wants to have sex.

"Are you insane? I am not about to have sex with you now because you are horny from looking at that devil in the flesh."

"Oh, you are going to give up that booty, you and your fat sexy ass." He smacked her on the butt and ran.

Diana had very strong convictions about being disrespected by Ron and was not about to let him start now. She ran after him yelling. Sheila, Tonya, Shantai, Cynthia, Christine, and Catarina got smacked on the butt by the men and they ran, and the women ran after them.

Leticia Wilson saw all this and laughed while she and her bodyguards walked away. They walked about a mile away to a secluded area with large boulders and tall trees. It was evening now and there was a cool breeze. Leticia's bodyguards gathered a few branches to make a fire. Leticia gripped one of the branches and it caught on fire along with the rest. They sat down in a circle and began meditating, and a few minutes later five handsome men approached. The women jumped to their feet and faced the men. One of the guys held his hands up.

"Relax ladies we did not mean to disturb you, but you caused a serious scene when you walked by earlier and we wanted to come by to hopefully talk with you."

Leticia looked at the women and smiled then looked at the men.

"Please gentlemen come on over. It takes a confident man to approach beautiful women and we like that. We know why you are here so let's not waste each other's time. This is a beautiful place, the timing is right, so let's fuck."

The guys looked at each other thinking this must be some joke but when the ladies removed their clothes, what little they had on, they knew it was no joke. The guys removed their clothes quickly and laid them out on the ground. Leticia walked away while her bodyguards began having sex with the men. They were scattered on the ground and leaned against trees having one mass orgy and the men were having the time of their life because the women allowed them to do anything to them. They were having intercourse, oral and anal sex. Everyone switched partners and had one big freak show. Suddenly, a loud howling sound caused the men to stop and look around. It was far too late. A large grey wolf with large teeth rushed towards the men, they tried to run but each woman pulled their knives out and cut their Achilles tendon. The men were on their stomachs crawling on the ground to get away, but the wolf leaped on one guy and bit his leg and arm off, and then leaped on another and bit a large hole in his neck. There was a lot of blood flowing and loud screaming. One man managed to stand and tried to run but the wolf leaped off one guy after biting his head off and then snapped off the rest and leaped on him. It sunk its teeth in his throat and snatched it off and changed instantly into a rat and crawled inside the man and burst out through his stomach. It transformed back into a wolf and stood on the man's corpse drenched in blood. It growled and looked around seeing the last guy leaning on the boulders with his hands out begging to live.

"Oh my God, please Jesus help me oh Lord. Don't let this wolf kill me."

One of the bodyguards walked up to him and put her hand on his shoulder.

"Now you want to call on God. Were you calling on God when you had your dick inside me? No! Were you calling on God when you were licking my ass? No! Were you calling on God when you had your dick in my mouth, saying, suck it baby, suck it? No! So don't call on God now when you are going to hell."

The wolf walked slowly over to the man while he was leaning against the boulders and stood on its hind legs with its paws on the man's chest. He was crying and pleading for his life. The wolf's head grew larger and opened its mouth with blood dripping from its teeth and covered the guy's entire head down to his neck. The wolf snapped his head off and walked away with the guy's head in its mouth. Blood shot out from his neck like fireworks going off while the wolf ate his head. The wolf transformed back into Leticia, and she called for the rats to come forth. The bodyguards stood back while the rats ate all the body parts. Loud smacking and bones crunching permeated the air while the rats ate everything and ran away. Leticia and her bodyguards were covered in blood, so they got in the water to rinse off and began having sex.

On the fifth morning, the routine was the same for most of them. They all met in the dining room of the hotel and ate breakfast together and then went their separate ways. Sandra was still upset with Luke, but they talked as they went for their walk. She realized his reaction was normal and the only reason she became upset was her feelings were deeper than she thought.

James, Catarina, Zechariah, Sheila, Rick, and Cynthia went shopping together and then went on a boat ride. Everyone was having fun, but Cynthia wanted more private time with Rick because she was horny and blamed this on him as usual.

Christine, Sonny, Shantai, and Shawn were on a forty-foot boat fishing for the very first time, laughing and having fun but the girls would not bait the hooks or touch the fish. The captain was operating the boat. Everyone wore shorts and T-shirts. It bothered Shantai to see Christine hugging and kissing all over Sonny because she is Ron's sister, and was supposed to be a Christian. She was not acting like it. They went below in the boat, and she heard them having sex. This disgusted her and she wanted to get off the boat, but Shawn talked her into staying. When Christine and Sonny came up, Christine wore a two-piece bikini and Shantai gave them the meanest look, but Christine did not care and asked Shantai to come below so they could talk.

"Shantai, I know you don't approve of what I am doing but will you do me a favor please, so I don't have to hear any lectures later?"

"What is that?" She stared at her.

"The favor is, what happens on this boat, stays on this boat." She caressed Shantai's face and kissed her on the lips and said things in a language she did not understand.

Shantai was shocked and could not believe what Christine did.

"I cannot believe you just kissed me. You know what, you are a church going closet super freak and we need to get off this boat while God is keeping me from turning your hot butt out."

Christine stood and pointed her finger in her face.

"It is you who would get turned out and you, Shawn, and Sonny together couldn't handle all this hot ass of mine. Do not forget what I said please. What happens on this boat stays on this boat." She walked away but pulled down her bikini bottom and flashed her butt to Shantai and pulled it up before she reached the top.

When Christine flashed her butt, many thoughts came to Shantai's mind and they were all bad. She had to pray and asked God to help and give her strength not to go backward. She was still in shock and could not believe everything Christine said and did. Shantai wondered what happened to this girl to get her like this. She served God for so long and was now a super freak. She sat there shaking her head when Shawn came down and sat next to her.

"Is everything all right down here? You look upset."

"You don't know the half of it."

"I am no one's judge and was not going to say anything but are you into women?"

Shantai leaned back and looked at him.

"Why would you ask me something like that?"

"Well, as I was walking around the boat I looked down and saw you two kissing, that's why."

"Oh God. No Shawn, that is not what happened. That is why I said you do not know half of it. She kissed me and I was shocked."

"Wow, okay church girl is freaky. That is nothing new and you know how it goes. You can find some of the freakiest girls in church."

Christine walked below.

"Forgive me for interrupting you too but I am so bored right now. Sonny is seriously into fishing more than he is into me right now. What kind of man would rather fish than get his dick sucked and get some hot tight pussy?" She looked at them like she said nothing wrong

Shawn and Shantai looked at each other with their mouths open not believing the words they just heard. Shawn waved his hand at Christine.

"I don't want to know about anything, and you are not getting me killed by your brother or Keith. I am gone." He walked up the stairs.

"You know Shawn is right, you are trying to get us all killed, I am gone." She stood to leave but Christine pulled her back and stood close to her.

"Where are you going? What happened to all that mouth you had? Talking about turning my hot butt out," She took her top and bottom off. "What happens on this boat stays on this boat. Now come get this hot ass of mine." She began caressing her breasts while staring at Shantai.

Shantai was fighting her deep desires and was doing well until Christine took her clothes off and started caressing her breasts. This was a setup because seconds later Shawn and Sonny walked in completely naked. Sonny grabbed Shantai and kissed her and Shawn grabbed Christine and licked her breasts.

"Sonny stop, don't do this I am trying to live right," She smacked him. "Please Stop!"

Christine walked over to Shantai and smacked her then kissed her.

"Where is all that mouth now? Stop smacking him because you know you want this." She pulled down Shantai's shorts and panties and took her T-shirt off and backed up.

Sonny was in front of Shantai, and Shawn was in the back kissing and caressing her body. They picked her up and put her on the bed. They sucked on her breasts and Christine licked between her legs then moved up to whisper in Shantai's ear.

"Now who is getting turned out? You are going to get dick in your mouth, pussy, and ass and love it." She moved down and started licking and sucking her clit.

Shantai was trying to get away from them, but their every touch was affecting her hidden desires quickly until she began moaning and her entire body was shaking. Every erotic sexual image and thought came to her mind until all of it was too much.

"Yes, I want it. Fuck me."

Shawn and Sonny had sex with Shantai in various positions making her scream and climax hard while Christine watched. Shantai sucked their dick and gave them her ass. All this was a dream and a nightmare for her, but she could not stop and at the time, did not want to. Christine wanted Shantai to herself, so they moved into a sixty-nine position giving each other intense orgasms. This went on for two hours until everyone was very satisfied. They took showers and the men walked back up first and Christine turned to face Shantai.

"Remember, what happens on this boat, stays on this boat. We all belong to each other now and I have some big plans for us that I will share with you later." She kissed her.

"I can't believe what just happened and it was so damn good. I don't understand how you can be this way, Christine."

"I got messed up and don't want to talk about it. Us four are one now. We will stay in our little group of four. None of that stupid jealousy garbage, we will protect and satisfy each other at any given time. We will have any kind of sex we want and we will all have lots of money."

Sonny and Shawn came back down and looked at them.

"So, you are trying to say," She grabbed Christine's butt. "I can have this fat ass of yours whenever I want?"

"Whenever you want however you want. My mouth, my pussy, my ass, and," Christine pointed to Sonny and Shawn. "We have two hard dicks waiting for us. We will be fucking good, and living good. From this day forward we will be MPAD. Money, Pussy, Ass, and Dick. To everyone else, MPAD stands for, Motivated, Persistent, Abundant, and Determined. We will start this business and go from there. Yes, I like that, MPAD, LLC."

They all joined hands and looked at each other and said at the same time.

"MPAD, Money, Pussy, Ass, and Dick."

They kept repeating this over and over and then walked up on the deck.

Seconds later, a cloud of smoke appeared where they stood. Leticia Wilson was dressed in all black mumbling some words. She lifted her head and sniffed the air and started laughing.

"I love this. You can smell the lust and evil spirits in the air. Stupid foolish people. They had it all living for God and now they want to do my will, I love it. MPAD, Money, Pussy, Ass, and Dick, damn that is me. I am taking all of them and their family straight to hell. When you remove the light all you have left is darkness and that is me all day every day and I am deceiving the world." Smoke appeared and she was gone.

When Christine walked into her hotel room, she was very tired from all the intense sex. She never felt like this before to this degree, so mentally, physically, and spiritually drained. She noticed the judgmental look Sandra gave her but was not about to get into any conversation with her. She took a long hot shower and went to sleep. Sandra noticed how tired she looked, and felt a strong lust spirit from her but did not say anything to avoid a big argument, but she prayed until falling asleep.

Saturday morning everyone was packed and ready to leave. They met in the hotel dining room again for breakfast. Everyone noticed something was different about Christine, Shantai, Sonny, and Shawn but did not know what it was. When Sheila hugged Christine before they sat down to eat, the spirit she felt from her almost made her vomit and she knew what it was. Evil was upon her daughter greatly and the other three as well and she feared Leticia Wilson was behind all of this. Sheila did not want to ruin this trip, so she did not cause a scene, but Zechariah felt her thoughts and held her hand under the table. All things considered, the atmosphere and conversation were pleasant at the table with everyone talking about the great time they had and looked forward to coming back again one day. Of course, Stacy mentioned Leticia showing up, but no one could understand how she was able to show up during their vacation time and how evil she looked regardless of her beauty. Luke said she did not look evil just oppressed and everyone stared at him. Sandra pinched him under the table.

The private plane took off and all were comfortable and still talking about the trip. Zechariah wanted to take this time to talk with Rick and tease him.

"My brother Rick I will continue to pray for your strength."

"Why is that, am I missing something?"

No sir, not all but you will need all the strength you can get for that young wife of yours. Keep working out and stay in good shape and may God bless you." He looked at Rick and laughed.

Rick could not help but laugh.

"You are right, but I thought about all that before marrying Cynthia and decided life is short and to enjoy it while you can, besides, she is a good friend, and we can talk about anything."

"That is what a relationship is all about." They shook hands.

The rest of the guys came over and started talking while the women did the same. Four hours and forty minutes later the plane landed at BWI airport and the limos were waiting to take everybody home. Their bags were put in the limo and everyone hugged and said goodbye. Christine saw the mean look Ron and Keith gave her when she approached Sonny to hug him.

"Sonny, to keep the peace for now please do not kiss me because Ron and Keith are looking at me like they are ready to explode."

"No problem baby. You know how I feel about you, but I am not crossing your brother and Keith."

She kissed him on the cheek and rubbed his chest.

"Don't worry about that I will handle it." She hugged him and walked to the limo with Sandra and Luke. She looked over at Ron and Keith and stuck her tongue out at them and got in the limo and it drove away.

# CHAPTER FORTY EIGHT
*The Meeting*

Sandra called Ron and Keith and ask to meet with them so they could talk. She was already in Baltimore, so they agreed to meet her at the steakhouse. Keith and two *Young Wolves* rode with Ron in his Bentley. All four wore business suits.

"Ron, do you know why your sister wants to talk with us?"

"I don't know but what I do know is I am not in the mood to hear any bad news and no foolishness. My instinct tells me it is about Luke the guy she has been talking to from church."

"I thought he was cool and Sandra seems to like him."

"It does seem that way but we know how that can go. Keith, I'm telling you my brother, if he did or said something crazy to my sister, well I won't say what I want to but let's hope all is well."

"Amen my brother."

They arrived at the steakhouse and saw Sandra waving at them. She wore heels and a dress. The *Young Wolves* sat at another table and ordered food. Ron and Keith hugged her and sat down to order food as well.

"Thanks for meeting me," she pointed to the *Young Wolves.* "Why are they here? Never mind, I don't want to know. Anyway, just for the record, you two are paying." She smiled at them

"No problem sis. So, what is going on with you, and what is on your mind?"

"Well, first I want to say thanks again for allowing Luke to come along to Barbados we had a great time. Time will tell what will happen in the future, but I like him a lot so far and want us to become closer. However, it will be difficult for this to happen if you two keep intimidating him."

Ron and Keith looked at each other because they had no clue what she was talking about.

"Sandra, I was not aware we were intimidating him at all. Why, what did he say?" Keith stared at her.

"Yeah, what did the cupcake say?" Ron got an attitude.

"See, that is what I am talking about. Why do you call him a cupcake Ron? Because he does not look like a thug or carry a gun. He is a genuinely nice gentleman and he loves the Lord, so stop calling him names and stop giving him mean dirty looks, like you two are about to do something to him. He respects me highly and that should be enough."

Keith looked at Ron and was irritated because he knew this guy was too soft to be with Ron's sister.

"Sandra, no disrespect but you are here defending this guy because he thinks we gave him bad looks. Tell me this is a joke." Keith shook his head.

She gave Keith her usual looks.

"Keith, I am not defending him. I am making a point and I have seen the way you two look at him, even in Barbados both of you could have been a little nicer to him."

"You are my sister, so you get much respect, but he is a grown man, yet cries to you about us not being nice to him. You have got to be kidding me. A grown man cries to his woman about dirty looks. Sounds like a female to me, soft cupcake."

"Ron, do not insult me, and I asked you to stop calling him names. I am not his woman, but you can still respect who I am with."

"Since you are not his woman then why are we even having this conversation?"

The waitress came and brought their food, and they began eating while Sandra looked at them frowning.

"Ron, you and Keith are married, and I would like to have someone in my life. So, stop doing the gangster intimidation thing to Luke and be nice to him please. Anyway, the spirit of intimidation is not of God but the devil. How do you expect to win souls for Christ if you two are operating in a devil spirit and then talk about Jesus? So, just stop it and if you do not stop, I am telling mom on you Ron and I am telling the Pastor on you Keith. I will tell him you too Christians are intimidating people and as Stacy would say, believe that!"

Keith looked at Sandra and laughed.

"Keith don't co-sign what she said by laughing. Before we got here, my instincts told me this meeting was about your boyfriend or whatever he is, and I was right."

Luke walked into the restaurant and saw Sandra, he walked over to her. She stood up and kissed him on the lips to irritate them. The *Young Wolves* mean mugged him from the time he walked in. Luke noticed them at the table but ignored them.

"Hi Sandra, I am late because I had to work overtime on a client's project." He sat next to her.

Keith and Ron looked at him like he was beneath them.

"So Luke, what do you do for a living my brother. We did not get a chance to talk that much in Barbados." Ron said.

"It was not the time to discuss business anyway, but I am an architect for one of the largest firms in Baltimore and I like what I do a lot."

"Good for you Luke. So, what are your intentions with Sandra? Are you serious about her or are you just trying to hit it and run?"

"Keith, I cannot believe you asked that and embarrassed me at the same time!"

"It's a good question but he beat me to it. So, what's up Luke? Are you for real with Christ or faking it to corrupt the girls in church?"

Luke knew a great deal about the O'Neil family but he was not about to be intimidated by anyone. He stared at Keith and Ron.

"I am just as real as both of you are supposed to be." He stared at Ron.

Ron became angry and jumped to his feet with Keith doing the same and the *Young Wolves* walked over to the table with their suit jackets unbuttoned.

"What is that supposed to mean?" Ron stared at him.

Luke stood up to face them and so did Sandra to de-escalate this situation because she knew her brother and Keith well.

"Ron stop it and I mean it. I see this was a mistake," She looked at Luke. "Luke come on before this situation turns ugly."

"Sandra, I am fine, and I don't need you to defend me."

She looked at Ron and saw the anger building in his eyes and knew what was about to happen.

"Yes, you do but you don't know it. Ron, I am surprised at you, and I am telling mom and the Pastor. Ron, you need to make up your mind to live for Jesus or the devil, because you cannot serve two masters, Ron" She stared at him and then grabbed Luke's hand and they walked out. Luke turned his head to look at Ron and gave him a mean look and wanted to do something to irritate him more. He put his hand on Sandra's lower back and his fingers touched the top of her butt and caressed it. He looked back at Ron with a smirk on his face and they kept walking.

Ron stepped in their direction, but Keith grabbed his arm.

"Don't sweat that partner, another time and place."

One of the *Young Wolves* stepped closer to Ron.

"Ron, do you want us to handle that for you, it won't be any problem because he crossed the disrespect line with the hand on her butt jester."

As angry as Ron was, he had to pray quickly and calm down so he would not do something he knew he would regret.

"I appreciate that but like Keith said, "Another time and place." I need to cool off, so I am going for a walk." He put some money on the table to pay the bill and walked out with Keith walking next to him and the *Young Wolves* behind them.

# CHAPTER FORTY NINE

*Keeping her Word*

The next day Sheila was walking in the park with Zechariah when she got the call from Sandra explaining everything that happened in the restaurant. Sheila was furious at Ron and Keith. She told Zechariah about the incident.

"Sheila, I understand your anger, but you have to understand he did what was in his spirit to do, protect his sister. I would not have done any different if it was you." He kissed her.

"You are sweet, but I am your wife, she is his sister and very much a grown woman who has to make her own choices in life, good or bad. That is how we learn."

"True that but you protect those you love and for some people and Ron happens to be one of them, this will never change."

"Well, Sandra did mention when they walked out Luke put his hand on her lower back and his fingers caressed her butt. She fussed at him about that later. He only did it to make Ron and Keith angry because they were bullying him."

Zechariah stared out into space thinking about that guy who almost knocked Diana down at the club and how protective he was of her. He thought about some guy trying to rub her butt.

"Sheila, men approach men and not use women as shields to hide behind and the butt thing he did was enough to let me know his true character."

She squeezed his hand and looked at him.

"You men are something. What is it that makes you go crazy over some butt? Women have a body and not just buttocks, you know the face, breasts, hips, and legs. You men see a woman with an unattractive face and talk about her but if she has a round derriere, you lose your mind. Okay, Luke should not have caressed her butt in public or private for that matter but he did not attack her, good God relax!"

"Okay, if some guy walked past you and patted you on your butt, how would that make you feel and would you expect me to say or do nothing? No, not happening Sister. I would catch a charge with no question."

Sheila could see this was a no-win situation and he was getting upset and it was ruining their walk.

"You made a good point. Anyway, Sandra also called the Pastor and told him what happened, and he wanted to see everyone in his office. Now, can we get back to our wonderful walk please and when we get home you can rub me all you want?" She smiled at him knowing this would change his mood.

"Wow, she told the Pastor. I feel for those two and yes I will be glad to rub your body anywhere you want me to."

Sheila stepped in front of him and kissed his lips.

"I am sure you will, and you do an excellent job sir." She kissed him again and they continued walking and held hands. Sheila looked at him smiling and felt so in love with this man.

# CHAPTER FIFTY
*A Wake up Call*

Ron and Keith were in Pastor Williams's office at church sitting in front of his desk as he talked to them.

"My brothers first let's have a word of prayer. Oh Lord, we once again come boldly and humbly to your throne thanking you for your grace and mercy on our lives. We ask that you bless this meeting for your glory, and we bind every spirit that is contrary to the Holy Spirit, in Jesus name, Giving you all the glory and praise, Amen."

"Thank you Pastor for the prayer." Keith said.

"Amen, Pastor."

"Brother Ron, I have known you all your life and your family. I feel like I am a part of your family in many ways and know so much of your life and history," He pointed to Ron. "You are truly called by God to do great things and I know this for a fact and so do you."

Keith looked at Ron and smiled then looked at the Pastor.

"Tell him Pastor, chosen by God, for God, and because of God. This brother is a walking living testimony."

"Brother Keith, so are you. The friendship you two share is a powerful one that has experienced its up and downs, but you have remained close friends, nonetheless. Most people do not have friends like this in their life. Sandra called and expressed to me what happened. I do not do, he said, she said conversations, so I will ask. Brother Ron, where are you in your walk with Christ?"

Ron knew this was coming and he could never lie to the Pastor even if he wanted to and he does not.

"Pastor you know how much I respect you and value all you have done for me and my family, and I will not lie to you. No, I am not out in these streets acting crazy as I did before. My walk with God is good but it could be better, and I am working on it. Pastor, it seems no matter what I do or how hard I try, my family comes under attack."

"My brother you should know by now these things will happen in your life and all who embrace Christ. Psalm 34:19 says, *Many are the afflictions of the righteous but the Lord delevereth him out of them all.* A high calling has been placed on your life and whatever the devil can do to try and destroy you, he will. The devil will use whomever and whatever to accomplish this."

"I know this pastor but why is it all the good people are killed, and the bad ones are committing all kinds of sins and getting away with it. My dad was killed, and my family has been under attack ever since. Sandra was in a coma, Christine is, well I don't know where she is but not where she should be, and Sandra has this cupcake trying to fool her into thinking he is so righteous."

The Pastor smiled and then laughed.

"Forgive me brother Ron for laughing but Sandra did mention you called brother Luke a cupcake. It is an old school term from long ago. Son, regardless of what other people do and how they conduct themselves, no one can deceive God. Either you are living for Christ, or you are not. I fully understand the protective spirit for your family and friends, you were born with that, however, God must get the glory son in all things, not us."

"So, what do I do in the meantime Pastor? Let people disrespect me and my family and turn the other cheek."

"No, you have to constantly pray and ask God to give you wisdom in all matters of your life. Brother Ron, always remember this, if you live by the sword you die by the sword but if you live for King Jesus you will never see death. In John 8:51 it says, *Verily, verily, I say unto you, if a man keeps my saying, he shall never see death.* The word of God is true and everlasting to everlasting."

Ron lowered his head because he knew everything the Pastor said was true.

"Brother Keith, where are you in Christ? In or out."

"Pastor I am in but dealing with things as all people do. Dealing with things in my marriage but it had gotten better. We pray more and talk more. As Ron said, the bad guys seem to keep winning. We have some very evil forces trying to destroy us. First, it was the drug Lord Victor Augular, and that devil Mr. Bones and now we have this evil lady Leticia Wilson out to kill us."

"I am aware of all you are saying, and I know of Miss Leticia Wilson and the very demonic evil spirit in which she operates. She is the devil incarnate but like all people who follow the ways of darkness, their fate is already doomed, and hell will be their home."

"So Pastor, what do we do in the meantime with all this coming against us?" Ron said with irritation.

"Good question my brother. Pastor, what do we do?"

"You become closer to God so you will walk in his anointing and power. You cannot fight a spiritual war with carnal means. So, your only answer is to be on the winning team regardless of how the devil makes it appear. You are on the winning team walking with the master builder himself, King of Kings, and Lord of Lords. God almighty in the name of Jesus, whom even the ground could not hold. Brother Ron, brother Keith protect your family and friends but you must respect their choices even if you do not agree with them. You cannot control another's individual's life, no matter how much you care for or love them." He stared at Ron when saying this knowing he will get the message about trying to control Sandra.

"Amen Pastor." Keith said.

Ron had his head down then looked at the Pastor.

"Message received Pastor and I will pray more and seek God for his wisdom. I thank you for your time and much needed prayers."

"This is how it should be in the body of Christ. We walk as many but in one spirit helping each other to remain strong in this journey. Remember his word in Proverbs 27:17 which says, *Iron sharpeneth iron, so, a man sharpeneth the countenance of his friend.* Now let's pray my brothers. Father, we thank you for your time, love, and protection. Guide our every step and keep us always, giving us the wisdom to make those choices that are pleasing in your eyes, in Jesus name, Amen."

They all stood and hugged. Ron and Keith thanked the Pastor again and left.

# CHAPTER FIFTY ONE
*No Competition*

The diamond mine in Mumbai India brought Leticia Wilson the best of diamonds. *Jubilee Diamond Mine,* located in the Republic of Russia, was the biggest diamond mine in the world. The mine was estimated to contain more than 153 million carats of recoverable diamonds. Leticia's diamond mine was producing the largest and most rare diamonds in the world. No matter where the miners dug they found diamonds and after hearing how much the diamonds were worth, they tried various ways to smuggle them. One miner swallowed four diamonds worth over ten million dollars and was leaving the camp. He almost made it out, but Leticia and her bodyguards approached him. Leticia swiped his brow with the back of her hand and two of the bodyguards stabbed him in the eyes and cut his stomach open and pulled out the diamonds. Leticia cut his head off with one swing of her blade and kicked his head down in the hole so others would see it and deter them from doing the same thing. Several miners began vomiting diamonds after they saw this and Leticia started laughing and walked away. Her bodyguards stabbed them.

Leticia accomplished in a fraction of the time what Victor Augular tried to do. She was on the cover of Forbes Magazine as the wealthiest person in the world. She was worth two-hundred and fifty-billion dollars with no one close to her equal in competition. Many successful businesspeople feared, hated, or wanted to have sex with her which she loved all the attention and power. In her mind, she was now a living unstoppable God that was only going to increase in wealth and power. Leticia had two major objectives left to accomplish. Kill Ron, his family, and friends then world domination. She stood in her home at the diamond site looking at the men being killed and loved it. She raised her arms in the air.

"World domination is coming and so is your death Chosen boy Ron. I hate you and your entire praying family and all Christians, I am taking everybody to hell. I am going to make the tactics of Hitler look mild in comparison to what I am about to do. There will be no bargaining or deals made when doing business with me. My way of business is amazingly simple. Seduction, intimidation, join me or die." She laughed.

The spirit of the devil possessed her entire existence and gave her incredible powers but she had one weakness, sex. She could not get enough of it which is why she had a daily sex ritual with her bodyguards. They engaged in the most perverted sex and transferred this spirit to as many people as possible. By demonic curses and giving them what they wanted.

"I love this wicked society with such corrupt values. The stupid politicians spend more money building prisons than schools and no real code of moral conduct. This legal system separates the families by any means necessary. If you separate the family, all that is left is spiritual confusion and global chaos which leads to world domination to the one holding the power. That is me of course, Leticia Wilson, an unstoppable God. I am planning an attack like the world has never seen or would ever suspect. First, the chosen Ron must die a very painful slow death but not before watching me and my bodyguards have sex with his hot wife Diana, repeatedly. Then we will cut her body up in little pieces and feed her to the rats." She began laughing while caressing her nipples.

# CHAPTER FIFTY TWO

*Desires of the Heart*

Christine knew the only way she could get things done according to the desires of her heart, was to be on her own and move out. She loved Sandra but their ways were different now. So, she talked Ron into helping her get a house by using the club as a business reference. She purchased a five-bedroom, three car garage one-million-dollar house in Bowie MD. She also purchased a new Corvette and a 2013 Bentley. Ron talked with her about his book and movie plans. Christine was excited about this and wanted to be a part of it along with being part of their movie production company. She gave Ron one million dollars for the house so she would not have to be concerned with making any payments. Sandra wanted to show how serious she was about her involvement in his movie, so she wanted to invest three million dollars. It was Ron and Keith who helped her get the money for the diamonds she found at the house in the first place. Christine knew how hard Keith and Ron worked and trusted them. She spent a lot of money recently but still had twenty-one million dollars left over for her business plans.

It took Christine a month, but her house was finally decorated the way she wanted, and she was ready to have a party to celebrate. There would be alcohol, loud music, and dancing at the party so Sheila, Sandra, Luke, and Derrick said they were not coming. Rick declined to come because it was not his scene. But Cynthia said she was coming and so was Tonya, Shantai, Sonny, Shawn, Keith, Stacy, and Diana. Diana did not want to come but Ron talked her into it. It was Saturday night Ron and Keith would be at their club but tonight it was all about Christine. Zechariah and the *Young Wolves* could handle everything at the club. To make sure this party did not get out of hand, a few *Young Wolves* would be there as and Christine did not mind at all and appreciated them. Alcohol makes some people say and do stupid things, but she knew they would shut down any negative situation in a hurry.

There were about fifty people at the party. Keith and Ron did not like this but said nothing and it was plenty of food and drinks. The house had three levels, and the basement was large and many people were dancing because the floor was hardwood and not carpet like most basements. Ron did not like seeing Christine dressed the way she was and dancing so provocatively with Sonny. She wore a top with no bra and a skirt that was too short to be dancing in. Keith and Stacy were dancing and having fun because he knew Ron was fighting a losing battle. His sister was a grown woman and would do whatever she wanted. Shantai, Shawn, Tonya, and Cynthia were dancing and having a great time. Three hours later, the smell of marijuana permeated throughout the house, and Ron, Diana, Keith, and Stacy walked around trying to find out where it was coming from. Keith and Stacy opened a bedroom door and what they saw made them angry instantly and very turned on at the same time. Shawn and Sonny laid on the bed naked smoking weed and Christine was naked riding Sonny and Shantai was naked riding Shawn. Shantai and Christine faced Keith and Stacy and smiled at them but never stopped.

"What in the world?" Keith yelled. "Is this a freak party?" He pointed to Sonny and Shawn. "I don't care what the situation is between you four but you two get out."

RONALD GRAY

Seeing the rage in his eyes, Sonny and Shawn got up and dressed quickly and walked out the room, and slammed the door behind them. Christine and Shantai walked toward Keith and Stacy still naked.

"I don't know what is going on with you all, but this is repulsive and wicked. Christine, it is your house so do your thing but put some clothes on." He stared at her with strong desire.

Stacy saw the look in Keith's eyes and did not like it and knew they had to get out of this room quickly.

A thin mist slid under the door and floated to the ceiling and covered the entire room and landed on all four of them. Stacy and Keith turned to walk away but Shantai grabbed Keith's arm and Christine grabbed Stacy's and pulled them back. Stacy slapped them, and they laughed and began kissing each other. Keith and Stacy looked at each other and walked out of the room closing the door behind them and leaned against the wall.

"I can't believe what I just saw, oh my God. How did Christine and Shantai get like this and be in church serving God? All of this is so wicked," She looked at Keith. "Keith, I felt so much evil and perverted spirits in that room, and it made me have thoughts I know should not be in my head."

"Well since you are being so honest, intense erotic thoughts and images rushed to my mind, but I prayed and wanted us to get out of that room quickly." He kissed Stacy.

Ron and Diana walked up to them.

"Have you two seen Christine?" Ron said.

Christine and Shantai were having sex.

"Oh, don't stop, lick this pussy." Shantai yelled.

They all heard this and before anyone could stop her, Diana opened the door a little and saw Christine's face buried between

Shantai's legs. She closed the door quickly and leaned against the wall in shock.

"Diana, what is wrong with you? What did you see?"

Diana did not know what to say to Ron, but she was not about to tell him the truth, so she looked at him and blurted out.

"Ron, Christine is in the room and is not to be bothered right now, so let's go." She looked at him in such a way hoping he would get the message.

"I got the message, let's go."

Sonny and Shawn walked down the hall.

"Damn those too can suck dick and fuck. Wow, two super freaks, but it's all good. Let's go finish this party." They laughed until they saw Ron standing by the door staring at them.

Ron and the others heard what they said, and he was the last person they wanted to run into. He looked at them in confusion and looked at the door and pointed at them.

"Sonny, if you and Christine are supposed to be so close, who is she in the room with?"

Diana pulled on his arm.

"Ron let's go baby, please."

He knew something was wrong and four *Young Wolves* walked towards them and one of them pointed at Ron.

"Ron, what's up homie? Is there a problem?" All four lifted their shirts revealing guns in their waist.

This was a mistake because Ron snatched one of the guns from them and pointed it at Sonny.

"I said who is she in the room with Sonny?"

The other three pulled their guns out and aimed them at Sonny. Ron was about to kick the door open when Keith moved in front of the door.

"Partner, we have been friends all our lives, trust me when I say, you do not want to go in that room my brother." He stared at Ron.

The door opened and Christine and Shantai stood there in shorts and T-shirts and they were sweaty. Ron was the last person she wanted to see.

"Ron!" She put her hand up to her mouth in shame. "Oh my God."

He looked at Christine and Shantai with disgust because anyone could tell what they were doing. He snapped and hit Shawn and Sonny in the head with his gun and started beating them with it. It took Keith and the *Young Wolves* to pull him off.

"Ron, stop!" Shantai yelled.

Stacy looked at her like she lost her mind and smacked her.

"Shut up! I will deal with you later."

Shantai looked at her and said nothing and held the side of her face.

"I told you to protect my sister Sonny and you two are trying to turn them into freaks, I am killing you both." He yelled.

"Stop Ron, don't do this." Diana screamed.

Somehow Ron got away and had the gun against Sonny's head about to pull the trigger.

Christine came to Sonny's rescue and smacked Ron hard.

"Ron please stop, don't kill him. I love him."

Diana put her hand on Ron's shoulder.

"Baby I know how you feel but do not do this Ron, you will go to prison for life, and then what happens to us?"

"They are not worth it Ron, do not pull that trigger." Keith said.

Ron backed up and leaned against the wall still holding the gun by his side and looked at Sonny and Shawn on the floor bleeding badly. The words from Diana and the others made him think about the consequences of his actions. Diana hugged him tightly and got the gun out of his hand and gave it to Keith. He pointed to the *Young Wolves*.

"Get these two fools out of here."

Christine moved in front of them with her arms held out.

"No, you all think I am stupid or something. They can stay and you all need to leave, or I am calling the police and I mean it, so get out." She pointed toward the front door.

Ron, Diana, Keith, and Stacy looked at Christine like she lost her mind. Diana and Stacy grabbed Christine and Shantai and pulled them back into the room with Christine kicking and screaming but it did no good. One of the *Young Wolves* helped them and closed the door. Four more *Young Wolves* came into the house quickly and ran over to them and dragged Sonny and Shawn out of the house and into a car then drove away. Christine looked out of the window and saw them leave. She fell to the floor crying but Shantai looked at her and laughed.

"Christine, stop all that stupid crying. We had some good times and the dick and tongue were good but damn, it ain't worth all that crying. We can always get some good dick, some new dick and hot tongue at that." She smiled at her.

Stacy rushed toward Shantai, but Diana pulled her back.

"Shantai I can't believe you can be so trifling and low life after all the things you have been through."

"Look who is talking. You two have no room to judge me and what I have done when you have done the same thing. Oh, how soon we forget. You hide behind the church when you know both of you are undercover freaks who miss licking pussy and ass."

Christine stood and stared at Diana and Stacy.

"What, you have got to be kidding me."

"Oh yes, they are undercover church freaks for real. Fact is, Ron thinks Diana is so pure and untouched. Please, Stacy's face has been all between Diana's legs and her fat ass, licking and sucking it good."

Keith and Ron walked in the room and Shantai looked at them ready to tell. That was all Stacy needed to see. Stacy balled her fist up and moved like a seasoned boxer hitting Shantai in the jaw, the stomach, and an uppercut. She hit the floor knocked out.

"Stacy are you crazy? Why did you do that?" Christine yelled.

Now she regretted it because she could not stop Christine from talking and she could not hit Ron's sister.

"Stacy, what's going on in here? You knocked the girl out." Keith smiled holding back laughter.

Stacy gave Keith that look and walked towards him and grabbed his arm and walked out of the room. She pushed Keith against the wall and whispered in his ear.

"Keith, Shantai was running her mouth and told Christine Diana and I were together and when you two walked in she was going to tell Ron, so I reacted and hit her."

"No, you did more than hit her, you knocked her out." He kissed her and started sucking on her neck.

Stacy pushed him off.

"Are you kidding me? All that is going on right now and you have your mind on sex. I cannot believe you."

"Baby, you are so sexy when you get upset and right now my dick is harder than a diamond." He smiled and kissed her again.

Stacy looked at him and tried hard not to laugh but she did and felt his dick and it was incredibly hard. This made her horny and she kissed him back passionately.

Diana and Ron walked out of the room and looked at them leaning against the wall kissing and rubbing all over each other.

"You two are beyond words, all this craziness is happening, and you two are in the hallway acting like dogs in heat, Lord have mercy. Ron, I had enough of all this, take me home please."

Stacy and Keith looked at them and laughed and Stacy tried to hug Diana, but she pushed her away.

"Girl don't hug me after you have been rubbing and grinding all over Keith."

"You two are very nasty people." Ron said laughing.

The party was shut down. Ron, Diana, Keith, and Stacy left. Christine was in the room with Shantai holding an ice pack on her swollen jaw. Shantai was very angry and told Christine all about what happened with her, Stacy, and Cynthia. Christine was shocked and very angry, but she would never tell Diana because it would destroy what they shared.

"You have every right to be angry at Stacy, but you cannot tell Diana, Shantai. Yes, I am tremendously angry at Keith and Ron, but I said some things I should not have said, especially about calling the police. For all I know, Sonny and Shawn could be at the bottom of a river somewhere right now. Ron and Keith saved my life and I love them both no matter what. Ron is my brother, so you have to keep all this stuff to yourself, please."

"Yeah okay. I do not know how but I am going to get Stacy. Somehow, someway I am going to get her."

"I know how you feel but you have to get all that hatred out of your spirit, or it will destroy you. Focus on positive things for your life and just be happy." She hugged and kissed her on the cheek.

"I don't feel very positive right now but having you by my side is nice. Thank you," She kissed Christine on the lips. You are the desire of my heart."

"So are you and I will take care of you. I promise you that but right now, show me I am the desire of your heart."

Shantai kissed her and they continued kissing and took each other's clothes off, got on the bed, and began having sex.

A mist returned to the room and hovered over them. The face of Leticia Wilson appeared in the mist watching them until it landed on their bodies. This only intensified their actions of sexual activity. They moved to the 69 position and had their finger inside each other's butt and licking each other's pussy at the same time.

# CHAPTER FIFTY THREE

*A hard Choice*

The next morning Sonny and Shawn drove up to Christine's house. Christine and Shantai were so glad to see them alive, they hugged them tightly, but they winced in pain. The girls noticed how badly they were beaten and it made them angry all over again. The girls bathed them and prepared a nice meal and they laid down to get some rest. Sonny and Shawn slept off and on for the next three days, needing rest and time to heal. In the meantime, Christine was not feeling the same and spiritual conviction was affecting her greatly. She prayed a lot and wanted peace in her life. She knew this was not the path to be on to get this done. Shantai was tired of hearing her complaining and praying, so she tried several times to seduce her, but Christine turned her away. Shantai wondered how Christine got this house, expensive cars, and a house full of expensive furniture but she figured Ron and Keith purchased it for her. Those two were living large for years and now it was her turn. She did not know how she was going to get it until Christine shared the details of what happened to her in Miami. Christine told her about the cash and the diamonds and the millions she had left, and this is how she was living so large.

Shantai was very horny and despite Sonny and Shawn's pains, she seduced them. Christine heard them having sex and it lasted for two hours. Usually, this turned her on greatly but now it was disgusting to her spirit. She took a shower to try and feel clean. When Shantai finished having sex with them she showered and walked into Christine's room wearing a towel to seduce her, but she was on the floor wrapped in a towel praying. Shantai was sick of this, and she knew how to bring her back over to her side of darkness and perverted sex. She helped Christine get on the bed and rubbed her head slowly. Shantai never told or shared with anyone what she was about to tell and show Christine. For the next hour, she shared every detail with Christine of what Stacy told her about all the times and places she and Diana had sex. She made sure to be very graphic with the sex details. Slowly she could see the change coming over Christine but this was not enough because she was still mentioning God and prayer. So, she showed her the cell phone video. The night she and Cynthia tricked Stacy into the hotel room and had a threesome, she set up her cell phone in a hidden place in the room and recorded the entire session. She knew one day this video would be an asset for her, and this was that day. She showed it to Christine who turned her head away because she did not want to watch it. She repeatedly said how repulsive it was but Shantai turned her head back so she would see it. At the end of the video, Christine was breathing heavily and was caressing her thighs while Shantai whispered every nasty and erotic thing she could think of in her ear. Christine could not take it anymore and removed her towel and practically jumped on Shantai and snatched off her towel. Their sex was so intense they screamed while having explosive orgasms. This brought Sonny and Shawn into the room and they watched them. Shantai waved for them to come over and they looked at each other and could not get undressed fast enough. They engaged in wild sex and Shantai smiled because she got Christine back to where she needed her to be, in darkness and deceived.

It was Thursday night, *Ladies Night* at the club and it was a long line of people waiting to get in. Sonny, Shawn, Shantai, and Christine walked into the club. The *Young Wolves* were given specific instructions to bring them to the office immediately if they came to the club. Christine and Shantai had heels on and skin-tight dresses that hugged their body with nothing on underneath. Sonny and Shawn wore dress shoes, slacks, and dress shirts. Zechariah was informed of what happened at Christine's party and he was glad he and Sheila did not go. Sheila was so hurt and angry with Christine and prayed constantly for her soul. Stacy was at Diana's because she did not feel like being at the club. Keith and Ron were in the office dressed in suits when Christine, Sonny, Shantai, and Shawn walked in with the *Young Wolves*. Keith nodded at them, and they walked out closing the door but stood close by. Ron and Keith had guns in their shoulder holsters under their jackets and it took every ounce of discipline in Ron not to shoot them. When he looked at the way Christine was dressed and her extra makeup, he became angrier. Keith was aware of this because he felt the same way, so he watched Ron very carefully because that was his sister.

"Shawn, you Sonny, and Shantai go have fun in the club, I need to talk with my sister."

Keith looked at Ron and walked out with them. Sonny and Shawn went to the bar to get a drink to relax while the *Young Wolves* watched them. Keith walked around the club but Shantai followed him until he turned around to face her.

"Shantai, what do you want, and why are you following me? You, Sonny, and Shawn no longer work at the club so why are you even here?"

"Keith, I know you and Ron hate us, but I need to talk with you, and we don't need your club or your money." She looked at him with a smug look on her face.

Keith was not into hitting women, but he wanted to smack that smug look right off her face.

"So, you three plan on pimping Christine and using her money. That is never going to happen, so you can forget that idea," He looked at her with controlled anger.

Shantai saw the intense anger in Keith's eyes and was afraid of what he might do to her, so she had to act quickly, and they were being watched so she needed to get him alone.

"Keith, give me a few minutes of your time and you never have to see me again, please."

"Yeah, okay. Let's go to the other office and talk."

She knew where it was of course and walked in front of him shaking her butt. Keith tried to stay focused but Shantai was so fine, with a tight curvaceous body and she knew how to walk to make it shake just right. He knew he should not, but wanted to be playful and smacked her on the butt. She looked back at him and smiled. They reached the office and sat down and Shantai pulled out her cell phone.

"Keith, you and Ron have been friends forever and are married now living a great life but there are so many secrets with all of you. I know Stacy and Diana were together many times, having all kinds of freaky sex."

"Get to your point quickly Shantai because I am getting bored with you and all this." He was beyond angry.

"No problem Keith. Did Stacy ever tell you she also had a threesome with me and Cynthia?"

He hit the table with his hand.

"You are lying! Yeah, I knew about her and Diana but that was a long time ago, and she would never do a sick threesome, especially with you." He pointed his finger at her.

She turned her cell phone on and pulled up the video then slid it to Keith.

"Watch this Keith and see for yourself."

He looked at her and stared at the phone wondering if this was a trick or possibly the end of his marriage. He had to know the truth. So, he looked at the video and watched Stacy have sex with Shantai and Cynthia like it was the best time of her life. Tears came to his eyes because of so much pain but he held them back and felt so betrayed. His eyes were red with rage as he looked at Shantai.

"What do you want Shantai?" He stared at her.

She was almost afraid to speak after looking at his eyes, but she came this far, and it was too late to back out now.

"This is not what you think Keith and please don't hit or shoot me like I know you want to. What I want is you. I want you to be with me for just one night and I will never bother you again in life."

"And if I do not?"

"Keith, you act like I am a repulsive ugly woman, damn I am fine, and any man would love to be with me, even for one night."

He hit the table so hard with both hands the table shook.

"And if I don't?" He yelled and stood up.

Shantai jumped up thinking he was going to hit her, but she was not about to run now.

"Keith, if you don't, I am telling Ron everything about Diana and Stacy. I know he could not take it and it would destroy his marriage. And I am showing him this video. You can smash this phone if you want but you know I have copies of the video and don't hit me." She stared at him in complete fear.

He looked at her and sat down not knowing what to say or do. She was right, Ron could not handle this, and it would probably destroy him and most definitely end his marriage. When he saw Diana and Stacy kissing and when she later told him everything, his instincts told him one day this would all come back to hurt them all. He looked at Shantai and smiled. She sat down.

"You know what Shantai? In all the years Stacy and I have been together and with all the temptations I have dealt with and still do; I have never cheated on her. But you are trying to blackmail me and willing to destroy others' relationships so you can have what you want. What does that make you Shantai?"

"Keith, I will not allow you or Stacy to judge me because you two have done so much dirt in your life to get what you want. Now you are judging me for doing the same things you two have done, only you all have done much worse. Besides, you know you want me, and you smacked me on my butt and you know I do not have any underwear on or a bra. You have looked at my nipples since we have been in this room."

"Yeah, okay. Even if I do what you want, what is stopping you from telling Ron afterward?"

"As I said, I only want you for one night and we are doing everything. Keith, I promise, you will not be disappointed, and it will be the best time you ever had with any woman." In Shantai's mind, if Keith would have sex with her he would choose her.

"I need to sit here and think."

"So, we sit here and think together."

Ron talked to Christine but not getting anywhere and he recognized the extreme rebellious spirit she operated in because he operated in the same spirit for a while. He hugged her tightly and said he loved her and wanted to protect her, but she would not let him.

"I know you love me Ron and you know I love you back, but it is time for me to live my life." She hugged him and they walked out together.

They walked around the club and saw Sonny and Shawn grinding on two girls on the dance floor. She did not like this but would not show it in front of Ron. She walked on the floor and began dancing with Sonny and Shawn provocatively. Ron walked away because he detested what he saw but realized there was nothing he could do about it. Everyone was right, she was a grown woman. He asked one of the *Young Wolves* where Keith was and he pointed to the office. He walked in and saw Shantai and Keith sitting at a table.

"What's going on?"

They looked at him and Shantai looked at Keith.

"We were just talking. So Keith, what is your answer to my business proposal?"

"I will call you tomorrow and let you know."

Shantai stood up and shook her head.

"It is imperative you call me tomorrow Keith." She walked out of the room and joined Christine on the dance floor.

"Ron, sit down partner I need to talk with you."

He sat down and could tell by the look in Keith's eyes whatever he had to say was profoundly serious.

"We have been friends for life Keith and been through some things most only dream about. So, talk to me, what's up with Shantai."

Keith lowered his head and thought. This was one of the hardest choices he ever made in his life. It was a no-win situation that would only get worse for everyone if he did not tell Ron. He was not going to be blackmailed by Shantai or anyone especially after all the things he had been through. He loved Stacy deeply. So, he started from the beginning and told Ron everything. He knew Ron would snap but he did not he seemed almost too calm. He shook Keith's hand.

"I know this was not an easy choice for you to make but I appreciate you telling me the truth. I am going home and pray before I go crazy." He walked out of the office and out of the club and got in his car and drove away with tears coming down his face.

Keith called Stacy and told her Ron was on the way home and he knew everything and asked her to go home, and he was on his way. She hung up and told Diana it was late, and she had to go. They hugged and Stacy left and drove home with tears in her eyes knowing everything about to happen was her fault.

# CHAPTER FIFTY FOUR

*Pain or Love*

$R$on wasted no time driving home but the drive gave him time to pray to ask God to give him instant peace and keep him from doing something to Diana he would regret. He walked into the house and Diana sat in the living room on the sofa wearing shorts and a T-shirt watching a movie on the big screen TV. She got up and kissed and hugged him and caressed his chest with her hand, but Ron did not hug her back. He stared at her eyes wondering how she could have deceived him for so long. Diana knew something was very wrong because his entire demeanor was cold and distant.

"Ron, what is wrong baby? Did something happen at the club tonight? Did a pretty hot thing try to talk to you?" She walked back to the sofa and sat down and looked at him. "I am not jealous and realize it's part of the business you are in, and I know how faithful you are to me and you love me deeply. My husband is also sprung on all this good loving he receives at home." She smiled and blew him a kiss.

He sat on the sofa across from her gripping the cushions hard as he stared at her.

"Yes Diana I am the faithful type even though I deal with temptations on a regular. We have known each other all our lives and you have threatened me so many times since then. Ron, you better not do this or that with some other woman," He smiled as he rubbed his hands together. "Diana, help me understand why and how you could live such a double life for so long before and after our marriage."

"Ron, what are you talking about? I am not and have not been living a double life and stop looking at me like that and asking me stupid questions. Have you been drinking?" Raising her voice at him and becoming irritated.

"Diana, you have been lying to me for years and you still are, very convincingly I might say. You are an exceptionally good liar. What about your sexual relationship with Stacy and whoever else? Please do not lie to me because I know everything now. Stacy told Keith and tonight Keith told me all the sick details of you and Stacy getting your freak on while Keith and I are not around. You are a bible quoting church going undercover church freak and a habitual liar! All this time, I believed you were so pure and untouched. Others made commits no one is that clean, but I always disagreed when it came to my precious Diana. You fooled me good Diana, you fooled everybody. I feel like such an idiot. You and Stacy had sex in our house where we pray," he laughed. "Nothing is sacred to you as long as you can keep this pure clean image going on and still get your freak on. I hope it was all worth it for you Diana."

As she listened to Ron's every word Diana's heart felt like it would explode because it was beating so fast, and she began sweating. Nothing could have prepared her for all this, and the fact is, it was all true. What could be said to defend the words Ron spoke, how do you defend the truth? It felt like she would pass out on the spot. Every time she opened her mouth to speak no words would come out, but she needed to say something.

"Ron please let me talk and..."

She never finished her sentenced because Ron let out a blood curdling scream and slid down to the floor crying and screaming.

"Noooo! I loved you so much. Noooooo!" He screamed louder as the tears came from his eyes like a fountain.

Hearing her husband in such incredible overwhelming pain and seeing it at the same time knowing she caused it all was too much for Diana to deal with. She got up and ran to her bedroom and laid on the bed crying hysterically.

Two hours later, Ron walked into the bedroom and Diana was still on the bed crying. But her tears did not affect him at all, the fact is, he figured it was all an act.

"Did you do all that crying when you had your legs in the air or your face buried between Stacy's legs and ass? Obviously, I was not freaky enough for you, so you had to get yours somewhere else. Answer this, how many asses have you licked besides Stacy, and how many dicks have you sucked and fucked? Are you taking it in the ass too? Yes you are because once you get turned out, lust demons make you want to do it all. Miss Jekyll and Hyde, two people in one. Good clean church going girl by day and a liar and freak by night. I feel like such a damn fool, you kissed all over me and still licked someone else's ass and pussy."

Diana's heart and spirit hurt so much, she felt very guilty for everything. Hearing Ron talk to her so degradingly like she was a slut on the corner made it worse. He was accusing her of doing things she has not done which made her angry. She jumped off the bed and got in his face and poked him repeatedly in the chest.

"That is enough Ron! I know you are extremely angry at me and yes, I am guilty of doing some horrible things I should not have but it is in the past and God has forgiven me. You are not going to stand here talking to me like I am trash or some hooker on the corner selling her body to anyone."

"I know you better stop poking me with your finger. You may as well sell that ass instead of giving it up for free. Make money with that hot body you walk around shaking so hard. For all I know, you gave Keith some of your ass too, or did you charge him? I always knew Stacy was freaky so maybe you, Stacy, and Keith had a three-way behind my back like you did everything else."

His words hit her heart like a brick and caused her temper to boil over. She slapped him so hard spit came out of his mouth.

"Don't talk to me like that Ron I am still your wife, not a hooker. You have every right to be angry, but you will not talk to me like I am trash."

"You better not smack me again. You know what Diana; I don't know who I married? Do you even know who you are? I am gone." He walked out of the bedroom towards the front door.

Diana did not know what to do. All the years they have been together and all the praying, now everything was a nightmare. She lost her husband, her only true love. No, she thought to herself and ran to catch Ron before he walked out of the door. She grabbed his arm and pulled him back.

"Ron please don't leave. Stay here and pray with me, please."

He snatched his arm away from her.

"Were you praying when you were licking pussy and ass? Or getting some dick. While I was licking your pussy and ass you were licking somebody else pussy and ass or sucking some dick and then came home and kissed me on my mouth. Do you know how nasty and dirty that is? Did you even use mouth wash?" He shook his head and looked at her with hate in his eyes.

Once again, he pushed her buttons and she snapped. Diana swung at him, but he ducked which is what she knew he would do. She kicked him hard in the knee causing him to buckle and started swinging wildly hitting him at times in the face and then Diana did something that surprised her. She snatched one of his legs from underneath him causing him to fall and began hitting him repeatedly.

"You are not going anywhere and stop talking to me like I am some dog." She yelled and continued hitting him.

Ron thought she went crazy, and he blocked most of her punches, but she did hit him in his nose, both of his eyes, and his lip was bleeding. The doorbell rang and Ron pushed her off and got up to answer it. Keith and Stacy stood there in sweats and they looked at each other then at Ron. Keith did not want to be here, but Stacy was concerned for Diana and did not want Ron to do something crazy to her. It looked like she did something crazy to him.

"Damn partner, what happened to you?" Keith tried hard not to laugh but he laughed anyway.

"Ron, no you did not beat up your wife. Where is she?" Stacy walked past him and saw Diana sitting on the floor, but she had no marks on her. She helped her get off the floor and they sat on the sofa.

Ron left the door open and walked into the living room and sat down on the sofa across from Diana and Stacy. Keith walked in closing the door behind him and sat next to Stacy. Ron's nose and lip were bleeding and both eyes were black. Keith looked at Diana and then at Ron.

"You two were fighting in here! Wow! Diana did all that to you. Partner, I do not know what happened, but she beat your ass. Boy, you are bloody and beat up." He leaned back on the sofa laughing and holding his stomach.

RONALD GRAY                                                313

Diana looked at Ron and felt so bad for attacking him for being angry at her for something she was guilty of. She went to the kitchen and got some paper towels and ice and put some in two towels and handed them to Ron. He looked at her and took the towels and placed one on his eye and the other on his nose. She sat next to him and wiped the blood off his nose while leaning him back on the sofa.

Stacy and Keith looked at each other and started laughing.

"Oh, so you two think this is funny. All the lies, deception, and Diana attacking me like some crazy woman for something she did. This is funny to you?"

"Partner, I know this situation is as bad as it gets which is why we are here. Fact is, no words or apologies can fix this because the pain runs too deep. I wanted to leave Stacy when I found out and I tried but as much pain as I was in, the love in my heart and spirit for her was greater. So, I stayed, and we worked it out. You can leave your wife and everything you two have been through would be in vain. It has not been easy for us, and we all have been in wars but by the grace of God Ron, we all are still alive. This means something because God does not make mistakes and you know the life we lived, we should be dead."

Everything Keith said made sense to him but how was he supposed to get past all this? How does he ever trust Diana again? How do they establish the powerful connection they shared for so many years? How does he ever look at Stacy and Keith the same? His pain was tremendous and thinking about love right now was the farthest thing from his mind.

Stacy did not want to speak because she knew Ron blamed her for all this and he was right, but she had to say something.

"Ron, telling Keith the truth was one of the hardest things I have ever done in my life, but the truth needed to be told and we have been blessed to become closer than before, thank God." Stacy kissed Keith on the lips.

Diana slid away from Ron and stared at him.

"Ron, no matter what I say to you it does not have any meaning because you are so angry and in so much pain right now. All I can do is ask you to forgive me and to tell you it will never happen again. It is the past and if I could change it I would, but I cannot. You have every right to leave me, and I deserve it but please know this, you will be leaving a woman who is deeply sorry for all the pain I have caused you. I will love you for the rest of your life." Not being able to keep it all in, Diana began crying again very hard until she started hyperventilating.

Ron stared at her and tried hard to ignore everything Stacy and Diana said but when Diana started hyperventilating, it concerned him because regardless of his great pain he did not want anything bad to happen to his wife.

"Ron don't sit there staring at her choking. Do something!" Stacy yelled at him.

He looked at Stacy then put his arm around Diana and held her. Tears came to his eyes, and he started praying despite how he felt. He prayed hard calling on God to heal his heart and repair the damage to his marriage.

Twenty minutes later, all four of them prayed and called on God, praising his mighty name for healing and restoration. A cloud hovered over the house and it was the cloud of God blessing them all.

# CHAPTER FIFTY FIVE

*Baller Lifestyle*

Two months passed since God restored Ron and Diana's marriage and blessed Keith and Stacy as well. Christine went by Ron's house and gave him eight million dollars to keep for her because she trusted him, and she knew her money would be safe. She sunk deeper into darkness and developed more of a rebellious spirit. She allowed Sonny, Shantai, and Shawn to move in with her. Christine purchased S600's Mercedes Maybach's for all of them. They did everything and went everywhere together, the gym, expensive restaurants, they bought clothes, went jewelry shopping, and took trips to various Caribbean Islands. They smoked marijuana every day, and the sex became more perverted, anywhere and everywhere they could get away with it. For Christine, the only things that seem to satisfy her were spending money and sex. She stopped going to church. Ron, Sheila, and Sandra spoke with her, but it did no good. She would become very emotional and cry but never turned from the dirty lifestyle she lived. Her spirit, mind, and body were severely poisoned and damaged after she met with Leticia Wilson.

She called and requested a meeting with Leticia wanting to know why she was trying to destroy her family. She went by herself. Christine went to Leticia's hotel, meeting her in one of the office suites. She wore a conservative dress and heels and Leticia wore on a white business suit. They talked for an hour while eating and drinking. Leticia walked behind Christine and put her arm around her neck and squeezed it while whispering curses in Christine's ear. Leticia's bodyguards came into the room and what happened next between them could only be compared to Sodom and Gomorrah. Christine, Leticia, and her bodyguards went to another suite and for the next three hours, they engaged in every immoral act one could imagine. They used their bodies and various sex toys. What Christine had not experienced before this, she did now, and it took her to a level of wickedness that only an act of God could deliver her from.

One thing that stood out for Christine that gave her more orgasms than anything else was after they took showers together, she laid on the bed naked on her back. Two women were between her legs licking and sucking her pussy and ass and fingered her ass as well at the same time. Two women were licking and sucking all over her breast and nipples, and others took turns tongue kissing her with incredible passion. All of this going on at the same time and the intensity was beyond measure. She climaxed so hard and so many times, it felt like her body was floating. And just when she thought it was over, Leticia put on a strap-on and fucked her extremely slow in various positions until she screamed from unbelievable pleasure.

Christine went home and slept for two days, except to eat and shower. Afterward, for the next two days she, Shantai, Shawn, and Sonny engaged in sex and never went outside.

The following day they flew to Puerto Rico. They went to several different clubs dancing and drinking and having a great time not realizing they were on a path so many before them walked, ball until you fall."

# CHAPTER FIFTY SIX

*Powers of Darkness*

Christine, Sonny, Shantai, and Shawn's plane just landed at BWI airport from Puerto Rico at eleven o'clock Saturday night. A limo waited to take them home. Driving on Baltimore Washington Parkway they sat in the back drinking and laughing.

"Damn Christine, I would have never guessed you of all people would be the way you are now, doing so many freaky things." Shantai said laughing.

"I know that's right. Christine, your oral skills are so good you need to be in the movies." Sonny said laughing and kissed her and they started kissing each other.

There were trees on both sides of the Parkway and for a Saturday night, the traffic was heavy. Five hundred yards ahead of them in the woods, close to the Parkway, was Leticia Wilson dressed in all black holding a grey cane. She hit the cane against a tree and mumbled some words. Suddenly, the entire ground and road on both sides began shaking and everyone thought it was an earthquake. Cars swirled all over the road crashing into each other. Their limo crashed into the back of an SUV and their driver was killed instantly. Christine, Shantai, Sonny, and Shawn were banged up but okay. Christine prayed and thank God for saving them, but the ground shook, and other vehicles ran into one another.

Squirrels, twice their usual size begin coming out of the ground by the thousands. They ran up poles and across the telephone lines leaping on top of vehicles scratching and biting their way through. Suddenly, there was a very loud screeching sound and large rats came out of the ground by the hundreds of thousands jumping on vehicles biting through the metal of the cars and getting inside. The ground shook hard again with dark smoke coming from the ground and all activity from the animals stopped instantly. Every squirrel and rat stopped moving and looked towards the smoke coming out of the ground. Howling was heard and packs of large wolves came out of the ground by the thousands and ran directly into the vehicle's windows and smashed through. Their teeth were huge and razor-sharp which they used to bite into the metal of the vehicles like it was paper and pulled it back and ran in. The wolves' bit large chunks of flesh from the people and ripped off individual's arms and heads with one bite.

On both sides of the Parkway, nine miles in either direction vehicle traffic came to a stop and the people had no clue as to why the traffic was so bad. After a while, people turned off their vehicles from frustration and became angry and began cursing. Others relaxed and listened to music. Some started smoking marijuana and others began having sex, not having any idea what was about to befall them. Hundreds of people were being attacked at the same time. They were screaming and yelling as the squirrels, rats, and wolves got inside their vehicles, biting them all over their bodies. Their arms, legs, and heads were being snatched off by the powerful jaws of the wolves and the rats and squirrels ate the rest of their bodies. People were kicking the animals trying their best not to be dragged out, but the wolves were far too powerful and pulled them out with ease as the rats ripped the flesh off their bodies. Many people with legs and arms missing were trying to run away after being attacked or crawled on the ground, but the squirrels jumped all over them biting out their eyes, and ears, and nose.

One couple was in the back of their SUV, kissing and caressing each other. The man slid her clothes off.

"This is so wrong what we are doing and have been doing for so long now. We are married and have been meeting each other to have sex. Okay the sex is great, but this is still very wrong. May God forgive us." She said.

"Oh please, don't start talking about God again. You do this every time you start feeling guilty, but it is only after we fucked each other's brains out. God, there is no God or Jesus or whatever you want to call him. That is another story given to us to control people and make us weak. There is no God. Weak people call on this invisible God when they get in trouble, what a joke." He kissed her and laughed and removed the rest of her clothes and slid inside her.

They laughed while having sex. Two wolves locked their jaws on the door handles of both sides of the car and pulled the doors open. The wolves' bit each of their legs and pulled them out on the ground. Four more wolves walked over with blood dripping from their mouths and they stared at the couple, snarling and growling.

"Oh God no! Oh, Jesus help us Lord." She said while crying and kicking her feet at the wolves.

"Oh Lord God, help me Jesus! Help us Lord don't..."

He never finished his sentence because a wolf bit his head in half and another bit off her head. The rats came and began biting and eating their bodies in seconds.

Many Police arrived in their cars shooting the animals, but they were too fast and too many. The Police got attacked as well.

S.W.A.T teams arrived after reports of a pack of wild animals attacking people. They jumped out wearing body armor and helmets carrying shields and shooting the animals with rapid gunfire and flame throwers. Squirrels jumped from tree to tree leaping on them, but they were being smashed to the ground. More rats came out of the ground as Leticia Wilson continued to call them up through the powers of darkness. The ground was now covered with rats for miles, and they ran and jumped on vehicles. A lot of people were having sex in their vehicles, men with women, men with men, and women with women but the rats got inside their vehicles eating them alive as they all screamed to God for help but only their bones were left. The cries of the people could be heard calling on God, but they still got ripped to the bones by the rats. Rats jumped in their mouths while they were having orgasms and ate their insides while they yelled. Some were praying and when the animals came to attack them, they turned and ran away, they were blessed with mercy and grace.

Several helicopters flew over the traffic with bright lights. They watched the slaughter of people by the animals. A swarm of bats appeared out of some dark clouds, and they covered the front and side of the helicopters so the operators couldn't see. They flew inside biting everyone, causing the operators to crash and the helicopters exploded sending metal flying everywhere. The bats flew back into the dark clouds. For nine miles, east and west, dead bodies, vehicles, and body parts laid all over the streets. Heads, arms, legs, and backs were scattered on the street, and it was covered with blood. Wolves dragged dead bodies and body parts into the woods with rats hanging on still biting and eating the flesh.

RONALD GRAY                                              321

The body of the driver of the limo hung out of the broken window with both arms and his head missing. Shawn and Sonny laid on the ground dead close to the limo with their faces bitten off and throats ripped out. Shantai and Christine laid on the limo floor crying hysterically and praying. They rose slowly on different sides of the limo and looked out of the windows that were smashed by the animals. As their neck was level to the windows ledge, two wolves leaped up and bit their heads off and their bodies dropped to the limo floor shaking. Blood squirted all over the limo. The wolves and squirrels and most of the rats ran back into the ground. Leticia Wilson walked over and looked inside the limo and saw their dead bodies and the girl's heads on the floor. She laughed and raised her hands in the air.

"Yes, I finally got one of you," she reached down in the limo and smacked Christine's head. "All that praying but you turned from God and now I am taking you to hell with me, you and your friends and every dead person on this road. I am the power of this world; I am all power." As she spoke, her voice changed to the voice of Mr. Bones and her voice, back and forth as she continued to laugh.

Many rats crawled on the ground eating the flesh of the dead bodies and crunching the bones. Leticia mumbled some words and stomped her foot on the ground and she turned slowly into a wolf. It walked around looking at the dead bodies growling and bit the head off the body. It ran away with the head in its mouth and the other rats followed.

# CHAPTER FIFTY SEVEN

*Tears of past and Present*

It was a warm sunny Friday afternoon and the weather was beautiful. A day you go to the park with family, friends, or loved ones and get the grill out to Bar-B-Que one of your favorite meals and listen to some music, laughing with friends, and having fun. But this was not one of those days because the video was still being seen on every major TV station in the Country. Of the carnage that happened last Saturday night on the Baltimore Washington Parkway. Most of the scenes were too graphic to show on TV but you saw from the helicopter's footage where the animals attacked the vehicles and people before they crashed. Never has something so horrible of this magnitude happened and was caught on film. It looked like a scene from a horror movie, but this was very real and talk was already underway concerning the movie.

The process of identifying the bodies was still taking place but it was an extremely difficult task because body parts were missing from so many of the bodies. Thus far, the count was two thousand people were dead and major damage to most of the vehicles. There were so many questions being asked as to what could have possibly caused this. Scientists were saying there was an extremely unusual electrical current from a storm that hit the ground causing the animals to attack the way they did. The public did not believe this, and many thought it was just another sign of the end of times. So many funerals were being planned or underway in the DMV area it has put a tremendous burden on families and the grief was beyond words of expression. One such burial was taking place today.

The O'Neil family was at the same cemetery where David O'Neil was buried and Christine O'Neil was being buried next to her dad. Shantai, Shawn, and Sonny were being buried close to Christine. Sheila, Zechariah, James, Catarina, Tonya, Derrick, Cynthia, Rick, Ron, Diana, Stacy, Keith, five *Young Wolves*, Sandra, Pastor Williams, and the church members were present. The mortician at the funeral home did a great job putting the heads back on Christine and Shantai along with fixing the faces of Shawn and Sonny but there was no open casket ceremony for any of them. Pastor Williams sat next to Sheila talking with her and he stood waving his hand to get everyone's attention.

"I thank all of you for being here today to comfort the O'Neil family in the loss of their daughter Christine and her friends. Death is a very sad occasion for family members and friends but whenever there is a tragedy such as this one that brings about death, it is overwhelmingly difficult to deal with. I have known the O'Neil family for many years and shared many different situations with them. But this one is extremely hard for me to speak on because of the circumstances with which all of you are familiar. Please keep the family in your prayers and continue to pray for one another. Now, Sheila would like to share a few words with you." He sat down.

Sheila and Zechariah stood and he had his arm around her waist holding her trembling body. She looked around the large crowd and managed a smile, but her heart was so far from it as she stared at Christine's casket.

"First, let me say I thank God in the name of Jesus for giving me and my family the strength to deal with this most heart-wrenching situation. So many other people are dealing with because of," she put her hand up to her eyes trying to hide her tears, but they flowed down her cheeks. "Forgive me, but it is so hard to remain strong when your very heart feels like it was ripped from your chest. My tears and pains are from the past and present. My ex-husband was killed and now my daughter Christine. No parent desires to bury their child and today I am doing just that but many other parents and children are burying their parents. I am missing my daughter beyond what any words could describe. May God keep us all and again thank you all for coming." Sheila sat down and cried as Zechariah held her closely, feeling her pain.

Pastor Williams exhaled and prayed to remain focused, he stood and hugged Sheila and shook Zechariah's hand.

"Allow me to leave these words with you. When you are dealing with so much negativity in your life and so much is coming against you, it is easy to blame God. My prayer for myself and everyone here is to remember this scripture. Psalm 50:15, *And call upon me in the day of trouble, I will deliver thee, and thou shall glorify me.* My brothers, my sisters, my neighbors, we are truly living in the last days. Do not put your trust in man but put all your trust in the Lord. God bless you all." He waved his hand to the crowd of people.

Everyone began hugging Sheila and the family members, but Sandra sat staring at the casket when her emotions became too much, and she broke down crying and screaming calling Christine's name over and over. Ron walked over and hugged her tightly as his tears fell down his face. Everyone was crying but still trying to comfort each other.

A long white Benz limo pulled up close to where the crowd stood in the cemetery. Leticia Wilson and her bodyguards stepped out wearing all white business suits and they walked toward the O'Neil family with Leticia in front. The crowd separated as she walked closer. Keith saw her coming and he became enraged. He walked towards her and so did Ron and the *Young Wolves* who opened their suit jackets revealing automatic weapons. Rick, James, and Zechariah moved forward as well. Sheila ran towards Leticia Wilson, but Pastor Williams moved in front of her.

"What are you doing here you walking devil? If God did not keep me, I would choke the life out of you right now." She yelled.

"Miss Leticia Wilson your presence here is not wanted and for the sake of everyone I am asking you to leave before this situation gets out of control, real fast." The pastor said staring at her.

"It is not my desire to upset anyone. I came here to give my condolences to the O'Neil family and if there is anything I could do, please let me know." Leticia spoke very softly but with no emotion and her eyes were black.

Sandra pointed her finger at Leticia Wilson and yelled.

"I know all this is your doing because you are evil, and I hope you burn in hell, you devil." She spat on the ground.

Catarina walked towards Leticia with the stride of a warrior.

"I know who you are and what you are, but your time will come to an end. May God have mercy on your soul." She looked directly at her eyes.

James stood next to Catarina and leaned towards Leticia.

"I suggest you leave while you can."

Leticia leaned closer to James and Catarina.

"You two are next she whispered." She and her bodyguards walked away but Leticia turned around and blew a kiss at everyone and continued walking. They got in the limo, and it drove away.

Leticia Wilson whispered her words but God allowed Pastor Williams to hear her, and he shook his head because he felt for her soul.

# CHAPTER FIFTY EIGHT

*Turn from your wicked Ways*

People looked at the white limo when it drove away, wondering what was going on with Leticia Wilson and the O'Neil family. All the church members finally left, and the only people left sitting down talking were Pastor Williams, Zechariah, Sheila, James, Catarina, Derrick, Tonya, Rick, Cynthia, Ron, Diana, Sandra, Keith, Stacy, and the *Young Wolves,* who stood looking around, always on guard. The cemetery workers sat away from everyone else. There were several limos and the drivers still waiting to take everyone else home. Thirty minutes later, a long black Benz limo pulled up and Leticia Wilson and her bodyguards stepped out wearing all black. Leticia had an old grey cane in her hand with a black cat with red eyes sitting on her shoulder. Everyone stood as she approached. The *Young Wolves* were ready to shoot Leticia and her bodyguards, but Keith told them to relax and see what was going on. Pastor Williams turned around to speak to his family members.

"I need for all you to listen and move quickly, please. I need, Sandra, Sheila, Zechariah, James, Catarina, Derrick, Tonya, Rick, Cynthia, Stacy, and Diana to leave now. No questions."

"Pastor, I know this is about to get serious but Zechariah and I can help." Rick spoke with confidence and irritation.

"No question Pastor. I can't leave my brothers here." Zechariah said and looked at the Pastor.

The pastor looked at everyone in a way that none of them have ever seen before.

"I said leave, now." He looked at all their faces.

As they started to leave Leticia Wilson and her bodyguards stood in their way and Leticia pointed her finger at them.

"Where do you people think you are going? The only place you are going today is in the grave because I am killing all of you praying fake people today. All you are a bunch of church going closet super freaks. Pussy and ass licking, dick sucking, ass stuffing perverted freaks. I know you can't wait to get home to..."

She never finished her sentence because the Pastor pointed his hand at her and yelled.

"In the name of Jesus, hold your tongue devil, and peace be still. May your tongue cling to the roof of your mouth until God allows you to speak."

The cemetery workers were watching this, and they ran to the edge of the woods close to the cemetery. As hard as she tried, Leticia Wilson and her bodyguards could neither speak or move. Everyone walked to the limos and they drove away. Ron, Keith, Pastor Williams, and the *Young Wolves* all lined up facing Leticia Wilson and her bodyguards. The pastor walked closer to Leticia.

"God is giving all of you one last time to repent of your sins and turn from your wicked ways and he will heal your hearts, minds, and spirits. You may now speak."

Leticia was furious and had never experienced not being able to talk or move. She stepped closer to the Pastor and her bodyguards moved away from her but stood close to each other and stared at the *Young Wolves*. They heard a lot about them and wanted to see what they were made of.

"Stupid man, you have no clue who I am, but you are about to find out."

With skill and incredible speed, the five bodyguards pulled out knives and threw them at the *Young Wolves* and Keith. Ron waved his hand at them.

"No weapon formed against us shall prosper."

The knives stopped moving in mid-air just before reaching their target and fell to the ground on fire. Keith and the *Young Wolves* pulled out their guns and shot the bodyguards in the body and head. They fell dead, and their bodies began turning into worms and decaying. Leticia looked in horror and screamed.

"Nooo! You killed my family. I am killing all of you." She mumbled words and tapped her cane on the ground repeatedly.

The ground started shaking and holes began opening all over the cemetery. Large black cats came out of the ground. The cat on Leticia's shoulder began hissing and screaming then leaped toward the Pastor's face.

"Touch not mine anointed and do my prophets no harm."

Lightning struck the cat burning it in the air. It was dead before it hit the ground. Keith ran and stood behind Ron and the *Young Wolves* stood behind the Pastor. They saw the powers of darkness right before their very eyes. Leticia Wilson mumbled some words and screamed very loudly at them and hit her leg hard with the cane. She dropped the cane on the ground and began to change into a large black wolf. Two of the *Young Wolves* got scared and ran and this was their mistake. The black cats leaped on them fast scratching their eyes out, pulling out their tongues, and ripping their flesh to pieces. They were dead in seconds. There were hundreds of cats walking around the cemetery and they all stood behind the wolf ready to pounce. Blood started dripping from the wolf's mouth and it was howling extremely loud. Pastor, Ron, and Keith spoke at the same time under the power of God.

"If God is for you, then who can be against you."

The wolf growled, the cats hissed louder, and they all leaped at one time toward them. Knives of fire came out of the sky striking and killing all the cats and the wolf burning their bodies.

Pastor Williams, Ron, Keith, and the Young Wolves looked around shaking their heads in total amazement at the evil that came against them but how God protected and saved their lives. The pastor laid hands on them and prayed, and walked towards their vehicles and drove away. Ron and Keith were in the same car.

"Partner, once again we have seen some incredible powers of darkness but thank God, he has all power in heaven and earth. This is MY CALL." Keith said.

"Amen my brother. This is MY CALL. Friends for life." They gave each other some dap and smiled, realizing they were blessed with another time of grace and mercy from God.

One of the cemetery workers walked from the edge of the woods and continued walking around until he saw the grey cane that belong to Leticia Wilson. He looked around making sure no one saw him and felt compelled to pick the cane up, looked around again, and ran holding the cane. He fell twice and the second time he hit his mouth on a headstone and knocked out six of his front teeth, but he got up with blood dripping from his mouth. He wiped his mouth with his hand, brushed his clothes off, looked around, then took off running with his head up high, still holding that cane.

# Coming Soon!

## My Call IV The Origin Of Mr. Bones